THE
LOST
BROTHER

A totally compelling psychological thriller
with an electrifying finish

SUSANNA BEARD

JOFFE
BOOKS

Joffe Books, London
www.joffebooks.com

First published in Great Britain in 2021

© Susanna Beard

Join our mailing list and become one of thousands of readers enjoying free Kindle crime thriller, detective, mystery, and romance books and new releases. Receive your first bargain book this month!

www.joffebooks.com/contact

We love to hear from our readers! Please email any feedback you have to: feedback@joffebooks.com

ISBN: 978-1-78931-602-5

For Carolyn

PROLOGUE

For a moment, when the shot rings out, everything freezes. The warm wind pauses, startled. Leaves droop; grasses stand straight, motionless. Reedbuck pose like statues, ears pricked for the slightest sound, while the rock rats pause their endless scrabbling, noses held high for the waft of danger. Lizards stand poised, one leg held high, on stony viewpoints.

With a sigh, the moment passes. Silence drifts back into the valleys, along the sweeping mountainsides, over the great grey outcrops, through the swathes of grassland. Heads dip back to the earth, resuming their browsing, and the dassies go back to work. Snakes curl their way onwards; lizards close their lazy eyelids against the South African sun. High above, a black eagle circles, watching.

The body lies relaxed on its bed of grass, the pool of scarlet syrup beside it darkening. A tent flaps in the breeze, spreading the stench of death. The blowflies have arrived already, laying their eggs in the wound, the mouth, the nose. They're busy at their task: they know how this is done. Soon Cape vultures will appear, but not before the flies have finished their business. Perhaps the jackal, never far away, will come too, take his chances and leave before the bigger predators get a whiff of the feast that awaits them.

For now, though, it's calm. Only the soft buzz of insects, the cry of a distant bird, the rustle of grass, disturbs the air. It will be a while before the humans arrive, with their hulla-baloo, the crashing of feet, the crackling of communication with the world beyond. Then the animals will fade into the African bush, as only they know how.

CHAPTER ONE

Leonora

"He's sending me away." He leans in the doorway, his thin shoulders drooping. His eyes are huge, dark shadows spreading beneath.

She sinks onto the bed to keep from falling. A shadow falls across the room — a touch of cold air wafts around the window. The sudden thump of her heart drowns out the rumble of the radio from the kitchen below.

"Away? What do you mean?"

"To boarding school. Boys-only bloody boarding school." She's never heard him swear before. It sounds strange, coming from him. He closes the door behind him and joins her on the bed, his legs folding under him. One of his socks has a hole — she can see a small, soft toe poking through.

"No — no, he can't," she says. "He can't do that, Ricky." She gazes at his pale face, willing it not to be true. Her only brother, her best friend, who knows her better than anyone in the whole world. He can't be going away.

"He can. I'm going away to school in December. I have no choice, he's fixed it all." His fragile fingers shake as he brings them to his head, burying them in his hair.

"Didn't you tell him? Didn't you say you couldn't — you wouldn't?" She hugs her stomach, hunching forward over her knees. Even as she says it, she knows that Ricky — gentle, compliant Ricky — would never stand up to his bullying father. "You're not going, Ricky!"

"I tried. But you know what he's like. He'll—" He breaks off, his lip shaking. "What else can I do? It's no use asking Mum."

In this house one man rules. What he says goes, and nobody dares to object.

Leonora picks at a loose thread on the bedcover, pulling it until the fabric puckers and strains. A voice in her head says, *No, no, no. This can't happen.* "But — why? Why is he doing this?"

"He wants me to toughen up. To get me away from you. He thinks being with you is making me soft." She opens her mouth to object but he carries on. "He has no idea. You're much tougher than me."

She jumps up and goes to the window, gazing at the narrow garden below, its edges flanked by brown fencing. A strip of unkempt grass takes the centre space, lines of tatty shrubs along each side. At the end, a tangle of brambles and weeds around a ramshackle shed. The garden is uncared-for, like the rest of their house.

She leans her forehead against the cool glass. She has loved her brother with a fierce passion ever since she first set eyes on him. How can she bear to live here without him?

"I'm twelve, and I'm a boy, and I don't like sport," he says, his voice flat. "I won't fight the other boys when they bully me. I like books, and school, and being with you."

"But what's wrong with that? You've never caused him any trouble, not like some kids. He should be glad about it, surely, instead of punishing you by sending you away."

"He wants me to go to a school where I'll learn to be a man. Like him, I suppose." He pauses, his mouth working. "I never want to be like him!" He spits the words out, his voice trembling with emotion, the knuckles of his clenched fists showing white through the taut skin. The radio downstairs falls silent, the house closing in on itself, waiting.

Leonora's head hurts, her throat swelling with the effort not to cry. "I can't live here without you. I hate him. How can he do this?"

"He's talked about it before, but I didn't really believe he'd do it. I don't have any choice. I'm sorry, Leo. I hate it just as much as you — more. I don't want to go away, even if it's the best school in the world. I don't want to leave you and Mum." His face crumples and he leans back against the wall, his eyes closed. A single tear escapes, making its way slowly down his cheek.

A thought occurs to her. "You could run away — we'll go together! We could—" But even as she says it, she knows it's hopeless.

"Where to?" he says. "We have no money. We're just kids. They'll catch us and make it even worse."

"Then I'll come with you! We can go to the school together, I—"

He shakes his head. "You're only ten. You have to be thirteen to go there, which I will be by December. Anyway, it's a boys-only school, Leo."

She throws herself onto the bed, thumping her fist into the pillow. "I can't bear it. Why does he have to do this? I'll die here without you."

"You won't. It will be okay," he says. He doesn't sound convinced.

"It's easy for you to say that — you'll be away."

"I'll be back in the holidays. You get long holidays at boarding school. And anyway, you're almost eleven now, soon you'll be at big school. You'll have new friends. You won't need me so much."

"You know that's not true." She looks at him, her eyes brimming. No friend could possibly take his place, ever.

He looks away, at the floor, starts to say something. A flash of pain passes over his face, like a tiny flinch.

"What?" she says.

"It's his old school, in South Africa. I'm going to school in South Africa."

* * *

She creeps downstairs in the shadows, peeping into the sitting room and the kitchen, just in case. No lights are on, the house damp with darkness. She tiptoes to her father's study, searching by the dim moonlight. On a low shelf, covered in dust, she finds an atlas of the world. Quietly she removes it and carries it upstairs.

At first, she stares at the map in confusion, the dim light of her torch casting an orange glow across the page. She thought he was going to the southern part of Africa. Now she realises it's a country called 'South Africa', flanked by others with strange names, all of them in a huge place called 'Africa.' School hasn't taught her much about the rest of the world, or maybe she just hasn't listened. She has a hazy memory of a project about African children, living in mud huts with thatched roofs, but it's all very vague. Geography is one of the most boring subjects at her school.

With a ruler she measures Great Britain, then compares it with the size of South Africa. It doesn't help, it just frightens her more, to see the size of it, the massive gap between the two countries. She's never been further than the edge of her home town, and that seems like a huge distance to her. What if something horrible happens to him? How will they know? Africa seems like a frightening, threatening place, with dangerous animals lurking round every corner. Something bad could so easily happen.

A sense of foreboding slides over her, like a snake silently tracking its prey.

* * *

She wakes off-balance, cross with everything, her pillow still damp with the night's tears. How can anything be right, when Ricky's leaving?

"The summer's ruined," she says, as they sit in the sun on the slope that looks onto the canal. She grabs clumps of grass from beside her, throwing them down towards the murky water. "He's done this on purpose, to stop us being happy."

"No, it's not ruined." Ricky leans back on the dry grass and props himself on one elbow. "It doesn't need to be, anyway. We've still got weeks before you go back to school, and it's months before I go."

He's right, of course. Leonora holds onto that thought, the summer holidays stretching into the distant future. She can barely imagine going back to school, it's so far away. And Ricky won't be leaving until December, which is for ever away. But he will still be going, and she can hardly bear to think about it. When she does, she gets a nasty feeling in her tummy and she can't concentrate. She shakes her head, to stop the thinking.

"It's weird, starting school in January," she says. "Why do they do that?"

He shrugs. "I suppose because, in South Africa, they have summer in our winter. So the long holiday is at Christmas, when it's hot. It's confusing."

A small white boat chugs past, children trailing their hands in the water, orange life jackets puffed up against their necks. Leonora watches, squinting against the sun. "What will you do until then, while I'm at school?"

"Dad's got them sending me some prep work. I'll be a bit behind in some subjects, but otherwise it's okay. There's reading and stuff to do."

"I still don't get why he's doing it." The patch of grass destroyed, she hugs her knees. "We never seem to have any money. Why is he sending you to a posh school?"

"You know why. He went there, and he thinks it'll be good for me, set me up for a good career. Anyway, let's not talk about it anymore, it's boring." He stands up, holding his hand out for Leonora. His legs are pale and thin beneath the frayed edges of his shorts. "I want to enjoy the summer holidays, like I said, and not think about it till it happens. Let's go and get an ice cream — I've got the money from my paper round. Up!"

She gazes up at him. He's always been her best friend, always there for her, backing her up, showing her the way. They've shared their toys, read the same books, played the same games. The fact that he's a boy and she's a girl has hardly occurred to her. It never seemed to matter.

Until now. It's not just that he's being sent away. Realising that she will be treated differently is a shock. She isn't worth a good education: that's the message she's getting — and it's hard to understand, especially when her results are better than her brother's.

She sighs, grabbing at his hand, and he waves it around, teasing her.

"You always do that," she says, frowning. "It's not funny anymore."

"Yes, it is," he cries, running down to the towpath. "Come on, ice cream!"

CHAPTER TWO

Leonora

The strange feeling in her tummy when she thinks about Ricky leaving has turned into a proper ache. It keeps her awake at night. Sometimes, when she imagines what it will be like when he's gone, she can hardly breathe. At school, she's tired and listless. She could stay home, get a note from her mum, but her dad would be angry. He wants Ricky to study.

Every day after school she hurries home, running upstairs to find him. He might be in his room or hers — they never shut each other out — and she dumps her bag on the nearest surface, grabbing the books she needs for her homework. He helps if he can, but usually she races through it without pausing. While the evenings are light, they walk to the canal, or into the town, making up games or just sitting, watching, comfortable in each other's company.

As the weeks go by, the house seems to hold its breath, the air stagnant with expectation. While Ricky tries to avoid the subject, his dad can't stop talking about it: how lucky he is to be going to South Africa, what a great time he'll have, how marvellous the school is. Leonora can hardly bear to listen, though she's expected to be pleased and excited for

9

her brother. Once their dad got angry with both of them for their lack of enthusiasm. Now they nod and smile, and repeat what he says. When their dad flies into a temper, it's not good for any of them.

One day in November, before he's home from work, Leonora finds her mum in the kitchen, doing the laundry. She turns away, but not before Leonora sees the redness round her eyes, the damp tissue in her hand.

"What's the matter, Mum?" Her mum has been so quiet recently. She doesn't smile much anymore.

"I'm just being silly, Leonora, it's fine," she says, with a watery smile.

Leonora notices a pile of Ricky's school shirts folded on the table. "Are you sad that Ricky's going away?"

"I'm going to miss him. But it's a great place, I'm sure he'll love it. All mums have to say goodbye to their children in the end."

A great bubble of emotion bursts in Leonora's chest. "Yes, but not when they're so young!" she cries, tears gathering. "Why does he have to go so far away, Mum?" She sinks into a chair as great, rasping sobs wrack her body, all the fear and pain of the last few months gushing from her.

Her mum puts an arm around her shoulders, pulling her close. "Listen, love, I know it's hard for you. But it's not that simple . . ."

Leonora stiffens, pushing her away.

"Yes, it is, Mum! He could go to some posh school here, in England, if he has to — or stay at home, go to the local school, where everyone goes, where I'm going. What's wrong with that?"

"Leo . . ."

"No! It's not right, it's so unfair! You don't understand. I hate Dad, I hate him!"

She turns and runs to her room, taking the stairs two at a time. She slams the door with all her might — purple flashes sparking and dazzling — picks up a pile of books and hurls it to the floor. They land with a huge grey-green thud, some flying open, pages bent and crushed beneath their weight. She doesn't care.

She'll never understand why they've done this, never.

* * *

Tomorrow, he's leaving, and there's absolutely nothing she can do about it.

Ricky meets her after school, and they walk the short distance home in the gloom of December, the cold, damp air seeping into Leonora's clothes like the dread that's entered her heart.

"Leo?" He glances sideways at her. "You okay?"

He always knows her moods. Right now she has nothing to say that she hasn't said before. *Don't go, please stay, don't forget me, what will I do, who will I talk to, how can I live without you here?*

She nods, avoiding his eyes. Letting him see her pain will only make things worse for him. He already feels bad, desperate to know everything will work out.

But it won't, and she can't lie to him. She bites her lip to keep it from quivering.

"Listen, Leo," he says. "I know I've said this before, but you will be okay, you know. You're strong, and clever, and you'll get new friends."

I don't want new friends. All I want is for my brother to stay at home.

She swallows the hard lump that's appeared in her throat. "I know. You're right."

"There you are — I am right, I always am." He grins at her, punching her on the arm.

"Ow. No you're not — I am." She grins back, pulling at his jacket. "Come on, let's have a huge chocolate milkshake at Burton's. Last one for a while! It's on you."

"Okay, but we'll have to share, I don't have much money." He flings an arm around her neck and they walk lopsidedly along the pavement towards the café. He's only an inch or so taller than her, so it's uncomfortable but she doesn't mind.

"Hey," she says. "You'd better not grow too much without me. I won't be able to borrow your sweatshirts anymore."

"You're welcome to the ones I leave behind," he says, laughing. "They're all in holes, anyway. Borrow away."

"I will — and your books? You can't take them, they're too heavy."

"Borrow what you want, I won't know. But make sure it's all there when I get back, eh?"

My kind, sweet soulmate brother. What will I do without you?

* * *

Their father is driving Ricky to the airport. She's not allowed to go with them. The horrible cramps in her tummy are worse today. Something's telling her she'll never see him again, and she's frozen with fear.

She crouches at the bottom of the stairs, biting her lip until it bleeds. She can taste the sweet warm blood on her tongue.

He steps forward to give her a hug, but she can't look at him, her body rigid with pain, every breath an effort.

Their father calls from the front gate. "Come on, Richard. We need to go."

He turns to their mother for a kiss. She holds him tight, a tear escaping from her closed eyes. He gently pulls himself away and with a last "Bye, Mum, bye, Leo," he's gone. The door closes behind him with a grey-blue click of finality. Leonora stares at it for a moment, disbelieving, then dashes forward, wrestling it open with shaking fingers.

"Ricky! Wait — wait." As he turns, she grabs his arm and whispers: "Write. Write to me. You will, won't you? I can't bear it . . ." He nods, squeezing her hand for a long, precious moment before he climbs into the passenger seat. One impatient rev of the engine and the car moves off, its square shape receding until finally it turns a corner and disappears.

Leonora stands in the street, desolate. Already the emptiness is gathering around her, seeping into her bones, making her shiver. It swirls around the street, follows her slow footsteps back into the house. Upstairs, it takes up residence in Ricky's room, in Leonora's bedroom, in the bathroom, in the empty space for his toothbrush.

She runs to her room and throws herself onto the bed, heaving great sobs into the pillow, pummelling the mattress with balled fists. He's gone — the person she loves and trusts most in the whole world is gone. To the other side of the world, to South Africa. It could be the moon as far as she's concerned.

CHAPTER THREE

Leonora

"I want to write to Ricky. I need his address."

Her father's head jerks up at the sound of her voice, his eyes boring into her. He sits at his desk, reading a newspaper, his glasses perched low on his nose. His look says: go away, little girl, I'm busy.

He says: "You can't. Contact isn't allowed for the first three weeks. Anyway, you should let him be. He's starting a new life. He doesn't need you bothering him." He shakes his newspaper pointedly, so it crackles in a shower of sea-green sprinkles. He turns back to it, the lower half of his face hidden.

She stays in the doorway, refusing to be dismissed, though her stomach churns, her hands sweating. "I want to write to him anyway. They can keep the letter until he's allowed. I need his address."

"What for? He won't be interested in your girly stuff. You're not good for each other, I told you. Go and — do something. Play, whatever."

She stands and waits, tense, feeling her jaw stiffen. A few moments pass. When he looks up again, she sees that look on his face. "Are you still there? Go away, I said. I'm busy." He waves a hand. "Get out!" There's a dangerous edge to his voice.

She steps forward, one faltering step into his study, almost as far as the rug that covers the centre of the floor. "I need the address of the school," she says, her voice shaking.

In one swift movement, startling her, he's out of his chair and around the desk. Fury oozes from every pore in his face. Despite her determination, she flinches, stepping back, one hand feeling for the safety of the door jamb. He looms over her.

"Leonora! What did I just say? Why must you always argue with me? You heard me — get out of here!" He grabs her shoulder and, forcing her around, pushes her roughly through the door and into the hall. "And don't let me hear another word from you about your brother." The door slams behind her, rattling the delicate stained-glass window in the front door with the force of his anger. A yellowish mist rises, then fades.

She stands for a moment, hesitating, looking at the closed door. She walks slowly down the hall to the kitchen where her mother stands, worry drawing deep lines on her forehead. "Why must you bother him?" she says, ushering Leonora in with fluttering hands. "You know you shouldn't go into his study — he hates that. Now you've made him angry. What's got into you?" Her voice breaks, distress in every feature of her face.

"I want to write to Ricky. Dad won't give me the address."

"I'm sorry, Leo. We need to give him a chance to get used to the place, so he doesn't feel homesick." She sighs, her voice softening. "All the boarding schools do the same. I miss him too. We just have to be patient."

She hates it when her mum says that. Patient is something she doesn't want to be.

"If you miss him, why did you let him go? Why did you send him so far away?"

Her mum sighs. A lock of hair escapes from the clip she uses to hold it in place in a twist at the back. Part of it is grey, almost white. "Your father set his heart on it, and you know what he's like."

"I have to write to him, Mum. Will you give me the address?"

"Not if your father's said no."

"So what if he said no? You're a person, aren't you? Do you always have to do what he says?" She wants to scream at her mother, but her father might hear. She knows what would happen then.

Her mother turns away, busying herself with the cutlery drawer. "So he said no and I can't go against it."

"You agree with him, then?" She already knows what the answer will be.

"You know very well I do." Her mother always agrees with her father.

"But Ricky's all alone, in a strange place — such a long way away, with nobody he knows. All I want to do is write him a letter, so he gets something from home — so he knows at least one of us cares about him!"

Her mother glances at the open door to the hallway. She whispers: "Don't let your father hear you. You'd best go to your room. Go on, Leo."

Leonora glares at her mother and runs.

* * *

She turns the music up loud, not so loud as to annoy her dad, but loud enough to fill her bedroom. Lying on the bed, staring at the flickering colours on the walls, she feels the music through her body, calming her, the anger slowly seeping away. She's still determined to write to him, though. He's going to need her letters, with all the strange things that must be happening to him: new country, new school, new friends. Sleeping in a dormitory with other boys. What if he doesn't make any friends, what if he's sad and homesick? Her letters will be even more important then.

After a few minutes she rises, taking an exercise book from her school bag. She'll get the letter ready, and work on the address later.

Thursday, January 31st, 1988

Dear Ricky,

It's horrible without you. I knew it would be. I hope it's better for you there. Are there lots of animals? I looked up South Africa on the map and in the Encyclopaedia at school. It's such a long way. Are there giraffes? And lions? What are the other boys like?

I don't know how I'm going to get this letter to you. They won't give me your address. I don't know why — you're my brother, after all. It's like they're jealous or something. Anyway I'm going to find it somehow, even if I have to raid his study. He'll probably kill me, so I might be dead by the time you get this. Ha ha.

I miss you. Dad is so grumpy with Mum and me, worse than before. He says I'm going to St Peter's secondary mod. It's where all the bad kids go. And the stupid ones. He must want me to fail, that's all I can say. Well I'm not going to. I'll show him he's wrong.

Sometimes I go down to the canal to read, like we did in the summer. There are lots of boats there now. It looks pretty but the people are quite scary, with dreadlocks and weird coats and stuff, but there's a man who plays guitar and sings, and the other day a woman started to talk to me and she was really nice. She said I could have a look inside the boat. I said no, I thought I'd better not, but I might change my mind. I might ask Kelly to come too.

Please write, as soon as they let you. I'll look out for the postman every day.

Kisses, (ugh)
Your sister Leo x

CHAPTER FOUR

Leonora

Leonora was six when she realised she was different.

Learning to read was easy. At school there were shelves stacked high with picture books, starter books for little children and more difficult ones for the better readers. The children were encouraged to borrow up to five at a time so their parents could read to them at bedtime. Leonora took five almost every day. But she didn't need to be read to.

She drank in the words on the page, thirsty for more, always seeking greater stories. Stories of adventure, fairies, monsters, animals who spoke. Happy families. Her imagination leaped with pictures and letters and colours and sounds, the words drifting through her mind as she fell asleep. At bedtime she'd race to get ready for bed, then once her mum put out the light, she'd pull her battered torch from beneath the mattress and read until her eyelids drooped. When the batteries ran out, she would raid the kitchen drawer for new ones and if there were none, she'd rummage around for spare pennies in the bottom of her mum's bag or her coat pocket. She would save them until she had enough. Luckily they passed the corner shop on the way home from school, and since their mum stopped walking them, they'd stopped by regularly.

Ricky. R is orange. His name is orange — a lovely rich colour, Leonora's favourite.

Colour is an important part of her life, a part she keeps close to her. Not many people know.

When the door closed behind Ricky as he left for South Africa, the click was a soft grey-blue.

She remembers sitting at the kitchen table with her spelling homework, her mother at the sink, bubbles up to the wrists of her yellow rubber gloves. Leonora was reading out the words on the list, enunciating them carefully.

"Giraffe, Mummy," she said. "Green."

Giraffes were her favourite animal. She loved their long curving necks, their huge eyes fringed with soft black lashes.

"Giraffes aren't green, Leonora, you know that," her mother said without turning from the washing-up. "Giraffes are brown, mostly, and cream. Grass is green."

"No, Mummy, giraffes aren't green but the G is green."

"Oh I see," her mother said. "G is for green, that's right." But she didn't see, because she was still at the sink, and anyway she didn't understand.

"Not G is for green," Leonora said. "G is green. And A is red." She pressed her pencil hard on the page as she wrote her name at the top of the sheet. "And L for Leonora is blue."

Her mum turned with a sigh, the washing-up finished, the plates dripping silently on the draining board. She removed the rubber gloves with a snap, causing pink swirls to float into the air around her. They faded slowly as she peered over Leonora's shoulder. "What do you mean, Leonora? They're all in black pen."

"I know. But I have colours for them."

"All right, darling." Her mother shrugged and turned away. But after that Leonora began to realise that it wasn't just her mum. Other people didn't see the colours she saw.

One day, as they sat playing in Ricky's bedroom, she asked what colour he thought letters were. He looked at her strangely and said: "Well it depends what colour crayon you're using. If it's ink, usually black, or blue. Black, in books."

This was frustrating — he didn't understand. "No, not the writing, the letter," she said, knowing she wasn't saying it right. "L for Leonora is always blue, and you're orange, for R. For Ricky. I like orange. And your middle name is pink. O for Oliver is pink. I don't like it so much as orange."

"Do you have colours for all the letters then, Leo?"

"Most of them."

"Does it help you remember them?"

"Yes, but I—" This wasn't what she meant. She tried a different tack. "When Daddy climbs the stairs, it's brown."

But Ricky had already lost interest, absorbed in a silent battle of plastic soldiers.

* * *

She knew instinctively that she couldn't tell her father. There were too many times when she'd said things he'd laughed at, not kindly. If he thought she was imagining things, his words dropped like stones from the sky onto her head.

One evening at suppertime, before she became wary and stopped talking to him entirely, she tried to describe to him what she saw in her bedroom at night — how the shapes she saw when the light had just been switched off would persist around the ceiling as she watched, fascinated. Only she didn't have the right words.

"There are beams," she said. "On the ceiling. I watch them when the light goes off."

"Beams?" he echoed, scoffing. "What beams?"

"I — I don't know. I thought they were called beams . . ." Already she felt beaten down, ridiculed. She glanced at her mum, who gave her a tiny shake of the head, then looked away.

"There are lots of kinds of beams. What kind of beams are you talking about? Wooden? Satellite?"

Her head drooped in shame. She had no idea what he was talking about. What was a satellite?

"Come on, Leonora, answer me — what beams?"

Wishing she'd never started this, she stuttered and mumbled: "I . . . maybe . . . I don't know." A tear threatened to fall from her lowered eyes. She willed it to stay put, so as not to make him angry.

"Light, Leonora! That's what you mean, isn't it? Beams of light!" The exasperated expression on his face turned to contempt as the tear broke free. "Oh, that's right, go on, cry. That's all you're good for, Leonora. In future, don't speak unless you know what you want to say. Is that understood?"

She nodded, unable to stem the flow of miserable tears.

"Is that understood? Yes or no?" His voice was low and threatening.

"Yes," she mumbled, her voice hoarse against the lump in her throat.

He stood suddenly, the chair behind him crashing against the wall, and with a snort he marched from the room, throwing his napkin on the floor. Leonora, cowed and shamed, flinched at every sound.

That was the last time she tried to tell him anything.

CHAPTER FIVE

Leonora

"What's up?" Kelly plumps herself down at the desk next to Leonora with a sigh, hefting a bursting satchel onto the surface. She catches an exercise book that threatens to escape and rummages in the bag, slamming textbooks down on the scratched desktop. The rummaging noise has a greenish tint, with white flashes, the slamming a scarlet glow.

"What?" Leonora drags herself into the present. The room was empty when she arrived and she's been cradling her head in her arms, thinking. When she thinks too much about Ricky not being at home she almost brings herself to tears, so she imagines herself there in South Africa with him, travelling around looking at the animals. Watching the giraffes as they browse. Sitting on elephants, playing with monkeys. It's a lovely daydream. But she has to avoid thinking about the lions and the buffalo, because they're dangerous and she gets upset again.

"Have you had a letter yet?"

Kelly is Leonora's best friend. She's probably her only friend — all the others are too stupid or stand-offish to be interested in the girl who likes to read and go to the library.

They even tried to bully her. That didn't work — Leonora is far too clever for them. She winds them into knots with her sharp tongue. They keep their distance. She keeps her eye on them.

"They won't let him write for at least three weeks. That's what Dad says, anyway."

"Why? That sounds like a stupid rule."

"Dad won't give me the address of the school. I've asked and he said no. So did Mum."

"That is weird." Kelly lets her satchel drop to the floor with a pale pink thump. "Anyway, I know how you can get the address."

Leonora looks sideways, wary of her friend's enthusiasm. "Really, how?"

"The teachers here know. They have books with all the schools in, even the abroad ones. I've seen them in the secretaries' office."

How could she not have thought of that? "Kelly — you're a star. Brilliant. But who can I ask? I can't ask Miss Lambrick, she'd only tell my parents." Miss Lambrick is the headmistress. Stern and old, with gnarled, knobbly feet stuffed into misshapen old-lady shoes. Leonora hates her feet, but she can't help looking at them with fascinated horror. She hopes she never gets feet like that.

"Ask Miss Stannard. She likes you because you're clever. And you smarm up to her."

Leonora flicks her pen at Kelly's hand. Kelly whips it away, laughing.

"I don't smarm up to her. It's just that everyone else ignores her. I think she's nice."

Miss Stannard is their class teacher. She's young, and kind, and the kids play her up badly. When she enters the room for the register, the blackboard is always covered in swear words, her desk messed up. She ignores it but Leonora can tell she's miserable. Miss Stannard will help, if she can.

* * *

23

"Your brother's school? Can't you get that from your parents?" Miss Stannard flashes her a smile, as if Leonora is joking.

"Well, yes, but—" Leonora doesn't want any questions. "I've forgotten the name and address and I want to send him a card — it's . . . it's his birthday soon and if I don't do it today I'll miss it, and he'll be upset. His school's in South Africa, so the post takes ages."

The lie falls easily from her mouth, sweet as honey. She doesn't like lying to Miss Stannard, but teachers are grown-ups, after all, and they stick together.

"Oh, yes, so he is. It's unusual, to send a child so far away. I expect you miss him."

Leonora nods, making her face look sad.

"I'll have a look in break time and see if I can get you the details."

"Thank you so much, Miss. So I can send it today?" She holds her breath.

"All right, Leonora. I'll have a look at last year's leavers' list, it'll be on there. Ask me after break, or at lunchtime. I'm on duty in the playground today."

She can hardly believe it's this easy. It may not be, still. If Miss Stannard asks Miss Lambrick, she might be told not to give her the address. Then Leonora will really be stuck — back to square one, and quite possibly in trouble. But she can't risk asking Miss Stannard not to mention it. That would be downright suspicious. She crosses her fingers behind her back.

"Thank you, Miss."

After lunch, Miss Stannard passes Leonora a note. It's the address of Ricky's school. Hardly able to believe her luck, Leonora draws a picture of a canal boat for Miss Stannard, who is delighted.

The letter's posted, the stamps on the top right corner bought with money taken from her mum's purse. There's no such thing as pocket money in their house. When she needs to buy something, she has to find a way. Leonora knows that other children get pocket money — granted, not many at her school get very much — but she's in the minority. She gets nothing at all.

When she asked about pocket money, a couple of years ago, having found that other children could buy their own sweets and books and even toys, her father said: "What do you need pocket money for? Don't you have everything you need — a roof over your head, food on the table? You're not wasting my hard-earned money on sweets and rubbish plastic toys."

And that was that.

She wonders how long the letter will take to get there, where it is right now. It's been a few hours since she took it to the postbox at the end of the road, extracted it from her school bag and placed it carefully in the rectangular hole, holding it for a moment over the void beneath and listening as it landed with a small pink ruffle onto the letters within. Perhaps it's in a sack, on a train, right now, thundering its way to — where? She knows it goes on a plane, because she stole the envelope from her father's desk, and it said 'Air mail' at the top. It took her a while to work out what that meant, imagining it fluttering, like a butterfly, high into the sky. Then she asked Miss Stannard and learned, to her surprise, that letters get put on planes to be sent abroad.

Perhaps it goes to London Airport first, and on from there. She likes the idea it's safely on a plane, like the ones that she sometimes sees overhead. Tiny silver arrows drawn across the sky, with their mustard-yellow rumbling sounds, homing in on their target.

She lies across her bed with her feet resting high on the bedroom wall, her head hanging over the edge. She imagines the letter landing at the other end, being loaded in its sack from the plane into a mail van (red, of course, because that's what they always are) and being driven off through the forests, past lions with their blackest roars and wildebeest running and all the other creatures she's seen in the South African wildlife book she borrowed from the library. She

25

worries that it might not make it to Ricky's school, what with all the things that might happen to it on such a long journey.

She grinds her teeth and crosses her fingers. She misses Ricky so badly, her stomach hurts. A new problem occurs to her. What if he writes back and her parents intercept the letter? Her dad will be angry. He'll probably destroy it without telling her, then punish her for defying him. She'll have to find a way to get the post before he does.

She bites her lip until it bleeds.

CHAPTER SIX

Leonora

Since Ricky left, even the cherry blossom hurts. Its blowsy beauty and obscene exuberance sting and tear at her. In her mind's eye, she turns it all brown, seizing each perfect ball of blossom, forcing dark poison into every delicate petal until the pavement below turns the colour of wet earth.

With every step she thumps her shoe onto the delicate confetti and grinds it with purpose until it tears and crumples. A woman passes her, looks with puzzlement at the destruction. Leonora swivels her eyes away, hides behind her hair.

It's six weeks since he left and there's still no sign of a letter from him. She counts the days on the calendar hanging in her room. Each day he's gone she marks with a cross, in black, with a big felt-tip pen. He's not coming back at Easter — their father won't allow it. He says he can't afford the plane ticket.

When he told her, Leonora screamed: "Why? Why did you send him there, then?" and he whacked her around the face, hard. It didn't hurt as much as knowing Ricky won't be home. Disappointment settled on her shoulders like a goblin, taunting her, never leaving her alone.

Her mum bathed her smarting cheek with cold water and told her to lie down with the flannel over the bruising. "You mustn't be so impetuous, Leonora," she said. "You know he has a temper, and he hates you answering him back. Try to hold your tongue, it will be better for us all."

Her brain hurt for days afterwards and her left eye turned black and purple. She didn't even try to hide it. She scraped her hair back from her face to show it off better, to make him pay. She held her chin high. The bullies saw it and left her alone.

When Miss Stannard asked her what happened, she told her she'd been hit in the eye with a tennis ball. Miss Stannard gave her a piercing look, as if she didn't quite believe her, but Leonora held her gaze and eventually the teacher sighed and let her go.

* * *

It takes her a while to work out the postman's route and his timetable. He usually gets to their house before she leaves for school, but not always. That's what she's scared of. She can wait round the corner for him, but if he doesn't appear in time she'll be late for school. Or miss him altogether — and she can't afford to do that.

Luckily for her, he's friendly. In the week or so after she posts the letter, she hangs around on the corner, out of sight of her house. When she spots him, she waits to see where he goes and in what order he does the houses on each side of the street. On other days she starts a bit further away so she can see where he comes from. He walks fast, rummaging in his bag every so often for the next handful of letters, sorting them in his hands as he goes.

One day, he almost trips over her feet as she leans on the low brick wall of the house around the corner. "Sorry," he says, as she retracts her feet hurriedly. "Didn't see you there. Did I tread on your toe? Clumsy oaf, I am."

She shakes her head, wanting badly to ask him to help her, but unable to frame the words with her lips. As he walks away, she stares after him in despair, knowing she should have said something, furious at herself. She forces herself to follow, unsure what she's doing but determined not to miss her chance. She's waiting at the gate of the next house as he leaves the path.

"You again?" he says, smiling. "Want me to tread on the other toes this time? Glutton for punishment, I'd say!"

"No, I—" she stammers, confused.

"Come on, spit it out, I won't bite you. But if I don't get this round done on time, I'll be in dead trouble." His face is round and kind, his cheeks ruddy from the cold air. His upper teeth stick out a little, giving him a comical look when he smiles.

She takes a deep breath. "Sorry. I'm hoping . . . I'm waiting for a letter from my brother."

"Gone away, has he? Well I'm sure he'll write soon. I'll be sure to deliver it when it gets here. What address is it?"

"No, it's not that." She takes a deep breath, willing him to be on her side. "My parents don't want us to write."

"Ah." He looks at her closely, his eyes narrowed. She notices the fan of lines around them, the blue of his irises.

"Why on earth not?" he says, then draws back, his face softening. "Never mind. I get it, you want me to look out for your letter? Not put it through the letterbox?"

She lets go of her breath in a rush. "Oh, yes please."

"What's your name, then? And the address?"

"I'm Leonora. Leonora Bates. 12, Wells Street."

"I know it," he says, with a wink. "Don't worry, I'll look out for your letter. I won't post it through the door, I'll keep it in my pocket until I see you."

* * *

She writes to him every day, hiding the letters in her school bag, using lined paper from her exercise books because she daren't steal any more from her father's desk. The money for stamps is easy — her mother never seems to notice.

Sometimes when Leonora returns from school, she can smell a strange tang on her mother's breath.

The postman smiles and says: "There's a letter from South Africa, but it's addressed to your parents. Perhaps there's a note to you inside?" He shows her the envelope. The stamp has a picture of an elephant's head, white tusks shining. The writing is definitely Ricky's. "Shall I give it to you, and you can pass it on to your mum and dad?"

"Okay," she says. Her hand shakes slightly as she stuffs the letter into her school bag. "Thank you."

"Don't go opening it and getting into trouble, now," he says, with a wink.

All day it sits in her school bag, like a hot coal burning a hole in the bottom. It's sealed tightly, the paper flimsy, and she can't risk tearing it. In the toilets she holds it up to the light and tries to see through, but she can only see blank paper. It must be the back of the page. She feels the thickness, looking for a sign — any sign that there's a hidden letter for her. But it refuses to reveal its secrets.

At break time she can't resist showing it to Kelly. "I really want to open it," she says. "But I daren't risk it — my dad will go ballistic if he finds out. What shall I do?"

"Well you could try steaming it over a kettle. I've never done it but I think you can do it and seal it up again so it doesn't show. You probably need to practise first on another envelope." This all sounds too long and complicated to Leonora. And far too risky to do at home.

When she gets back, she takes it straight to her mother, who is dozing in front of the TV. Leonora touches her shoulder, careful not to startle her. "Mum. Mum, look — there's a letter from Ricky. Can we open it now, please? I want to see if there's a letter for me. Mum!"

Her mother's eyelids, puffy with sleep, flutter and open. She rolls her head to squint at Leonora and makes a feeble effort to smile. "Oh Leonora, it's you. What time is it?"

"It's four thirty, Mum. Look — open it! It's from Ricky . . ."

Her mum raises herself onto an elbow, peering at the envelope. "That's good, love." She shakes her head, smooths her rumpled hair. Her fingers tremble a little. "But we can't open it before your father gets home. He opens all the post."

"But Mum . . ."

Taking the letter from Leonora's hand, her mum pulls herself to her feet, sliding them into a pair of shabby slippers. She stuffs the envelope into her apron pocket. "I said no, Leonora. I don't want any trouble. I'm going to get supper started."

The pale cream shuffle of her feet in the hallway fades as tears of frustration start in Leonora's eyes.

As soon as he's home, her dad takes the letter without comment and sends her to her room. It's opened without her, and try as she might to listen in, all she can hear from her vantage point on the stairs is a soft murmuring in the kitchen.

She longs to know more about the school. She has no idea what the school looks like: whether it's in a town, or out in the bush, standing alone in isolated splendour. Perhaps it's so remote he can't smuggle his letters out, or maybe there are no postboxes. Maybe the teachers are cruel, perhaps he's being bullied. Starved of his presence, she has to imagine the place he is in, the people he meets, his thoughts and feelings. Without that picture, he might fade away, and that would be terrifying.

Though she pleads and cajoles, her mother won't discuss the letter — she won't even say if there was a message for Leonora. "Your father says no, and what he says goes, as you well know. I don't want to hear any more about it."

Leonora runs to her room and screams into her pillow.

The wondering and the waiting are so hard. She spends hours in her room, alone, reading, doing her homework, listening to the radio, daydreaming. When she can, she eavesdrops on her parents' conversations. One evening, hearing Ricky's name, she creeps onto the stairs and leans her head on the banister to listen as they eat their supper.

"I'm not happy with his report. What are they doing with him? They're supposed to be teaching him, not pandering to him. It's not good enough." Her father's voice is hard with anger.

She can hear her mother moving about the kitchen, the lemon-yellow clatter of pans and crockery.

"Perhaps he just needs time to settle. If it's a good school, they'll help him out." Leonora can imagine her anxious face as she tries to mollify her husband. She's too scared even to defend her children when his anger's rising.

"Of course it's a good school — the best! He's had plenty of time to settle. He's a lazy boy, they need to crack down on him. I'm going to have a word. We're paying enough money, for God's sake."

She hears the plates go down on the table with a beige thud, the purple scrape of the chair across the floor as her mother sits down. That'll be it, then, end of conversation.

She needs to see that report.

CHAPTER SEVEN

Leonora

His desk crouches in the centre of his study like a toad in mud. The house holds its breath, the air stuffy as she creeps across the carpet, her feet bare. It's taken a while to get here. She waited for what seemed like hours for her mother to disappear into their bedroom, then for her father's heavy purple tread on the staircase. Another hour and the reddish clouds of his snoring drifted into the shadows beyond her open bedroom door. It was safe to make her move.

She's extra careful not to be found out when she visits his study. He still doesn't lock the door or the desk. He underestimates her, thinks she wouldn't dare to enter. More fool him. When she goes, she picks her moment, takes her time. She replaces everything, double-checks all is in place before she leaves. Not so much as a hair on the seat, on the smooth leather desktop.

She knows where he keeps his papers, prays that the drawer will open smoothly. Kneeling, she curls her fingers around the moulded curlicues of the metal handle. It resists. Her heart stops — she holds her breath. She can't afford for it to release with a crash. She keeps the pressure constant, it starts to move and she breathes out. A slight squeak and her body freezes again, her ears straining for movement on the stairs. But there's nothing new, the same blanket of silence draping heavily over the house.

When the drawer is fully open, it drops down an inch or so, but she's ready for that and lets it down gently. It's crammed with files, mostly thick beige manila folders, but one stands out. The name of the school is on the outside, in her father's spiky writing: Savoy School.

She eases it out, taking it to the window, where an orange glow from the street lights filters through. It's just enough to see what's in there, but anyway she's come prepared with her torch. The light is dimmed, the batteries about to expire, but that suits her well. It's enough for her to read the report on the top of the file.

March 1988
Term overview from the Headmaster
Richard Bates:
Unfortunately Richard has struggled to settle in at the school. In his first weeks he has had trouble making friends. He needs encouragement to sit with his peers at meals and to eat.

He is quiet in class and will only speak when specifically asked. However his work is handed in on time and it's clear that he's a bright boy with good intellectual ability. English is his strong subject and he seems to enjoy reading and writing creatively. In maths and the sciences he grasps the concepts well and keeps up with the class.

Richard is not a sportsman. When he arrived at the school he had little or no experience of team sports such as rugby and football, and although he made some efforts at the beginning, his hand-eye coordination is poor. He has experienced some difficulty with the other boys because of his lack of sporting ability. The Head of Sport has excused him from team sports for the rest of term as a result, though he is required to continue with gym work and athletics. He's also taken up shooting, one of our optional sports. It's hoped he will settle better at school over the coming months and we expect that once he begins to grow he will improve at team sports.

Richard has declined to join any extracurricular clubs or activities, preferring to read in his room, or to wander in the grounds (within the boundaries, of course). The staff have gone out of their way to encourage him to participate, without success to date. We will continue to urge him to join in with team activities and hope that he will come out of himself as he grows more used to the school.

We believe it's best for him to return home during the holidays, and urge his family to give him the love and support he needs to gain confidence and benefit from all this school has to offer.

Individual class reports follow.

* * *

"Mum?"

Her mother sits at the kitchen table with a mug of tea in her hands. It's late afternoon — the best time to talk to her, before she has to start cooking.

The radio blares an afternoon play. Leonora knows her mum's not listening, that it's just a habit she's got into. The mornings are for housework and shopping (a trip to the local corner shop). The afternoons are for rest and relaxation. In other words, for working her way up to cooking supper for her husband, which makes her anxious and on edge.

"Yes, what is it?" Her mother's eyes are reddened around the lids. She rarely bothers with makeup, and when she does, it's a smear of lipstick around her mouth. There seem to be very few occasions that warrant it.

"Is Ricky happy at school?" As soon as she's said it, she knows it was the wrong question.

Her mum's eyes flit around the room. "Of course he's happy. How could he not be? It's a wonderful school, all that space to run around, and the animals . . ." Her voice sounds false, the cheeriness of her words forced.

"What I mean is, how is he getting on? Has he made friends, what are the teachers like?"

Her mum looks at her now. Leonora sees the sadness in her eyes, belying the smile on her lips.

"Ricky's fine, you don't need to worry. You'll see when he gets home in December — he'll be a proper young man."

But Leonora doesn't want him to be a proper young man.

CHAPTER EIGHT

Leonora

Often, after school, she and Kelly walk along the canal, where the narrowboats linger. Though it's not yet winter, the afternoons are dusky and the boat people have hung lights across the roofs. A smell of wood burning hangs in the air. The girls walk slowly, making the journey home last as long as possible, avoiding doing their homework.

Not that Kelly is too bothered with it. She's bright, but like many of the other children, she doesn't care about school. Her family lives on the other side of town from Leonora's, in a small semi-detached house bursting with children and animals. Kelly is the oldest of six kids, and is used to looking after the little ones as well as two cats, a dog and the chickens that live in a coop in the back garden. Her parents are chaotic and loving. They are kind to Leonora, letting her stay for tea when she wants. Kelly's mum seems to understand and she doesn't ask awkward questions.

Kelly's father is the polar opposite of Leonora's own. He's called David, which means 'beloved.' She learned that in RE, when they were reading about David and Goliath. Her own father's name is Dennis, which means 'the god of wine', according to a book of baby names she stumbled across in the library. It doesn't suit him. She can't think of anyone less like a god.

When she first met Kelly's dad, he was playing with his two youngest children in the garden, a made-up game that seemed part-football, part-tag, part-charades. He ended up on his back, rolling around with two children sitting on his chest and stomach, laughing so much he couldn't speak while they tickled him, their squeals of pleasure a joyous cloud of yellow around the little squirming group.

Leonora had stood there open-mouthed, thinking there was a mistake, this couldn't be Kelly's father. He was too young, too smiley. And dads don't play like that with their kids. When he noticed her, he extracted himself with difficulty from his pinned position on the grass, stood up and grinned at her, hand outstretched.

"I'm David," he said, with a flash of purple. This flummoxed her even more. Fathers never used their first names with children, and they didn't shake hands with them either. But in her experience fathers never did any of the things she'd witnessed in the first two minutes of meeting Kelly's dad.

"You must be Leonora. Good to meet you. Lovely name — always loved Leonora." He almost sang her name, giving it a special turquoise-blue lilt she'd never heard before, and she adored him.

Through Kelly she gets glimpses of how it must feel to be part of a loving family. Sometimes this makes her sad, but sometimes it helps, knowing there's a better way.

Now Kelly and Leonora know the boat people better, the ones with dreadlocks and tattoos and floaty Indian clothes. In the summer the man sits on the roof of his boat strumming his guitar, his music and the sound of his voice floating on the breeze in a twinkling shower of gold and orange and silver. Once a woman waved to them and approached. There was a gold ring in her nose and her arms jangled with multicoloured bracelets as she moved. She had biscuits. They were delicious.

* * *

It's months before the first letter comes. But it explains it all. It arrives one day in the hand of Fred, her faithful postman. She's almost given up her daily vigil of waiting for him before school — some days she just can't face the disappointment — but this day, for some reason, she goes automatically to her normal waiting place and stands looking at her shoes, lost in thought. A shout at the end of the road alerts her. He's waving at her! A white envelope is clutched in his hand and his face is transformed by a brilliant, toothy smile. She rushes towards him and almost barrels into him in her excitement.

"Woah, steady on, girl! It's for you — from South Africa. At last, eh?" he says, laughing. He has practically broken into a run to get to her, despite his heavy bag.

"Thank you, thank you!" She almost hugs him in her joy. Her hand shakes with anticipation. The envelope feels thick and heavy, the stamp on the front brightly coloured, with a picture of an exotic flower. She would know his writing anywhere.

There's no time to read it before school. She places it in her bag and runs the rest of the way, happiness and expectation singing in her ears. All day she fidgets, urging the minute hand on the classroom clock to click onward, as if by sheer force of will she can make it move faster. Miss Stannard gives her a quizzical look, but says nothing. Leonora doesn't care. She hugs her secret close and longs for the moment she can be alone.

When the bell rings at the end of the day, she races for the gate, running all the way to the canal, not caring when her feet slip in the sticky mud of the towpath. There's a tree where she and Kelly sit on summer days when the weather's good, and they've carved out a couple of small steps beside it and placed flat stones there so that they won't get their skirts muddy.

She throws herself down and pulls out the letter, examining the thickness of the paper, the writing on the front, the colourful stamp, savouring the moment.

Dear Leo,

Thanks so much for all your letters. I guess you haven't seen any of mine, so I've invented a secret system to make sure you get them.

At the school, we have regular letter-writing time, when we have to write to our parents, but we can only send one letter at a time (they're quite strict here). At first I put a separate letter (sealed with glue) to you in the one to M and D, but I soon realised you hadn't got it.

I wasn't sure if the school would tell on me, so I waited for the holidays and got my friend Michael to post this from where he lives, near Durban. I don't have lots of friends here but I do get on with Michael. We both like books, and he's no good at rugby, like me. Rugby is important here, unfortunately for us!

It's school holidays now, though I'm not sure it is with you? Everything here is so different, I've almost forgotten how it works at home already. The first few weeks at school were weird. We sleep in dormitories with four or five other boys, and they make us go to bed early and get up very early. At first it was hard to sleep and I missed you badly. I got a bit sick, but Matron was very nice and I got better quite quickly. Now it's not so bad — I get on with the other boys most of the time. I think it would all have been much easier if I was sporty, but I'm not. Though I'm not too bad at shooting now — yes, with real guns, though we don't use live bullets and we shoot at a target. I've even got into the B team!

Everyone here has a nickname. Some people have a pretty bad time of it. Mine is Butts (a play on Bates ha ha — not). It could be worse. There's quite a lot of bullying, and we each get assigned to one of the older boys who bosses us about. Mine's not too bad, though he made me clean his toilet the other day when I forgot to bring him tea.

Lessons here are OK. Our English teacher, Mr Bassett (nickname Lickers — Liquorice — get it?), is quite nice and he lets me use the library when I want. At first I spent a lot of time there, but the best thing here is the outside — there's so much space, and all sorts of bugs and animals to look at. I'm beginning to learn about bush survival and medicinal plants, and the monkeys and antelope that roam around the grounds. There are lots of creepy-crawlies, which I'm not sure you'd like, but they're really interesting. The sun shines A LOT here, and it's warm most of the time. That bit I like.

*How are you? I hope school is OK. You're clever and strong —
more than me. I know you'll get those exams. It's good you have Kelly
and can go to hers sometimes. I hated leaving you. Is Mum OK? Dad
says I can come home this Christmas but not in between, as he can't
afford it. It seems such a long time. Are you still using the den in my
room? You can, if you want.*

*I have to go now. You can write to me at this address and my
friend will bring it in for me. Keep smiling, Leo. See you in December,*
Your best brother, Ricky x

She lies back, the letter clutched to her chest, gazing at
the spreading branches of the tree. Relief flows through her
into the damp grass beneath her body. She mouths his name
and an orange mist forms and hangs, glistening. He's okay
and he's still her brother who loves her.

CHAPTER NINE

Leonora

All day in class she sits by the window, staring up at the sky, watching as clouds form and reform over patches of perfect blue. Every so often a plane passes like a silver fish in a clear pond, and she imagines her brother getting closer every minute. She can barely wait for the end of the school day.

Her dad's going straight from work to the airport to get Ricky. The first person from the family to see him for a year — a whole year! — is the father who sent him away. She would have loved to go and meet him, but she had to go to school.

Anyway it would have meant being alone with her father in the car for a long time. That would have been almost unbearable. When she has to travel with him, she sits as far away as possible, staring out of the side window, holding on to the door handle. He doesn't bother to talk to her.

Her mum wasn't allowed to go to meet Ricky, either. She wanted to, but she was overruled, as usual. These days, her mum shrinks from any kind of confrontation, and whatever vitality she once had has trickled away. Leonora can hardly blame her. Her father is at best bad-tempered and silent, at worst violent and terrifying. If Leonora were her mum, she would take the children and leave. But her mum's too frightened of him. Perhaps before, she might have found the strength. Before he broke her.

When Leonora looks at her mum — really looks — she sees a shadow of the person she once knew. The once-smooth skin on her face is grey and lined, with a permanent puffiness around her eyes, while her slender body is properly thin, her dress hanging limp around her hips. When her husband is around, she hangs her head as she scuttles around the house, pandering to his demands, flinching at his carping.

* * *

Her dad is first through the door, his key scratching in the lock with a flurry of blue zigzags. Leonora sits high on the stairs, at the point where she can just see him coming through the door.

He carries Ricky's battered bag, which looks heavy. He drops it with a grunt and a flash of green in the hallway. There's a pause and there, at last, is Ricky. He closes the door carefully behind him. Behind his father's back, his eyes lift and he spots her. An orange glow hangs in the air around him as a slow smile creeps across his face. Ricky. Orange is for light, and happiness, and Ricky.

She smiles back, their eyes connecting in silent understanding. He looks the same, but different. Somehow she'd forgotten that he would grow. He's still very slight, but he's a couple of inches taller, and his hair, always thick and unruly with curls that won't be flattened, is darker and shorter around a face that has lengthened. His jaw is more defined, his eyes deeper, more knowing. She wonders if he's thinking the same about her.

"Come on, lad! Come on in and see your mother, tell us all about it! She's waiting to see you."

Ricky's shoulders lift in a barely perceptible shrug to Leonora as he follows his father to the kitchen. His eyes say it all. He's home and he's still her brother. There will be time to talk, to catch up, to be themselves again. Leonora turns and steps quietly back to her room.

When at last Ricky puts his head around her door, she bounds off the bed with joy, scattering school books and the contents of her pencil case in her wake. He stands there with a stupid grin on his face, enduring her squeals, while she hugs and bounces and bombards him with questions.

They close the door and put the music on to drown out their voices. They kick their shoes off, flopping onto the bed in the same poses as they've always taken, she at the top of the bed, he halfway down, his back against the wall. They grin at each other and there's a moment of awkwardness as they both start to speak at once, then they collapse with laughter at the sheer ridiculousness of it.

"There's too much to ask," Leonora says. "I'm bursting with questions, but I don't know which one to start with."

"There's way too much to tell." Ricky grimaces. "Some good, some bad. I can't say it's good to be home, but it's great to see you. You survived the first year, then . . ." It's a statement of fact, not a question.

"So did you," she says, eyeing him. "You look . . . different. Older."

"Thanks. You look . . . weird."

She aims a pillow at him, which he fends off with a raised arm and chucks back at her.

"Your letters were great," she says. "I still don't understand why Dad's so mean about us writing to each other."

"Nor me. Have you kept the letters?"

"In the den, in the tin box. I'm pretty sure they don't know about it. Mum never cleans back there — it's really dusty."

"He'd be angry if he found them."

"I don't care. He can't do anything about it now. Your plan is working!" She grins at him, her chin on her chest. He smiles back, reaching over to pull her toe.

"How has he been, really?"

44

"Oh, the same. Worse, if anything. I just try to keep out of his way. And Mum's . . . not good. Sometimes she has a drink in the afternoon, before I get home from school."

"What? What sort of drink?"

"Vodka, I think. It's not coloured, anyway. I've seen the bottle and I've smelled it on her. She puts it in her tea. She misses you a lot, Ricky. And he's horrible to her — she's scared of him."

"I wish—" Ricky's smooth forehead crumples into worry lines.

"What?"

"I wish I could get enough money that she could leave him. That we could leave him, now."

She grins and sits up. "Wouldn't that be great? Hey, wouldn't it be just wonderful if we could live in South Africa? With all the animals around us?"

"It would be the best thing . . . but it'll never happen. Mum won't do anything. And how would we get the money? We're still just children." Perhaps his voice is starting to change, or it could be frustration causing the catch in his throat.

Leaning forward, she whispers: "I'm going to get some money when I'm older."

"How?"

"I'm going to go to university. Then I'm going to get a really good job, and earn lots of money."

"University?" He sits up too, then. "What do you know about university?"

"Miss Stannard told me. She went to university, some-where, and studied English. You go when you finish school and you all live together, like boarding school but not nearly so strict — and you only get a few lessons a week. You don't even have to go to lessons if you don't want to. You're treated like a grown-up."

He smiles, then shakes his head. "But he'll never let you. He thinks women should be at home and jobs are for men."

"That's old-fashioned. It's not fair, either."

"I know. But it's hard to argue with him."

"Well, I'm cleverer than him and I'm going to show him." She feels the frown on her forehead, the muscles bunching so hard they give her a headache. "I *will* do it, whether he wants me to or not."

"But how?"

"I'll get the grades and go to university, like I said. My teachers will help me, even if he won't."

"You're so determined. I bet you will do it. I wish I was more like you." A shadow passes over her brother's eyes, a sadness that makes Leonora want to hug him. But she knows he's too old for that.

"But look at you — you're kind, and clever and you've got away already!" she says, scrambling onto her knees on the bedcover. "You don't need to come back — you could stay over there. Then I can come and join you! It's a perfect plan."

But her enthusiasm fails to lighten his mood. "I don't know. I suppose . . ."

"Well, what do you love doing? What would make you happy?"

"I don't want to come back here and work in some boring job in London, that's for sure. Actually—" He pauses and the shadow lifts from his face. "What I really like is being out in the bush, with the animals and the birds and the bugs, and the sun . . ."

"Well you could do that, couldn't you? You said you're studying it! Surely there are jobs doing — *that* — aren't there? It would be perfect!" She bounces on her knees and he laughs, so she tickles his feet and, for a while, the sadness is gone.

* * *

Their father is always on Ricky's back. He makes him do a paper round in the mornings, in the dark and the rain, the frost and the snow. He insists he studies for three hours every day, even though Ricky's teachers have told him to rest and enjoy himself.

But their dad can't be there the whole time and when he's at work, they shut themselves away in Ricky's bedroom and talk.

They play Leonora's tapes incessantly on an old cassette player they rescued from the dustbin. Michael Jackson, Duran Duran, Whitney Houston. The battered machine barely works, the tapes crackling and hissing, but she doesn't care. The music hums with colour, filling the room with velvety tones of burgundy, royal blue and purple. She tries again to describe what she sees to Ricky, who listens this time, asking what colours she sees when she hears different instruments, what colour attaches to which letter of the alphabet. He and Kelly are the only people she's talked to about her colours since her failure to explain it to her mum.

With Ricky at home, she feels safe.

When Ricky's not there, Leonora is in the habit of eating her supper early, before her father gets home. She helps herself to bread and whatever she can find to put on it — sometimes she buys food on the way home from school so that she doesn't have to bother her mother. She takes a sandwich up to her room. Five o'clock is a stressful time of day: her mum panics over the oven, checking the food obsessively, burning her hands, cursing. Once Leonora found her weeping quietly as she set the table.

She wants to help and at the same time she doesn't. With her in the kitchen her mum becomes more frantic, so Leonora retreats to her room anyway.

She does her best to avoid her father.

But when Ricky's home they all eat together as a family. He sits at one end of the table, their mother at the other, the two children facing each other on either side. Normally they eat on the bare Formica table top, to save the extra washing, but for these occasions her mum brings out a tablecloth. Meals are more formal when Ricky's home — it's like he's an honoured guest.

This is not the time for conversation and discussion, though. As far as Leonora can tell, their father uses mealtimes to berate and badger his family. Now Ricky is at a posh school, the fees making a dent in the family income, he bears the brunt.

"I didn't send you to that school to enjoy the scenery, you know," their dad says, repeating himself almost daily. His voice is loud and harsh. He uses it like a stick to beat them with.

Ricky keeps his gaze steadfastly on his food.

"You're there to work, to get the best advantages in life. Yes, to prepare yourself for a successful future — a career in the City, or politics, like the best of them. You may think you're too good to play rugby — oh, yes, I know you're not joining in—" Ricky looks up, startled. "It's not good enough. You need to get in there, learn the sport, stand up for yourself. All the best men play rugby. When you're finished with school you'll be glad of it. It will teach you to be a man, take you to the top of the tree."

They don't understand what he means by this, and they're not sure he knows himself, but the last thing they're going to do over the supper table is question him. Their job during the evening meal is to sit there quietly, nod when it's expected and get it over with. After each grim meal of greasy shepherd's pie or undercooked lamb chops, finished off with cheap ice cream or tinned fruit — never both together — they ask politely to leave the table, clear the plates and disappear upstairs again.

Sometimes Leonora is left to wash up on her own, Ricky being a boy and not expected to do menial tasks. Their dad strides off into his study, closing the door firmly behind him, and their mum fades into the sitting room, her daily ordeal over.

As soon as her dad has left the room, Leonora grits her teeth, muttering under her breath, calling him all the rude names she's heard used by the canal people, and some of her own.

CHAPTER TEN

Ricky

Now that we've found each other again, Leo, I can tell you my story. I've saved it up for you, kept it safe in the dark recesses of my mind, through all the years we've been apart. Nobody else has heard it.

There are some moments that might shock you, but I can see from your eyes, hear in your voice, that you're even stronger now you're grown. It's so good to see the woman you've become, the success you've made of your life, despite the misery of your childhood. My own journey to this point has been a rocky one, but I know you'll want to hear it, so here it is.

I never told you how bad it was at first.

How could I? I was the lucky one, I'd got away. The privileged kid, the one who was going to make his father proud, to get the best education he could afford. To attend his father's alma mater, to follow in his footsteps, to shine. Go to university, get a star job in the City — that was my destiny. Just because I was a boy.

You were the one who had to stay: the unfavoured child, the useless girl. You had to contend with a bad-tempered father, a helpless mother and a second-class education. Yet you were always the clever one, the one with hopes and ambitions. There was so much I couldn't tell you about my situation because I knew that yours was so much worse. And you deserved so much better.

My school, Savoy School, was in KwaZulu-Natal province, on the eastern side of South Africa. It was, on the outside at least, every boy's dream. Flanked by cricket pitches, rugby grounds and, incredibly, a safari park with giraffes, monkeys, impala and other wildlife, it would be hard to believe anyone would have a difficult life there.

As I was escorted up the magnificent front drive of the school, sitting in the back of a Land Rover with three other new boys in our crisp new uniforms, the sleeves too long, the collars too large on our skinny necks, I felt nothing but fear, sweat breaking out on the palms of my hands. The grandeur, the sheer luxury of the place, was intimidating and I knew immediately I would never truly belong here. The contrast with our home town was stark: like comparing silk with sacking, as far as I was concerned. But I had no choice — this was to be my new home.

A sixth-former whose name I forget shook our small, damp hands with a terrifying grip and showed us around the school, speaking in a flat, laconic voice in that odd South African accent that I could barely understand. I was too nervous to take much notice, which I soon regretted. I was overwhelmed by the scattered classrooms, the sheer size of the place. I had never seen anything like it in my life before.

The moment I walked into my dorm I knew it was going to be tough. There were already five boys in the room, lounging around, the contents of their bags spilling onto the beds, the floor. They all looked bigger than me, and met my meek "Hello" with blank stares as I shuffled towards the spare bed with my battered bag. The sixth-former introduced me: "This is Bates. Be nice," and he was gone.

"The name's Flick," a tall, fair-haired boy said, bashing me on the shoulder. "After my flick knife. So nobody messes with me, right?"

The other boys laughed uneasily and told me their names, which I forgot immediately. One or two of them shook hands. I'd never shaken hands with a boy before.

"Everyone has a nickname here, did they tell you?" Flick was smirking. "Hmm, Bates. You can be Butts, then. Suits you." He turned to the other boys, laughing. They fell about.

That was my introduction to the dorm.

The first weeks at the school went by in a daze. While most of the new boys found their way around easily enough, made new friends and entered with gusto into team sports, I found the scattered classrooms confusing and my classmates noisy and aggressive. My skills on the sports field were woefully lacking.

My first rugby lesson put me off team sports for ever. I wasn't the only newbie who'd never played the game, but I was the smallest, and probably the most unfit. I was kicked, punched, pushed around and spat on, the bigger boys laughing at my lack of skill, my pathetic efforts. As I walked back to the changing room afterwards, bruised and miserable, I knew it wouldn't finish there. It wasn't long before I was the punchball, the easy target for the bullies, and I was punished every day for my weakness.

My nickname was soon shortened to Butt — inevitable, really. It was certainly appropriate. I was the butt of everyone's joke in those early days, and I lost count of the times I was whacked on the arse. They found that joke hilarious every time. I nursed a lot of bruises until I grew bigger.

Unsurprisingly, Flick turned out to be a bully and a troublemaker. Everyone was scared of him, even his mates, because he was nuts. He'd lose his temper over nothing — he was big for his age and pretty stupid so it happened a lot. I was terrified of him, and he knew it. He got the others to do his dirty work for him, and they made my life hell.

One night, only a few weeks after the beginning of term, I went to use the toilet before bed, only to find they'd barred my way.

"C'mon," I said, trying to make light of it, my heart pounding. What were they up to now? I really didn't want trouble. "I need a piss."

"Really?" Flick's arm was across the doorway to the toilets. Two of the other boys were flanking the door, in case I made a dash for it.

"Yeah, really," I said, trying to push past him.

"That's a shame, because the toilets are closed," he sneered.

"Just let me in."

"No. You'll have to piss in your pants."

I knew the prefect would be along soon to check on us and I was running out of time. Also, my need was getting worse. I couldn't go to another boarding house, or even another floor — I'd risk getting into trouble — and I didn't want to get physical with these boys. They were strong and aggressive and I wouldn't stand a chance. If I tried it, I would end up with my head down the toilet.

So I turned and went back into the dorm room, opened the window and pissed out of it. I figured it was harmless — our room was on the first floor and it would land in the flowerbed.

"Ugh, disgusting, Butt's pissing out the window!" Flick said, as the other boys howled with laughter.

I never lived it down. And for the whole of that first tricky year, they didn't stop.

They put all sorts in my bed. They messed up my clothes, put stuff in my shoes, and got me into trouble with the older boys who monitored us. I tried telling a teacher about the bullying, but it just made things worse.

I hardly got any sleep in those first few weeks. I missed you horribly, Leo — I used to think of us together in the den, with our favourite things. I'd put the pillow over my head so the others couldn't tell that I was crying.

Meals were bad too. It wasn't the food, it was the boys. They wouldn't sit near me, they said I smelled (like a butt, ha ha) and they laughed at me behind my back. Luckily Matron, who knew all their tricks, saw what was happening and took me under her wing. I don't know what would have happened to me if she hadn't.

Apart from Matron, two things saved me in those early weeks and months. I took up shooting, as I'd withdrawn from team sports — and to my surprise I found I was quite good at it. The teachers let me shoot when the others were playing cricket, or rugby, or whatever other sports they were doing, and because I practised so much — partly to keep away from the other boys — I improved pretty quickly. When I started entering competitions and winning, I finally got some respect, though that was much later on.

The other thing was the wildlife. The countryside around the school was teeming with it. When I wasn't in class, or in the library reading, or out shooting, I was studying nature. And the weather was perfect. Most days were warm and sunny, and the sunsets were brilliant, literally — the sky turned pink, and red, and orange and purple by degrees.

* * *

"My name's Luke Harris, but everyone calls me Luke." The man standing in front of us didn't look like a teacher. He was young, compared with many of the other teachers we'd met, with wild curly hair and a big smile. His arms and legs were tanned and his eyes had a mesh of lines around them. He wore khaki shorts and a T-shirt with the school's symbol on it, and his feet were encased in stout, not very clean walking boots.

"I lead a small team of conservation staff who look after the reserve here, and you'll all be working with me on Estate Activities. The Estate has a diverse range of habitats and is home to many species of trees, plants, and birds. We've got giraffe, zebra, wildebeest, impala, warthog, and many reptiles and invertebrates. You'll be studying all manner of different things, and helping us with our ongoing research into rare species.

"All of us here are passionate about wildlife and conservation and we hope you will be too. Our job is to make nature come alive for you. We'll teach you about bush survival, tracking, medicinal plants, creepy-crawlies, birding and more. If you have a particular interest in wildlife you can really take it as far as you want to. Some of our boys have used their experience and knowledge gained here to prepare for their future career."

I was enthralled. I knew immediately that this was why I was here. This made sense of everything.

Estate Activities soon became my best subject, Luke my hero. I loved the wildness of the estate, the strange creatures we came across, all the wonders that opened up to me. I'd never experienced anything like it. The closest I ever got to nature at home was walking by the canal, where the slopes would be scattered with wild flowers in summer. I could scarcely believe my luck.

Our classes with Luke were always taught outside, with the subject matter right in front of us and the sun beating down on our khaki-clad heads. With him I understood at last what education was all about. It wasn't about books crammed with facts and figures, stuffy classrooms and rote learning. It was life, everything around us, the sky, the earth, the plants and the animals. I memorised the names of strange insects and medicinal plants. I studied the details of a starling's feather and learned to track creatures from their droppings or from the signs they left in the grass and the bushes.

When I got time to myself I would go outside and sit for a while in the manicured gardens that surrounded the school buildings. We weren't allowed into the reserve on our own, but I found a secluded spot where I could look down into the valley where the animals were free and the grasses grew long. There I would listen to the calls of the birds, trying to identify each one and remember it. I would track the progress of bugs crawling across the grass towards the plants, sometimes placing obstacles in their way to see how they dealt with them. When I looked up, I could sometimes see an eagle or two, circling high above me, watching for prey.

Often there were monkeys around, always curious and on the prowl for food. We had to be careful not to leave anything edible around our rooms, because they were wily and they'd get in an open window and ransack the place, to the annoyance of the staff. We of course found it hilarious, except when we discovered they'd used our beds to crap on.

But sometimes, when I sat outside in my usual spot, a couple of braver juvenile monkeys would come and investigate, venturing up close and bounding away if I moved. I loved being close to them, listening to their chatter, watching their intelligent eyes, their wizened old-man hands. It was far better than any TV show I've ever watched.

I knew then that I'd found what I wanted to do with my life.

CHAPTER ELEVEN

Ricky

It took me a while to get the letter-writing sorted out. I knew you would be waiting, and I tried hard to find a way, but they kept us busy at the beginning, and I was so shocked by the whole leaving home, moving countries and changing schools thing, I could hardly breathe. I also needed to see if Dad would pass on my letters to you — I didn't think he would, but it was worth a try. He didn't, and I had to wait for your first letter to confirm that. I'm sorry for that.

Luckily by the time the first school holiday came along, when everyone else went home, I'd made a friend, Michael. Yes, just the one — but he was in the same boat as me, not a rugby player, not boisterous or aggressive, and actually interested in learning. It was a relief to find an ally. So he posted my letters to you from his home in the nearby town and off we went.

I cried when I got your letters, I admit. I hid in the shower room and locked the door so I could read them in peace.

You tried so hard to be upbeat, but I knew how hard it was without me at home to back you up. You were always strong-willed, but I knew it would take a lot to survive being a teenager with parents like ours. I worried for your safety, knowing you were too brave — reckless, even, sometimes. You would confront Dad when I would have faltered, and sometimes you just didn't seem scared of him. But I knew what he was capable of. I was worried for Mum, too, of course, but you were so young and vulnerable.

I wasn't allowed home for the holidays until Christmas. In the other school holidays I was forced to stay with my guardians, the horrible Mr and Mrs Crow, who only did it for the money, and I felt loneliness and abandonment like a deep shame in my heart. It was only your letters and the wildlife that kept me from despair.

The Crows were miserable people, who clearly hated children. How did anyone allow them to become guardians? I wasn't permitted to talk at mealtimes, and I had to eat everything on my plate, even if I wasn't hungry. Mr Crow would say: "Eat up, young man. Others are starving while you have food on your table every day."

Like many white South Africans, they had a cook and a maid and a shared gardener. This didn't mean the Crows were rich — it was simply what the white population was used to. All the staff were black South Africans, who were given orders and treated like servants. Which they were, I suppose. I found it awkward and embarrassing. I went out of my way to be kind to them, though they treated me with suspicion. At first I tried to get to know them — I wanted to learn more about their lives — but my clumsy efforts seemed to scare them and I soon gave up.

Mrs Crow directed operations in the kitchen. Her menu choices were limited, and the cook's repertoire seemed to stretch only as far as a standard British-style meat-and-two-veg. I'll swear I always got the worst cut of meat and the stalest bread. In the evenings the Crows sat watching TV and drinking sherry in the sitting room. I wasn't invited to join them.

To be honest I was glad they left me alone. I spent most of the time in those holidays reading in the garden or in my room. They didn't organise anything for me, no trips, no company, nothing. Not that I would have wanted to go anywhere with them. They made it very clear that I was a nuisance and should stay out of their way.

Then, thankfully, after that first horrible year, Mr and Mrs Crow moved away and could no longer have me in the holidays. To my enormous relief, Luke and his wife Sally offered to have me stay.

It was the best thing that had ever happened to me.

That first year, after holidays with the Crows, I was more than relieved to come home for Christmas. When I arrived at our front door, it felt as if I'd been away for years, though it was just under a year I'd been away. It was brilliant to see you, Leo, but the gulf between our relative situations seemed enormous, and I was full of guilt that you were living with him in that gloomy house while I enjoyed relative luxury at my smart school.

But I was happy that we were still close. There were many reasons why we were. I was not a 'boyish' boy and I had no problem spending time with you. We both loved books and reading, and our family situation had drawn us together. I imagine that other siblings, separated by distance and lifestyle, would have grown apart, but we didn't — at least we hadn't by the time I got home that Christmas. I was thirteen and you were eleven — neither of us typical teenagers, neither of us little children either — but it was like we'd never been apart. I tried to play down the good parts about South Africa, instead describing the bullying at school, the problems I had with all those team sports. But none of it seemed anywhere near as grim as your situation.

I noticed how much Mum had aged in one short year. She looked worn down, as if she didn't care what she looked like, and if anything she was even more timid around Dad than before. I tried to ask her, when he wasn't around, how she really was, but she waved me away and said she was fine, just a little tired.

I was acutely aware of the contrast between my school and my home. I saw the dust, the balls of fluff gathering beneath the skirting boards, the stains in the bath and toilet. The cooker was caked with dried-on food, the tiles in the kitchen spattered with grease. Perhaps I'd just not noticed it before, but it seemed to me that our home was neglected, sad. Mum wasn't coping well.

Dad did his best to keep you and me apart that holiday, which was no surprise, but I did my school work diligently, took on the paper round and behaved myself. I had little choice and I didn't want to make things any worse for you than they already were. I bit my tongue, kept quiet and did what I was told, and I managed to keep the peace for those few short weeks.

He wasn't so bad at the beginning, when we were little. We didn't see very much of him, but he seemed more benign then, and Mum was relaxed in his presence. While he was at work, she would play with us and take us to the park, where we went on the swings and the roundabout and fed the ducks in the pond. We had some happy days. We even had some good times with him — he took us to the cinema a few times, even bought us ice creams. He was all right, then. I recall playing football with him, too, though it didn't happen often.

Mum would read to us at bedtime when I was small and you were just a baby. We'd snuggle up together on my bed, and I would look at the pictures while you tried to turn the pages or played with Mum's hair. Dad never read to us — it was always Mum's job to get us to bed.

It was only later, when I was about eight and you were six, that he began to get really bad-tempered. At first it was just some days, when he got home from work. But gradually it got to be all the time. When he was in the house, Mum became quiet and nervous, and we were supposed to behave ourselves. Often we were ordered out of the kitchen or the sitting room and we would disappear to my room, or yours, and make up our games together, only going downstairs for meals, or when Dad was out of the house.

As a boy, I thought that this was how all families were. But you, Leo — you knew from the start that all was not as it should be. With your strange insight, you knew that our parents were supposed to love and comfort us, and provide us with a caring environment. Once — I don't know how old you were, but you were quite small — you drew a picture of our house. It was brown, with no other colours. Mum was inside, looking out of the window with a sad face. You and I were upstairs, hiding under the bed (it was like a doll's house, you could see into the rooms) and Dad was out in the street in his coat, carrying his briefcase. You coloured in his coat, also brown. His face was oddly blank, without a mouth. Then you drew Kelly's house. The whole family was smiling, with their arms around each other, and the sun was huge and golden in the sky. In the garden there were animals and flowers and bright colours.

I remember you used to say you would look after me for ever, and I would say it back to you, as if we were orphans.

We might as well have been, for all that was lacking in our parents' idea of family life. Though that's probably unfair on Mum, who had made the mistake of marrying an unkind, controlling man who punished her for his own shortcomings.

The thing was, he always thought he should have been rich and successful. Growing up in South Africa to wealthy parents, going to a smart school and a posh university in the UK, he always expected life to be easy. And when it wasn't, he blamed our mother, because he'd married her, stayed in the UK and found himself tied to a boring job and a family. He could have got out, I suppose, but he was fettered by convention. So he ended up bitter and cruel, with a family who feared rather than loved him.

I always knew you were different, Leo. You were my little sister and special to me, but there was something about you that set you apart from other people, which I didn't fully understand until I grew up.

Your synaesthesia was a big part of it.

We didn't know the name for it at first. I came across it in an English class, when my teacher started talking about poets from the 1800s who combined the experience of sound and colour in their work.

I stuck my hand up. "Do people really see sounds like colours?"

"They do indeed," the teacher said. "It's something called a sensory condition — it's to do with the senses — and it's known as synaesthesia." She wrote the word on the whiteboard. I copied it down carefully to show to you.

"There aren't many people who experience it and it affects people in different ways, too. Some see colours related to sounds, some to letters. It's not a bad thing to have; it's as if they have an extra sense. Does anyone know what the other senses are — the ones we all have?"

You were delighted to find it had a name and that other people had similar perceptions of the world to you. Did you think it was only you? I suppose you'd kept quiet about it in case it got you into trouble.

As soon as I understood, I was fascinated by the colours you attached to certain sounds, or to letters of the alphabet. The letters seemed to be more fixed. R was always orange, for example, so you thought of me as orange, for my name. You were blue, for the L in Leonora.

But the sounds, to me, were unpredictable. You would talk about the door slamming as yellow, the seagull screech as purple. The sounds didn't seem related to what you liked or disliked — they just happened, and you saw them as they occurred. As you grew older, you began to see more subtle distinctions in the colours, and you learned new words for them: ochre, lilac, olive green, dove grey. You tried to describe to me what you saw, particularly when you 'heard' a colour, but it was hard for you to put into words, and even harder for me to imagine. There seemed to be bubbles, clouds, shimmering, flashes, puffs, sometimes a blaze of many hues.

I envied you your colourful visions and I think you gained comfort from them, rather than feeling isolated by them. They were your happy secret.

CHAPTER TWELVE

Ricky

Being around Luke and his family kept me sane. The more time I spent with them, the more I began to understand what you and I were missing — had always missed. A loving family. What enormous power and joy that can bring. It made everything else bearable, gave me the confidence to stand up for myself against the bullies, helped me realise I was clever and I was worth something.

Luke and Sally were more like parents to me than my own ever were, and I loved their children Meg and William, who were six and eight, like my own siblings.

I was just fourteen the first time I stayed at Luke and Sally's. When I walked through the door with my ancient backpack, Sally surprised me with an enormous hug. I was so unused to it, I stood there like a statue, my body stiff and unresponsive. I honestly didn't know how to respond.

Their house was a single-storey villa with an airy veranda along the sides. We walked straight into a large living room, with comfortable sofas and cool tiled floors. Everywhere there were animals: carved rhinos, stone hippos, pictures of antelope of various kinds. Comfortable armchairs and sofas were arranged around the centre of the room, and two collie-like dogs came to greet me, licking my hands and leaning on my legs to be stroked.

Meg and William bounced about me, pulling at my hand and my trouser legs.

"Come and see your room, come and see," they cried, pulling me along the corridor past walls decorated with photographs of lions and elephants, butterflies and caterpillars. I wanted to stop and look, take in the beauty of those pictures, but the children dragged me past.

I almost wept when I saw my bedroom. It was large and bright, with colourful cushions on the bed. More animal photos decorated the walls. Shelves of books on nature and South African wildlife waited for me to browse at my leisure.

"Look," said William. "Look what Dad's left for you. I'm not allowed my own proper ones yet, but you're big enough to have his old ones."

On a little desk by the window was a pair of binoculars. I looked at Luke, unable to speak. "Go on," he said. "They're yours now. You can use them to help me with my research."

I put them to my eyes, pointed them at the window and adjusted them like he'd shown me. Focusing on a tree in the middle of the lawn, I spotted a loerie, its plumage glistening in the sunlight, its head bobbing. I could see the curve of each individual feather on its wing, the gleam of its marble eye.

"Wow," I said, my voice shaking with emotion. "Just — wow."

Luke and Sally grinned.

"Thank you so much," I stammered. "This is . . . I'm — it's just brilliant."

"You are so welcome," Sally said. "This is your home in South Africa now."

The kids liked nothing more than to follow me around, teasing me and playing tricks on me as I pretended to fall for their games. The family looked after a menagerie of animals: a young impala, a couple of turtles, a loerie with a broken wing — the one I'd spotted in the tree — as well as two dogs and a guinea pig. The young impala slept in the kitchen with the dogs, the loerie wherever it liked, the turtles in a shady pool under the tree in the back yard, and the guinea pig in a small enclosure in the shade. The yard was fenced to keep unwanted predators out.

We'd never been allowed pets at home, and this array of animals strolling around the house was a delight to me. I particularly loved the dogs, who followed me everywhere, and I was soon recruited into feeding and looking after them, as well as the impala and the guinea pig.

Sally was lovely. She worked at the local nursery school part-time, ferried the children around and helped Luke when she could on the reserve. She was a wonderful cook, and from the first day I learned that meals as a family could be both delicious and fun. We all helped prepare the food, including the kids, who stood on chairs stirring the pans or chopping vegetables under one or another of the adults' watchful eye, and during the meal we talked about everything and anything.

I think it was the first time in my life that I experienced proper conversation. I learned the questions to ask: how was your day, what happened in your science class, how is the injured parrot doing, how is the fence repair down at the stream coming along?

How are you feeling?

At first I was tongue-tied, it was all so unfamiliar. But it was impossible to be quiet for long; the kids wouldn't allow it, even if the adults would. I soon learned to join in, and I cherished those evening meals.

I wanted to stay there for ever.

* * *

Dear Richard,

It's a couple of weeks now since you've been back at school and I trust you've settled in and have been working hard. I hope, too, that this term, now you've grown a little, you'll do better at rugby. Team games, as I said, are character-forming, and rugby will teach you to take the knocks in life like a man. Work on your fitness, listen to the coach and stand up for yourself. One day you'll thank me for this advice. As you know, your school has a huge amount to offer a young man (as reflected in the fees) and you need to take the best advantage of every facility.

Since your visit home I've decided it is best for you to stay in South Africa for every school holiday, including Christmas. As you know, the flights are expensive and money is tight. In addition, I feel you will benefit more from being with your guardians than with your sister, who distracts you from your school work. I have communicated this wish to the school, who will ensure you continue to study through the holidays, which will be vital if you're to get the best grades. There are only three more years before the final exams and I'm urging you to get your head down and focus on your key subjects. You might even get to Oxford University — think of that! Keep working, son.

Your mother sends her love,
Dad

I wasn't surprised when Dad said I wasn't coming home the next Christmas, though I didn't believe he was short of money. He was still working, and never spent anything on the house or holidays, like normal people.

I felt bad for you, Leo, having to face the holidays, as well as term-time, without me. You must have felt very alone when you heard I wasn't coming back — it must have seemed like you'd lost me for the rest of your childhood. I could only hope that you'd be able to spend time with Kelly and her family, or make new friends you could hang out with to get away from the grim atmosphere at home.

For me, though, it was a relief to know I didn't have to go back. I could relax and enjoy my holidays with my new family.

When I wrote back to him, I didn't mention the holidays at all. Most of my letters to Mum and Dad were pretty bland: how the subjects were going, what play we were putting on in the drama group, what books I was reading for English. I never told them how I felt about anything, or what my plans were, or about my passion for wildlife.

But I blamed myself for not standing up to Dad. I missed you and Mum. I was worried for you both, and frustrated at my helplessness.

In those middle years at school, when I realised that with Luke's help I'd be okay, I grew stronger. Although I still spent a lot of time on my own in the library or outdoors with my monkey friends, I began to get along better with the boys in my dorm. Not well, exactly, but there were fewer incidents. A couple of times, I even got the better of the bullies.

My success at shooting was a crucial factor. When I was fifteen, I entered the under-seventeen competition for the whole of KwaZulu-Natal, and to my surprise, I won. This resulted in an accolade in assembly, and then the whole school knew that I was an excellent shot. It did wonders for my reputation — especially when Luke gave me my own gun, a bolt-action rifle. I had to get a licence for it, and it was kept at his house, in a proper gun cabinet. I was enormously proud.

One day, my nemesis, Flick, who by then had developed a taste for sticking young boys' heads down the toilet, squared up to me in the corridor, a couple of his mates hovering behind. He had the habit of standing in front of you to block your way, and then if you pushed past, he'd knee you in the groin, leaving you doubled up with pain. But this time, he hadn't reckoned on me having my gun — it was on my shoulder but he didn't notice at first. As I got closer, I saw his eyes register the weapon and the flicker of uncertainty was enough for me to prepare myself. I slipped the strap off my shoulder, holding the gun under my arm, pointing down. It wasn't armed, but it was a clear signal. He stopped in his tracks and sneered.

"Well look at you, big shot."

I could tell he was unsure so I stepped closer to him, put both hands on the weapon and said: "What?"

His face registered surprise at my unexpected bravery, but he tried to brazen it out. "You think you're a man now, do you? We'll see about that when you haven't got that thing with you."

He was tall — at least four inches taller than me, and heavily built — but my confidence had grown by then and I'd had enough of his taunts. I squared up to him and stuck out my chin. "Well that would be stupid now, wouldn't it?"

"Are you threatening me, Butt-arse?" The sneer turned into a laugh, and his mates joined in, thinking he'd got the advantage and I would back off.

But I took another step closer and tilted my face close to his ear. "You need to respect a person who has a gun." He drew his head back, blinking with surprise.

"Don't forget you have to sleep, shithead," I said loudly and pushed past him without looking back.

He got the message, sure enough. It was the last time he gave me any trouble.

I didn't tell Dad about the shooting — I didn't want him to be proud of me. I suppose he found out from my reports, though, because he started to ask about it in his letters. But once I had won the battle with the biggest bully in school, I began to gain confidence. I was growing tall and strong. I swam regularly for the second team in my year and I had to train hard for shooting competitions. Perhaps I was already taller than Dad. Though in my heart I still quailed at the thought of standing up to him, I began to think it might be possible. Perhaps I could save Mum and you from him before it was too late.

CHAPTER THIRTEEN

Leonora

Leonora feels Ricky's absence like a physical pain. Losing him after Christmas is almost worse than the first time. For days she sobs into her pillow at night, her stomach cramping, only emerging, white-faced and exhausted, for school. In the daytime the sense of loss settles into a dull ache that never goes away.

The year without him stretches ahead of her relentlessly. School is a distraction, but at the end of lessons she avoids going back to the house and the empty space where Ricky should be. Her mother is no company. In her own world of suffering she is increasingly vague, often sleeping, barely speaking on bad days. Sometimes Leonora gets home to find her mother still in her dressing gown, her hair uncombed, in a panic because there's no food for supper. On those days, Leonora, tired and hungry herself, turns back around and goes to the shop. There's no question of letting her father come home to an empty table.

But term-time is better than the holidays, when the days stretch endlessly before her. Her only escape then is Kelly and her family. She spends most days with them, going home at the last minute, often arriving moments before her father's heavy step in the hallway. Though he pays her little attention, he insists she stays with her mum. Nobody tells him that her days are spent elsewhere.

When she's not with Kelly she spends long hours in her room, writing letters to Ricky or listening to music, transfixed by the colours that dance around her room with the tumbling notes and deep drumbeats. She counts the days, obsessively marking them off in her home-made diary. The weeks and months until Christmas seem like a lifetime.

Ricky's letters, when they do arrive, are a joy and a lifeline. She can tell from the moment she sees the postman if he's got something for her — he walks towards her with a jaunty step, his smile lighting up the street.

The contents are deeply satisfying, with long descriptions of school life — the lessons, the teachers, the library and, most of all, the school's estate and its rich natural life. Sometimes he sends a photograph — a termite mound, a snake curled beneath a tree, the head of a kudu, its horns outlined against a blood-red evening sky. Once he sends a picture of himself with Luke. The long, curved neck of a giraffe is just visible in the background. She imagines how wonderful that must be — to be close to those majestic, gentle giants in your daily life.

Leonora sits by the towpath, a letter on her lap, savouring the moment before she reads. Across the water, along from the boats, a heron stands motionless, one leg poised under its belly, its eye glinting as it gazes at the water. She watches it for a while, wondering how long it can stay without moving, but it's like a statue and she's impatient to read Ricky's news. She rips the envelope open messily, discards it on the grass.

Hi Sis,

I don't have much time so this is short. Sorry, but I promise I'll write properly in the next couple of days. All's well here but there is something you should know, and I'm pretty sure Dad won't have told

*you. He's written to say I'm not coming back in the holidays at all —
not even at Christmas. So it'll be another four years before I'll see you,
unless something changes. I know you'll be upset, but there's nothing
much I can do about it. I'm really sorry — I know how much you
look forward to us being together, and Christmas will be even worse
for you now.*

*It probably doesn't help you or Mum, but really it's OK for me.
Dad says he can't afford the flights, which is rubbish, as he never spends
anything and still has his job, and also that you distract me from my
work, which is also rubbish. He made me do far more than I needed to,
anyway — the school wants us all to get a decent holiday in the summer, not carry on studying. I'm going to try to get work in the holidays
(Luke says he'll help) and start saving money for you and Mum to get
away. If I can make enough, perhaps you can visit, or at least I can
get home to see you.*

*As far as I'm concerned, South Africa is my home now. I want to
work here, with the animals and nature. Dad's going to go mad, but I
can't live my life according to his rules. I'm not going to tell him yet —
no need — but when I finish school, I'm staying.*

*Leo, you must try to get Mum to leave him. If she won't do
it, you should get away. Could you live at Kelly's for a while? At
Christmas I realised how bad it really is at home, and I'm worried
about you both.*

*Perhaps talk to the doctor about Mum? There might be charities
that could help, and they'll know who to contact. Glad you've made
friends with the canal people, they sound great.*

Sorry, got to go now. Keep smiling,
Hugs, Ricky.

She throws the letter to the ground, rests her forehead
on her knees. Tears trickle through her eyelids and drip gently onto her skirt. Four years. She will barely know him after
all that time, even if they write every month. It's unbearable.
All the joy at hearing from Ricky has poured away, leaving
her limp with grief. Her life seems to stretch before her, unre-
mitting, hopeless, nothing to look forward to. She sobs until
her eyes dry up and her throat aches.

When she looks up at last, the early evening sun shines bright on the dark waters of the canal, soft ripples catching a golden gleam.

She takes a deep breath, squares her shoulders and walks towards the gentle sound of guitar music floating from the open door of the narrowboat where her friends Maria and Pete live. The colours drift and dim as she approaches.

CHAPTER FOURTEEN

Leonora

She kicks the front door closed behind her in a shower of pleasing yellow raindrops. The stained glass rattles grey in its frame. There's a cry from the kitchen like a repeating pattern in her ears: "Please don't slam the door, Leonora—"

She mouths the words as if reciting a poem, adding her own lines: "If the glass breaks, there'll be hell to pay. Your dad . . ."

She throws her bag to the floor and stamps upstairs, shedding her school tie and her shoes as she goes. In the bedroom she rips off her shirt and skirt and grabs a jumper and jeans, trying to ignore the pull of the marks on her arms and legs. She puts her loudest music on, throws herself onto the bed and watches the rainbow shapes flow and ebb as the music whirls around the room.

"Leonora!" Her mum's voice penetrates the closed door of her bedroom from the hallway below. But she won't come up, she's too defeated. Now Leonora is fifteen, she is stronger than her mother. She only wishes the same applied to her father.

With the door closed and the curtains drawn, she opens a drawer. The drawer. She chooses a razor blade, her favourite implement. She has scalpel blades and a knife, too, but they are for a different kind of feeling. Not this one.

She got top of the class in English. Eighty-eight per cent. She should be feeling joy, but all she feels is anger and frustration, the unfairness of it all. What good is it, getting top marks when nobody cares?

She unzips her trousers and studies with interest the criss-cross pattern on the white skin of her left thigh.

* * *

Fifteen. She's still too young. She needs to be eighteen and away. Then he can't yell at her or do any of that other horrible stuff. She'll no longer lie trembling at the brown thud of his stockinged feet on the landing.

It gives her huge satisfaction to imagine his fury when he can no longer control her. All his stupid non-plans for her, in pieces. In law, she'll be an adult, his equal.

Her own plans are beginning to crystallise.

She hugs the knowledge to herself. In her heart she's grown-up, already away, with a proper job, living independently. Broken free.

But three years is too long to wait. Things are getting worse. Her father grows angrier all the time, takes it out on her more and more. Her nightmares are painted the colour of filth — the thump of his footsteps follows her everywhere. Her mum is too scared to help. Her drinking is getting worse. She tries to hide it, but the scarlet flash of the bottle landing in the bin outside alerts Leonora every time, and it's getting more frequent.

If only Ricky were here. She could talk to him, make a plan. Lucky Ricky, he'll be eighteen soon — and he's in Africa. All he has to do is stay.

Perhaps she'll do it at sixteen. A thrill of fear rises in her chest — that's just a few months away. She's going to have to get going.

She doesn't yet know how she's going to do it. But she has a great advantage. One thing her parents have done for her — God knows there are very few gifts coming her way from them — is to give her a decent brain. She's going to use it, despite the rotten school they've sent her to. Even in that dispiriting place, where the teachers are ground-down, sorry creatures with the poorest qualifications — even there, she can learn, absorb, get an education while others daydream or fight, yell and get into trouble.

She's going to show her father that she's worth more than he could ever have imagined.

* * *

She waits, leaning against the bare brick of the corridor wall. It's open to the air and when it rains, a puddle forms along the edge of the walkway overlooking the bare quadrangle where they spend their break. At least that's where they're supposed to spend their break time. Those of them who don't want to be under the teachers' eyes have found other, better places. Places where they can smoke, sleep, even fuck if they feel like it.

Leonora doesn't do any of those things. She goes to the library where she can be alone and read, or study, or do her homework.

She's early for English as usual. But this is her best class, the one where she learns most. This teacher, Miss Archer, is old-school, strict and shouty but not stupid. Miss Archer has found Leonora out — she has detected a brain in her class, to her immense surprise. And Miss Archer is clever enough not to make it obvious to the other kids. She simply gives her more advanced work, keeps her busy, points her in the right direction with subtle hints and notes in her exercise book when she returns an essay. None of the other teachers have spotted the difference, that one child in thirty-three has an outstanding brain — and, against all the odds in a school like this, wants to learn.

The wind whips through these corridors with a mean yellow wail and Leonora's hair whirls around her face, catching in her mouth. What sort of vindictive person designs a school with open-air corridors? Did they smile a cruel smile when they thought of queues of children waiting outside classrooms in bitter temperatures and driving rain? Some posh architect who gave no thought to the people he was really designing for, his eye only on the money. She pulls her cardigan around her, hunching her shoulders against the chill.

"Hey." A voice interrupts her thoughts. It's Kelly, who's been sent to this godforsaken place as well. Kelly cares even less now about school — this dump does that to people. She's there because she has to be, but her ambition stretches only so far. Get a job, preferably in a clothes shop, get married, have kids. She's counting the days to leaving school. She doesn't understand Leonora and her plan to squeeze as much advantage as she can from this limited educational resource. Kelly has grown into a good-looking girl, tall and healthy. She's popular with the boys and can take her pick.

"God, it's bloody freezing," Kelly says, sticking her hands in her pockets, a worn backpack over one shoulder. The side seam of the bag is ripped and a thread hangs temptingly. Leonora wonders if the bag would fall apart were she to tug at that thread. But that's what other kids would do, not Leonora. What's the point? It's not that she wants to be liked, only that she has a plan and bullying isn't part of it.

CHAPTER FIFTEEN

Leonora

It wasn't always this horrible, being her.

For as long as she can remember, she and Ricky looked after each other. From the start, they were perfect playmates. There was never a feeling of rivalry. Though dissimilar in temperament — she brave and questioning, always in trouble; he sensitive, quiet, the peacemaker — they were devoted siblings.

They built the den behind the drawers in Ricky's bed when they were small. It was their own little sanctuary where they could hide when their father was angry.

They found it one day when they were playing hide-and-seek. One of the drawers, only half-full, had come right out and Leonora crawled through to the wall to find a perfect hiding space, big enough for two children to sit in with a pillow if you half-opened the other drawer. They took a torch, their teddies and a blanket and set up their private space where nobody could find them. They would creep in when their father was on the rampage, waiting without making a sound until the house was quiet, only venturing out when they knew he was settled in his study and the coast was clear.

When their mum was out, their father not yet home, they sometimes got scared on their own. They'd retreat to their den, certain that no burglar could track them down.

Because their mother did leave them, even when they were very small. Not for very long, usually — just enough time to go to the corner shop — but there were times when she didn't come back for what seemed like hours.

She never asked where they got to when they hid. Perhaps she knew. Certainly she must have known why.

In their early years, they didn't see much of their father. He left the house early and returned after their bedtime. He was a remote figure, spending many hours in his study with the door closed.

His hobby was painting tiny metal soldiers. He had armies of them lined up on the sideboard, their uniforms painted in meticulous, authentic detail, categorised by historical era. The children weren't allowed to interrupt him while he was alone in his study with his paintbrush, but on occasion, Ricky would be invited in to watch the process, as he was a boy and it was assumed he'd be interested. Leonora wasn't asked, which irritated her, but Ricky said he wasn't allowed to do anything, he just had to sit there and listen to his dad talk about his armies and their manoeuvres, which was boring, so Leonora didn't mind so much.

At the weekends, strangers would arrive — men with loud laughs and big bellies — and they would all retreat to the garage at the end of the garden, where a tabletop was laid out to represent the fields of war. Hours later, they would emerge, having strategised for hours with their tiny battalions and regiments. It all seemed very mysterious and uninspiring to Leonora.

Every evening after supper their father walked slowly to his study and closed the door. It was supposed to be his private den, though sometimes, after school, before he was home and while their mother cooked, the children would venture in, their hearts beating hard with fear and excitement.

Silent in their socks, they creeped around the huge wooden desk in the middle of the room. They opened each drawer in turn to check the contents, which were invariably disappointing — papers, the odd letter, bills. They knew not to touch the newly-painted soldiers lined up on newspaper to dry, but would take down some of the older ones on the shelves, handling them with care and making sure they put them back just so. There was a high-backed leather chair that Leonora loved to climb into and swing around, a couple of threadbare armchairs where, presumably, their father's friends would sit when they visited, and a pile of newspapers in the corner, ready to be used to light the fire in the sitting room or to be taken to the dustbin outside.

These provided fascinating reading for Leonora. At first she studied mostly the pictures, finding the stories too difficult to grasp. But as she got older she loved reading about other people's lives, exotic cultures and conflicts in countries she'd barely heard of. She was always careful to fold the papers exactly as they were. It wasn't worth being found out.

Faded photos decorated the wall, of their father as a boy in Africa, animals, people with black faces, a man with a gun and his foot on a dead lion's back. Leonora hated that one. There were other artefacts too: a carved mask propped on the bookcase, an antelope's horn, an elephant made of wood, its tusks smooth and creamy, its glass eyes empty and staring. Ricky loved these, but Leonora found them threatening and tried not to look. She thought they were evil — perhaps the reason her father was so frightening. In her darkest imagination he would use them to cast a spell over his children, to make them behave.

* * *

After school she waits for Kelly, who always seems two steps behind the rest of the class. It's early spring, the clocks have changed and the world along the canal has opened up again.

The boats always leave for winter before it gets too cold, only returning in spring, and Leonora and Kelly have missed their regular visits to the towpath. During the winter Leonora spends many long hours at Kelly's house, where they curl up in her bedroom, listening to music, playing with the younger children and the family's menagerie of animals, eating Kelly's mum's delicious cakes.

Leonora is in love with the family dog, Cookie, a small golden terrier with one ear floppy, the other cocked, as if he's always at the ready. To her delight, the little dog adores her. When she's there, he's always on her lap and she's entranced when he falls asleep, confident that he's safe in her arms. She loves his warmth, the soft fur around his ears, the curl of his hind legs. She vows one day to have a Cookie of her own.

Today, as it's sunny and feels like the first day of spring, they decide to collect Cookie from Kelly's house before making their way along the canal to where their friends' narrowboat is parked. The dog runs ahead, knowing where he's going, his tail wagging incessantly, every new smell delightful to his sensitive button nose. Still in their uniforms, the girls have discarded their school bags and their ties at Kelly's house, undone their top buttons and rolled up their skirts at the waistband.

There's a gentle breeze by the canal, bringing fresh smells from nearby fields. Leonora's struck by a new sense of possibility as they approach the brightly coloured barges moored along the towpath. These will probably stay all summer, though they'll be joined by an ever-changing variety of leisure craft and other narrowboats over the next few months.

The girls are friends with this small community of free-thinking people. Last summer, when the sun shone for what seemed like many weeks, they got to know Pete, the man with the guitar and the golden voice, Maria, the woman with jangly bracelets and a ring in her nose, and most of all Jack, her son. Jack left school last year and spent the whole of the summer on the canal, swimming, canoeing, hanging out with whoever was willing to spend time with him. To Leonora he was the perfect boy, with his dark curls reaching his shoulders, his way with words, and the carefree manner he talked to everyone, even the people who'd frown and hurry by on the path, disapproval clouding their faces.

The girls haven't seen Jack yet this year. He's found work on a farm nearby and the hours are long, but Maria and Pete are already there, the roof of their barge bright with painted pots ready for planting with geraniums for the summer. Cookie is ahead of them, already on board by the time the girls step down onto the platform and bend down to see who's home. A Bob Marley song creates a floating rainbow of colours as Leonora drops down into the kitchen where Maria greets them with kisses on both cheeks and a waft of musky scent.

"Hey, girls," she says with a smile. "Want some tea and biscuits? Freshly baked." She passes them a loaded plate and they take it back outside with them, holding it high and laughing as Cookie leaps and bounds in hope of a treat. Maria follows, bringing with her blankets and cushions and spreading them out on the grassy bank.

"What's new then, Leo?" Maria says. The canal people are the only ones apart from Ricky and Kelly who ever call her Leo, and Leonora loves it, even though they didn't ask permission. If other people do it, she corrects them. It's only for special people.

Kelly answers for her. "Leo's clever. Top of the class in English. Pretty close to top in everything. She's really going places."

Maria smiles. "Well done, Leo. Your parents must be proud of you."

Leonora makes a face.

"Well they jolly well should be. I'm proud of you, anyway." Maria gives her a little squeeze and a warm feeling. "And you, Kelly?"

"I'm doing okay. Can't wait to leave and get a job."

"School's not for everyone, that's for sure." Maria always says the right thing. "I didn't like it either, but luckily I met Pete. Then I didn't need to worry. He's looked after me since I was seventeen."

Leonora is fascinated by Pete and Maria. They must be only a few years younger than her parents, but they're

80

completely different. Nothing they do conforms to her parents' view of life — her father's, anyway. Their home on the boat is small and scruffy, but it seems more like a proper home to Leonora than the dark space of her parents' house. It's warm and welcoming and she feels more relaxed there than she ever does in her own home. Pete often disappears in the evenings to play in a band, and on the boat he spends long hours singing and strumming his guitar. Maria bakes, creates beautiful drawings of flowers and plants in the summer, and paints pots in the winter months.

It's not clear how they survive, but while they buy very little and what they have is reclaimed from junk shops and bring-and-buy sales, Leonora has the impression they have enough money and they don't want to live any other way. To her knowledge neither of them has what her father would call a 'proper' job. In the winter they leave the narrowboat — Maria can't bear the cold — and retreat to a cottage in Wales. Leonora imagines a cosy, warm place where chickens roam freely outside and milk and cheese come from the local farm.

"I'm going to find someone to look after me," Kelly says, taking another biscuit. "He can work while I have lots of children and dogs." It's said lightly, but Leonora knows she means it.

"How about you, Leo?" Maria asks. "Not the life for you, I imagine?"

"I'm going to look after myself. I don't want to rely on anyone else for money."

"She's going to university," Kelly says, digging Leonora in the ribs. Leonora fends her off with a smile.

"Are you now?" Maria smiles. "That's a great thing to aim for. What will you study?"

"English, probably. I'm going to be a journalist." Leonora has never said or even thought this before, but as she says it, she knows it's true.

CHAPTER SIXTEEN

Leonora

When she can, she takes the international pages from the newspapers in her father's office, scouring them for news of South Africa. What she reads — stories of inequality, unrest, poverty and violence — does little to reassure her, though it seems to have little bearing on boarding-school life. She worries how Ricky will fit in, in the real South Africa. Now she's had the time to consider Ricky's news, she knows it's best for him, and despite the sadness of knowing she won't see him, she's happy for him. Not only has he got away, he's found a life he loves.

Returning a paper to the pile, she checks the desk drawers as usual, hoping to find a letter from Ricky. She hasn't heard from him for at least a month.

She opens the drawer with her mind elsewhere, riffling through the papers, finding nothing except the odd electricity bill. As she reaches into the corner, though, her fingers alight upon something new and soft. She draws it out gently and finds to her surprise that it's a small velvet pouch, dark blue in colour and tied with a delicate ribbon. It holds something small and round, its surface uneven beneath her touch.

Though she knows her mother is asleep in the lounge, she turns to the door and listens intently for sounds of life in the house. There's nothing, the dusty weight of the air in the study undisturbed except for her own light breathing.

She places the pouch in the palm of her hand and unties the ribbon, then slips her fingers inside and draws out the contents.

It's the brooch from her mother's jewellery box. Memories crowd in as if they've been waiting for their moment. As a little girl, Leonora would sit on her parents' bed while her mother got dressed. She would empty out the large wooden box, her fingers caressing the polished lid with its delicate marquetry. One by one, with extreme care, she would lay out the contents on the bedspread.

Each item was an object of wonder to a small girl. There were long strings of beads in different colours, a necklace of iridescent pearls that shone with warm creaminess, its clasp glistening with tiny diamonds. There was a silver chain bracelet with intricate charms — a ballerina, a house, a hat — and an array of earrings, placed in a special compartment for safekeeping. Her mother didn't like her touching those, in case she dropped them on the floor and they disappeared.

And there was this brooch. When Leonora was little, the brooch didn't live in a pouch, it was just part of her mother's jewellery collection. She remembers every sparkling detail of the brooch. It's shaped like a flower, with small white jewels set into curves to form delicate leaves around a central stone that glows pink from its centre. Leonora was always fascinated by this stone — she could never see where the pink was coming from. If you looked at each side of the jewel, you'd be sure it was colourless, or white, maybe, but if you compared it with the other, smaller stones, it flowed pink from its very core. She used to turn the brooch in all directions to see if she could see through, but the stone never revealed its secrets to her.

Why does her father have the brooch in his study? Leonora remembers the day her South African grandparents came to visit, when her grandmother promised the brooch to her mother. Leonora was only four or five, but it stayed in her mind. It was the first and last time she met her father's family.

"You must pass it on to little Leonora when the time comes," Grandma said, stroking Leonora's cheek. "It will make me happy to think of her wearing it one day."

She was excited to think that one day she would own such a beautiful thing.

These days, Leonora never goes into her parents' bedroom — she can't remember the last time she did. She certainly hasn't opened that jewellery box for many years. She doesn't even know if it's still there. Her mother doesn't seem to wear any jewellery anymore, except for the simple gold band of her wedding ring. Even her engagement ring seems to have fallen out of use.

Leonora studies the brooch for a moment more, then takes a decision. She puts it back into the little pouch and, closing the drawer carefully, places it in her pocket.

As she shuts her bedroom door, she wonders what she's done. It was a spur of the moment thing, it felt right — it's her mother's property, not her father's, after all. And ultimately, it belongs to her.

She sits on her bed and takes the pouch from her pocket, emptying its precious contents into her hand. There seems no good reason why her father would take the brooch from her mother's jewellery box, only to hide it away in his desk. She thinks back to when she last checked the drawer. It was only last week. Why would he have taken it — and why now? Something strange is going on.

She studies it again. Somebody made this with skill and artistry. Each delicate petal is different, with a swirl of tiny jewels swooping towards the central stone, but the overall effect is symmetrical, true to the nature of a flower. The setting looks like gold, though she has no way of knowing.

Perhaps her father took it for safekeeping — but that would be giving him the benefit of the doubt. No, Leonora thinks, he's not like that. He stole it from her mother because it's valuable and he wants it for himself. Perhaps he's even going to sell it without telling her.

Well, he's not going to now.

She freezes as the front door slams. Time has slipped by — her father's home. Her hand folds instinctively over the brooch and she sits for a moment rigid, listening for his feet on the stairs. But he heads for the kitchen as usual, where her mother will be standing over the cooker, trying to focus on the evening meal. She hears his gruff greeting and her mother's soft reply before he heads for his study and closes the door behind him.

She fumbles the brooch back into the pouch, her fingers slow and awkward, her heart pounding. If he looks in his desk and finds the brooch missing, she can't imagine what will follow. She has to hide it — and right now. With him in his study, she has probably five minutes to get to the den and put it with the letters. It's not a great hiding place if he decides to search properly but it will have to do for now. She creeps into Ricky's room and pulls out the drawer, her hands trembling. Scrambling into the tiny space, she opens and closes the tin box with her eyes squeezed shut as if it will be quieter if she can't see it.

She prays that tonight he won't check. She has to find a better place.

It's midnight before she can breathe properly. Her parents are sleeping at last, as far as she can tell. She heard them climb the stairs, her mum's pale blue shuffle a few minutes before his heavy brown tread. That was more than an hour ago, as she lay in the dark under the bedclothes, rigid with fear.

Their bedroom door is closed and her father's snoring sends reddish flares into the darkness as she treads softly out of her bedroom and onto the landing.

She reaches the back door without incident and gently unlocks it, drawing back the flimsy bolts top and bottom before slipping out into the cold night. A pale moon emits an eerie glow that slips and slides across the garden, draining colour from grass and flower beds. Shivering in her thin pyjamas, her feet still bare, she glances up at the back of the house, where the window to her parents' room stares like a single eye across the garden. The curtains are closed — no light seeps round the edges.

A narrow paved path leads from the terrace at the back of the house down the garden to a tangle of apple trees and a ramshackle wooden shed where her father keeps his lawn-mower and gardening tools. Her first thought was to hide the brooch there, under a loose floorboard or among the profusion of junk thrown haphazardly into the corner. But that's too obvious, and it would be hard to retrieve anything unnoticed if she needed to find it urgently. Also it's her father's territory, and his alone, like the garage. She needs to find a better hiding place. Looking around, she notices her mother has placed a number of small jam jars along the back wall. Perhaps, long ago, she had dreams of making jam — or more likely, she couldn't bring herself to throw the jars away. Her husband is so tight with money, she's taken to saving everything in case it comes in useful.

Leonora shivers as she bends to retrieve the smallest jar. It looks like a honey jar, squat and solid, and she has a fleeting memory of how, as small children, she and Ricky would sit on the garden bench on a sunny day with slices of bread and honey, swinging their legs.

Its lid, rusty and bent with misuse, fights against her but she wins the battle and screws it back and forth to loosen it as best she can before placing the velvet pouch inside. She tiptoes down the path until she reaches the old apple tree that stands like a sentinel at the edge of the lawn. At the back of its gnarled trunk, at the junction where two branches meet, there's a large hole where birds sometimes nest in spring. She's hidden things in there before and knows that it narrows and closes as it descends into the trunk. Her precious goods will be safe there. She makes sure the jar is upright and secure, flashes another look up to her parents' bedroom — the window still blank and empty — and runs, her feet light on the path, back to the house. To her relief, everything's quiet as she creeps upstairs, her father's snoring still loud and regular.

In her dreams he chases her, the sound of his stockinged feet getting louder, faster as she crouches, trembling, in her hiding place. She wakes with a jolt, her heart racing, but he's not there.

For the next few days she trembles at her father's key in the door, his step in the hall. Expecting him to discover his loss at any moment, she thinks of little else until the door closes behind him in the mornings. At night she lies awake imagining the scenario: the roar of fury, the crashing around in his study, her father's shouts, the note of desperation in her mother's voice.

She doesn't fully understand her spur-of-the-moment act. The moment the brooch fell into her hand, she knew its presence in her father's possession was wrong, in that unforgivable, never-to-be-forgotten way. And somehow, though she's frightened for her mother and for herself — because surely her mother will claim her innocence, even if she doesn't go as far as pointing the finger at Leonora — there is no going back. Whatever he does, she won't return the brooch. She won't tell him where it is. She won't give him the pleasure of finding her out, whatever the cost. It's a small gesture, but it could be the trigger for a huge event. Well, if it is, so be it — it's about time something changed around here. If she ends up out on the street, she'll be glad.

But she is worried for her mother.

CHAPTER SEVENTEEN

Leonora

She's almost home when Mrs Clark from next door hurries out, her arms flapping, her cheeks pale. Leonora's heart begins to pound.

"What's happened?" she says, as Mrs Clark grabs her arm and pulls her up the path.

Inside, there's no sign of her father, no sound from the kitchen. In the hallway, she steps on something — the unmistakeable powder-blue crunch of broken glass — and when she looks down, there's a dark red patch on the grubby beige carpet. Is that blood? She gasps, frees her arm and faces Mrs Clark. The woman shakes her head and works her lips, as if she's struggling to find the words.

"It's your mum, dear," she says at last, taking Leonora's hand and pulling her into an awkward embrace.

"What? What about my mum?"

"She's in the hospital. Your dad—"

"What's he done to her?"

"It seems he hit her, with a bottle," Mrs Clark says. "We heard shouting and screaming, someone running down the stairs, then thump, thump! Knocked her out cold, he did.

We all heard it. We banged on the door, me and Mrs Collins from over the road — and in the end he opened it. She was slumped on the floor, here. We called an ambulance straight away."

"Where is he? Did he go with her?"

"No, dear. He just left, didn't even wait for the ambulance. Pushed past us, he did, his face like thunder, all red and sweaty. Swearing and cursing, yelling all the way down the path. Had a terrible temper on him, scared the wits out of us."

"Did you call the police?"

"They came, waited for the ambulance, asked a few questions — but he was long gone. Your mum's at the General Hospital, she has a nasty gash on her forehead. You should go see her."

"Yes." She sinks onto the bottom step of the staircase, her mind racing. "I will. I just need to — check something first."

"Will you be okay? Want me to come with you to the hospital?"

"No, no — I'll be fine. I'll go as soon as — I'll go in a minute." She turns to the door and opens it for Mrs Clark, ushering the protesting woman out as quickly as she can without actually pushing her. "Thank you, thank you. I'll let you know how she is."

The front gate clangs shut in a haze of grey and Leonora bursts into action. She runs into the kitchen, where the remains of supper still stand on the table, the two place settings waiting to be cleared. A dirty pan tilts on its side in the washing-up bowl, and her mother's apron, still wet, hangs from the back of a chair.

In the front room everything looks normal. She gives it only a cursory look through the open door. The study door is closed, and though she knows her father's not here, she still feels a stab of fear at entering where she shouldn't. The door swings open slowly — the light is still on. It reveals her worst fears. Her eyes are drawn straight to his desk in the centre of the room. It's always so regimented in here, no mess, no work in progress, the chair always pushed under the desktop, everything neat, buttoned-up, like her father. But not now. Drawers hang open obscenely, their contents spilling this way and that, papers littering the floor.

She runs up the stairs, skirting around the ominous stain at the bottom, halting at the door to her parents' bedroom to take a deep breath. As she flicks on the light, she gasps. Everything is thrown about. The bedclothes have been torn off, the mattress hangs sideways from the frame, clothes litter the floor, her mother's underwear is scattered around like confetti. The wardrobe door stands open, but all the clothes on hangers have been thrown towards the bed, some falling short, strewn around like dummies from a shop window waiting to be displayed.

She steps gingerly through the chaos, careful not to tread on any of her mother's clothes. She touches nothing. Then she sees what she's looking for.

In front of the heavy wooden chest that her mother uses as a dressing table, her mother's jewellery box lies open, empty.

* * *

The smell of the hospital hits her immediately. As the door swings closed behind her, her nostrils flare at the unfamiliar stench of bleach, mingled with an acrid tinge not unlike human sweat.

She's struck by how shiny it all is. The floors, polished and buffed, reflect the gloss of many layers of paint on the walls and the ceiling. Blobs of paint the colour of rancid butter fill every crack and dent on doors and walls — every Victorian window frame is frozen in place with gobs of ancient buttermilk, and every inch of every surface reflects the brutal glare of artificial lights placed with heartless precision along every ceiling. Even the chairs shine brightly, their blue plastic made brilliant by years of use, rubbed smooth by the backsides of sick patients and their families.

Swallowing hard, she removes her coat — it's stifling hot in here after the winter chill of the street — and joins a short queue at what looks like a reception desk. A nurse with a clipboard seems to be having an argument with a man in a threadbare tweed coat. They talk in hoarse whispers. The man turns his back on the people waiting behind them so they can't hear. As she waits, Leonora looks around, wondering if she's doing the right thing. Perhaps she should just march in and find her mum. Nobody seems to be policing the corridors; it would be easy enough.

But then suddenly there's no one ahead of her and a nurse looks up and says, with a smile: "Can I help you?"

"Yes, it's my mum, Sandra Bates. She was brought in earlier, she — she's injured." She wants to shout — to everyone, so they know, if he comes: "My bastard father beat her up!" but it's not the nurse's fault and she swallows the urge with difficulty. She'll save it for later, for the police, for whoever will be on her side.

"Sandra Bates. Ah yes, Ward 10. It's not visiting time—" she glances at her watch "—but you can go up. Ask the nurse on the desk if it's okay, though; she may have gone to surgery."

"Surgery?" Leonora whispers. Of course, there was blood, perhaps they're having to sew her up. She has no idea how long her mum's been here, or what condition she's in — she hadn't asked what time it all happened and the bus ride to the hospital was agonisingly slow. To Leonora's horror, her throat swells and she begins to shake. She whirls round and stares at the signs, searching for Ward 10 through stinging tears.

The nurse comes out from behind her desk, puts a hand on her arm.

"Let me take you there, it's a bit of a confusing place, with all these corridors," she says. "I'm going there myself anyway."

The simple act of kindness causes the tears to flow and Leonora stumbles unseeing after the nurse, her head down.

In a side room distinguishable from a line of others only by its proximity to the stairs, her mother lies behind a flimsy curtain that stops a full twelve inches off the floor.

There are four beds in total in the room. One is empty, its bright white sheet stretched tight across as if to bar unwelcome visitors. The other two are occupied, the first with a sleeping figure on its back, the blankets pulled up to cover the face, a tuft of dark hair on the pillow. A drip attached to a tube disappears under the covers. A half-eaten meal lies congealed on a wheeled tray at the end of the bed. The other occupant is a large silver-haired woman reading a magazine, looking far too healthy to be in a hospital bed. Leonora avoids her gaze and slips behind the curtain as fast as she can.

Her mum's body is curled tight. She's facing the wall, the loose ties of a hospital gown trailing at her neck, the skin of her back pale and thin so the hills and valleys of her spine stand out in sharp relief.

"Mum?" Leonora whispers. She puts her hand out to touch the bony shoulder. Though she barely makes contact, her mum's body reacts immediately, tensing and recoiling as her head lifts up. Leonora's hand drops as she registers the terrible damage on her mum's face.

Her nose is clearly broken. Strips of white tape stretch across the bridge, pulling sharply against the skin on either side. In her nostrils are dark patches of dried blood. Her upper lip is swollen so badly on one side that her mouth is distorted into a grotesque sneer and there's a bruise beginning to bloom on her left jaw.

Her eyes are even worse. One eye has disappeared in a puff of angry purple skin — on the other, a cut on her brow, at least two inches long and stitched with ugly black twine, looks like an evil centipede crawling towards her hair.

"Oh, Mum." It's all she can say. She takes the thin grey hand that reaches towards her and sinks onto the chair beside the bed.

Her mum's head falls back against the pillow, her eyes on Leonora. Her mouth twitches.

"No, don't try to talk. I'm sorry, Mum. It's all my fault."

Her mum's right eye opens a fraction wider. She mumbles and waves her hand at the beaker of water with its plastic straw on the side table. Leonora holds it for her, pushing a pillow behind her head to support her neck. The water dribbles down her chin and Leonora reaches for a tissue to wipe it away.

"It was the brooch, wasn't it?" she says, already knowing the answer. Her mum's head inclines — there's an urgent question in her functioning eye. "It was in his desk" — her mum flinches — "yes, I went through his drawers. It's yours, not his. So I took it back. I didn't mean . . . I should have warned you. I'm sorry, Mum."

Her mum shakes her head, squeezing Leonora's hand and wincing with pain. "Yours," she says, her voice a dry croak through her damaged lips. "Don't tell me where it is. Keep it safe." Her head falls back to the pillow as if all her energy has gone into talking. A sheen of sweat glistens on her forehead and Leonora leans forward to wipe it away.

"Okay. But Mum, you can't go back to him. He's going to keep on hurting us. You must leave him. We must both leave him. I'll help you."

It's hard to see her mum's reaction through the devastation of her face. But she goes still, her one visible eye glued to Leonora's face. "It's too late for me. But you — you must go."

CHAPTER EIGHTEEN

Leonora

Mrs Clark's shepherd's pie is a lot better than Leonora has ever tasted and her sausages and mash are downright delicious.

Leonora finds the first dish on the doorstep when she gets back from the hospital, with a note that says: "Leonora, hope this helps until your mum gets back." Still warm from the oven, it's wrapped in a large striped tea towel. She takes what she wants up to her room, leaves the rest on the kitchen table. She pushes a chest of drawers against the door of her bedroom and waits for her father's step in the hall. While she waits, she welcomes the release of a carefully chosen razor blade to her forearm.

Thankfully he shuts himself in his study for the rest of the evening.

But the following morning she can't escape. She trembles at the brown thump of his feet on the stairs, waits for the sound of the front door closing behind him. When it doesn't come, she hangs back as long as possible, then, not wanting to be late for school, creeps down the first few steps. The outline of his coat is the first thing she sees through the banisters. She's about to turn back, thinking she'll clamber out of a bedroom window rather than confront him, when he says, his voice harsh: "Come down, girl, I know you're there."

Biting her lip, she descends another two stairs until she can see his upturned face. "Right down here," he says, pointing at the floor, and his stare chills her to the bone. She reaches the bottom of the staircase, leaving one foot on the last step as insurance. She keeps her eyes on his chest, ready for a sudden movement. "Your mother's not well," he says. "I'm expecting you to keep the house running until she's back. Do you hear me?"

"Yes," she says, in a low voice, keeping her eyes down.

"That means you clean the house, do the laundry — properly, mind. I need a shirt ironed every day. No loitering after school. You get back here and get supper ready. D'you hear?"

He takes a step towards her and she recoils, both feet now on the bottom step. "Yes." She senses his hesitation, prays he won't ask about the brooch. Against him, a big bulk of a man with a terrifying temper, she has no chance — she'll be joining her mum in a hospital bed if he decides to lash out. But he steps away with a growl of frustration, opens the door and is gone in a shimmering cloud of yellow.

She sinks onto the steps, shaking.

Later, she goes next door to say thank you. To her surprise, Mrs Clark takes her hand in a warm grasp. "It's not for him, it's for you. You've got enough to think about, what with your mum, and school, and your brother away. It's the least we can do. Mrs Collins will help too, we have to cook anyway. What's a bit extra when someone's in need?"

Leonora finds herself surprised and overwhelmed by this act of kindness. Mrs Clark leans forward conspiratorially. "I know your mum has her problems with the drink. Don't blame her, living with him." She jerks her thumb towards some unknown place where Leonora imagines her dad feeling his ears burning. "He's a bad one, always has been. Your brother's well out of it. You need to get going too, I reckon."

Leonora nods, struck dumb. She had no idea other people knew about her family. "I . . . thank you," she mutters.

"You make sure your mum stays in that hospital as long as she can," Mrs Clark says. "She needs to build up her strength."

Leonora knows this is true. She can't blame her mum for her dad's violent behaviour. Perhaps now there's a small chance to change things, to get her mum away, perhaps to show her that a better life is possible. But if she refuses to leave, then Leonora knows what's in store. She will be forced to leave school, stay at home and take care of her mother.

Not to mention her father — and that thought is unbearable.

* * *

At the police station, a young officer with spots on his forehead and thin, bony fingers takes notes in a lined notebook. His boss, a white-haired man with a large stomach and a jovial manner, tries to persuade Leonora that she's making a big fuss.

"It'll blow over, love," he says. "Bit of a domestic — it happens all the time." Stained teeth and fingers indicate a heavy smoking habit.

The air in the room hangs heavy with years of human stories.

She can feel the anger begin to brew, deep in her belly. "Please listen to me. He almost killed her. I'm not exaggerating. Ask the doctors — they'll tell you how bad she is. Next time she might die, then it will be murder. You must do something to stop him!" Even as she says it, she knows it's hopeless. This man is like her dad: arrogant, selfish, proud. His word is law. His wife probably cooks and cleans and keeps her mouth shut the same as her mum. Women everywhere, resigning themselves to a life in the shadows.

"We can have a word, but it's best to leave it. Believe me, we've seen it before. Your mum and dad will make it up before you know it." He pushes his chair back, closing the discussion. "Gordon will see you out."

Gordon, closing his notebook with a snap of scarlet streaks, springs to attention and leads her through to the front of the station. Opening the door to the lobby, he pauses. "I know it seems bad now," he says. "But he's right, you know. Usually it turns out okay."

She stares at him, wondering how old he is, if he still lives at home, if his parents are normal. The anger bursts out at last. "But it's never been okay. It's never going to be okay. Nobody listens to me!" She pushes the door open, shoulders her way past him and runs into the street.

For the next few days she goes home only to do the chores, before her father gets back from work. She checks the coat rack in the hallway when she goes in, to make sure he's not there.

She does his washing, not bothering to separate the whites or check the temperature. She hangs it to dry in the garden, irons a few shirts, makes his bed. Shortly before he's due home, she leaves his meal on a low heat in the oven and goes to Kelly's. There she sleeps on an array of cushions on the floor of Kelly's bedroom with Cookie, burying her nose in his warm fur.

Kelly's parents know what's happened but don't question her beyond asking how her mum is. Kelly lets her talk if she wants to, but mostly they sit quietly together doing their homework or listening to music. Leonora is grateful for their quiet support while she works what to do.

Her mum is getting better, though the bruises make her face look worse for a while, the black turning to livid purple, green and eventually yellow. She's found a way to smuggle vodka into the hospital (a friendly porter with a penchant for a tipple) and spends her days dozing behind the curtain. She won't talk to Leonora about leaving home. She waves her hand and turns her head to the wall when Leonora tries to broach the subject. Talking to her back, Leonora pleads and begs and comes up with all the reasons she can think of to make her mother change her mind. But her mum is adamant and Leonora has to concede defeat. She walks home with a sick feeling in her belly. Despite everything, her mother will never leave home.

Leonora is going to have to go without her.

CHAPTER NINETEEN

Ricky

When I heard about Mum, it was already two weeks after it had happened. Something visceral took hold of me. I raged, yelled obscenities, punched and kicked everything in sight. I was so mad with anger, I frightened myself. Luckily I was on my own in the dorm, but when I calmed down there was a gaping hole in the door.

Later that day, I was hauled up in front of the headmaster.

His name was Mr. Carter, and he was a rather remote man with narrow gold reading glasses and a permanent frown on his face. He ruled the school firmly and on the whole fairly, but still I was terrified of what he would do. Violent behaviour was among the worst violations of school rules and expulsion was on the cards.

I couldn't believe how stupid I'd been. The thought of being sent home was unbearable, and being expelled would be like the wrath of the heavens on my head.

I'd never been inside his office before. A picture window on one side framed the best part of the gardens, like a huge vivid painting, the golden sunlight contrasting with the faded furnishings of the room. It was spacious and comfortable.

Framed certificates and old black-and-white pictures of the school were dotted around on the surfaces and hundreds of books lined floor-to-ceiling shelves.

I was ushered in by a frosty secretary to find him sitting at a large wooden desk reminiscent of my father's. He waved a bony hand vaguely at the seat in front of him. There followed an awkward silence while he looked through some papers, which I assumed were about me. His expression was stern, bordering on angry.

My stomach clenched. I felt the blood drain from my cheeks. Sweat broke out in the palms of my hands.

"Well," he said, looking up. It wasn't a question, so I stayed quiet. "I'm surprised to have you here for this reason, Bates. You must know, this isn't behaviour that we can tolerate at this school."

I felt the flush of shame rising from my chest, the hairs on the back of my neck bristling. I swallowed, clearing my throat. "No, sir. I mean, yes, sir, I understand, and I'm sorry. It won't happen again."

"It certainly won't. We're going to have to pay for repairs to that door as it is."

"Yes, sir. I really am sorry."

"Can you explain yourself?"

I knew this question was coming and yet I was unprepared. Despite everything my father had done, I still felt a vestige of loyalty to him. Or perhaps it was shame: I didn't want the headmaster to know how utterly despicable my father was. I dropped my eyes, muttered: "There was . . . an incident at home. My mother was hurt and had to be taken to hospital. I — I was upset . . . and angry."

Mr Carter stood up and wandered over to the window, where he stood for a moment, contemplating the garden. I sat, quivering inside, certain I was going to be expelled.

"Sir?"

He turned. "Is there more?"

"I just — I'll try to pay for the repair, sir, if you'll let me stay. I can't . . . the school, my education — they're really important . . ."

He stopped me with a gesture, sat down and placed both hands on the desktop.

"I know they are, Bates, and I'm not thinking of expelling you, if that's what you're worried about."

My relief was palpable. I'd been holding my breath without realising, and the puff of air that escaped from my lungs lifted the papers on the edge of the desk.

"Thank you, sir."

"No need to thank me. I've had a conversation with Luke, your guardian. He tells me life at home is not as it should be. I'm very sorry about your mother. It must be frustrating, and worrying, not to be there for her at a time like this."

To my horror, I felt a rush of tears to my eyes. But he carried on as if he hadn't noticed.

"Bates, you've always been a diligent student. Your grades are good, you're progressing well, and we're proud of your success with the shooting. You've never behaved badly, unlike some of your contemporaries. So I'm going to treat this as . . . an aberration. If I thought you could help with the cost of repair, I would ask you to, but I know you don't get much in the way of an allowance. So I'm going to ask you to do extra hours to help Luke instead. He will give you a schedule of work and you'll do it in your spare hours, without pay. Does that sound reasonable?" He looked at me with something like a smile playing around his lips.

"Yes, sir, thank you, sir," I said, trying to control the huge grin that threatened to break out on my face. "I really appreciate this, sir."

"Yes, well," he said, waving me out, "off you go."

* * *

Hi Leo

When I heard what Dad had done I went mad, and I nearly got expelled. But it's all OK now, so no need to worry.

I don't understand, though — can't the police see that he's dangerous? What does he have to do for them to arrest him, for Chrissake? It was brave of you to go to them on your own. At any rate they'll have a file on him now. If it happens again, he'll be in real trouble.

You must have known it would be trouble, taking the brooch, though I didn't in a million years think he'd go so far as to beat Mum up. Isn't that illegal? I feel really bad that you had to deal with that on your own. Thank Christ Mrs Clark was there to help, and Kelly's family.

Anyway, I'm glad to hear Mum's home and getting better, though I'm worried for you both in case it happens again. Aren't there women's refuges and things for beaten wives? I know Mum wouldn't want to go but we could try to persuade her. Should we find out? Perhaps Mrs Clark would help.

I had a letter from Dad. Can you believe it? He didn't even mention what happened with Mum. What a tool he is. He's obsessed with me getting my exams, going to university and making lots of money. He's never even asked if it's what I want.

But I don't know, Leo, perhaps I should do it. At least I could support you and Mum, maybe even get you both away from him. Only thing is, it will be years before I have any money and I don't know if you and Mum will last that long. What do you think? I really want to stay here in South Africa. Now it looks like they're abolishing military service, which I definitely don't want to do, I'm thinking it's a real possibility. But with things as they are at home, I don't want to leave you and Mum to deal with it.

What have you done with the brooch? I hope you've stashed it somewhere safe, where he'll never find it. I'd like to know if it's worth anything. It could help Mum to escape, or you to get through university. If I was coming home, then I could bring it back here for safety — but it looks like that's not going to happen, at least for the next couple of years. If we could just get it here, I'm sure Luke and Sally would help me get it valued, and we'd know if it could help us. But I don't trust the post here, things get nicked, so don't just send it through the normal post. Don't do anything yet, I'll think of something.

Write soon and keep smiling, Leo, we'll be okay.
Love,
Ricky

I figured the brooch was our big chance. I asked Sally if she could get it valued, if we could get it over here. I was still only seventeen, a schoolboy, and I wouldn't know if I was being ripped off if someone decided to be dishonest. Sally looked dubious about the chances of it arriving safely in South Africa, even if you did manage to send it, but she was fine about having it valued. She said she'd take it to a proper valuer who knew about these things.

I worried about it getting lost in the post from the UK to South Africa, but not as much as I worried about Dad finding out you'd taken it.

So, to my plan. I know you think I never planned anything, and compared with you, I was a novice. But yes, I had a plan.

When I told you I wanted to stay in South Africa for ever, it was true, but at first it was only a dream. It seemed out of the question, what with Dad and his ambitions for me. But as time passed and I grew older and stronger, I began to think the unthinkable. Perhaps I really could stay in South Africa after I finished school. I could train to be a ranger, work with animals, make a life for myself out here. I was sure Luke would help me — we talked about it a couple of times in a roundabout sort of way, when I allowed myself to contemplate it. I even imagined you and Mum joining me here, getting away from Dad once and for all. I had no idea what I would need to do about visas or permission to stay. I was young, and such things did not cross my mind, but even if there had been a small chance, it would have been worth almost anything to pursue it.

My stay in South Africa had spanned a time of huge change in the country's politics. Nelson Mandela had been freed and the end of apartheid had begun. When I reached my final year at school, it seemed as if anything was possible. The country felt dangerous, but exciting, with new possibilities, huge political change, arguments and discussions. For me, though, perhaps selfishly, the key was the end of conscription. Previously, conscription in South Africa meant a year of rigorous military training, followed by deployment in South Africa, Namibia or Angola. After that came several years of annual short-term 'camps.' There was no way I could have survived it. I would rather have come back to England and done battle with Dad than gone through that, so it was a huge relief, and timed perfectly for me to stay. It seemed like serendipity.

"Sure, you should stay," Luke said. We were out in the bush, checking the fencing around the perimeter of the reserve. It needed checking regularly as the animals would test it from time to time, and sometimes there were gaps and broken posts that needed fixing. "You would do well as a ranger, you're a natural. You can learn from me while you're still at school, then go and get a diploma in Nature Conservation, like I did. Or you could even do a degree."

"There are degrees in Nature Conservation?"

"You'd probably do Natural Sciences, then specialise. Lots of places offer them. If you're serious, I can help you apply."

"I'm serious. It's what I want to do."

Luke stopped the Land Rover by the next stretch of fence and we jumped down. I was thinking about what he'd said, wondering if it could ever be possible, knowing I would be deserting you and Mum. Not to mention how I was going to deal with Dad's reaction.

It must have shown on my face, because Luke stopped testing the fence and said: "Look, Ricky, I know you feel guilty about your family. But you must do what's right for you. Your mum and your sister would agree, I'm sure. They'll want what's best for you. Anyway, things change — anything could happen before then. Let's plan this future for you, and deal with what comes along as it happens, eh?"

"Okay," I said, my heart lifting.

"Okay. I'll have a word with the Head, and we'll get you started on that path."

At that moment, probably for the first time in my life, I felt I could make something happen. My future was up to me and I could decide.

CHAPTER TWENTY

Ricky

Hey Ricky!

I've done it! The brooch is winging its way to you (separately) as I write. Fred (my lovely friend the postman) was brilliant. He said the best way to do it was to send it through the special post, which would guarantee it was protected, and that he would make sure it got to the right place. I even went to the depot with him, where we wrapped it up in lots of tissue and put it in a little box, then covered the whole thing in brown paper and tape. Fred's got some system where employees get special treatment or something. He may be making that last bit up to reassure me, but anyway it's on its way, and if anyone can make sure something arrives, it's Fred. I gave him all the money I had, which wasn't very much, but anyway he wouldn't take it. He just wanted to know what it was all about, when it was okay to tell him (obviously I didn't tell him everything, just that it was something really important and I needed to get it to you safely). He's a very kind man.

I'm not sure how long it will take to get to you, but if you could write just really quickly to let me know when it gets there, then I'll know and I won't worry it's got lost or stolen in the post.

Fingers crossed! Let me know,

Your cleverest sister,

Leo xxx

Sally was cooking breakfast and Luke was trying to round up the children, who were out playing in the sunshine. It was Sunday morning and I had the brooch clutched in my hand. Though it had arrived the day before, I'd been at a shooting competition all afternoon and hadn't had time to come down to their house. When I put it under my pillow that night, it felt as if it was radiating heat, and I hadn't slept well for worrying over it. What if it wasn't valuable at all, just a piece of well-designed plastic, worth a few rand? I couldn't help it, I was relying on this trinket to release Mum and Leo from their unbearable lives.

"What is it, Ricky?" Sally could see from my face that I was bursting to tell her something.

I opened my hand, and the brooch seemed to glow with a strange iridescence.

"Will you look at that." Sally wiped her hands on her apron. "Can I see?"

I held out my hand and she took the brooch gently, turning it from side to side to catch the glimmer from the stones.

"It's beautiful," she said. "So Leo managed to get it to you?"

"Luckily, she's made friends with the postman, Fred. He's been very kind to her."

"Hm," she said, studying the brooch again. "I'm no expert, but the stones look real to me. But listen, don't get your hopes up, I could be wrong. I'll take it into town as soon as I can and get it valued."

My face must have fallen because after a moment she said: "Okay, I'll go tomorrow, take the kids after school. I've got a couple of things to get anyway."

"If it's no trouble."

"No trouble at all. But I will probably have to leave it with the jeweller. Don't worry, I'll get a receipt. And this person I've got in mind, he's been a friend for years. He's honest. I promise he'll look after it, and do a good job for you."

I gave her a huge hug and she pushed me away gently, smiling. "Now come on, help me get these kids in for breakfast. And Luke, now he seems to have disappeared too!"

* * *

When Sally came back after picking up the brooch, she had a strange look on her face. She got me to sit down and took it out, very carefully. Apparently her friend the jeweller was shocked when he saw it. He needed a few days to ascertain its background, take pictures, and talk to other experts. But he had recognised it, and by the time he'd checked all the stones he was pretty certain it was a well-known piece. If so, the central diamond, the pink luminescent one, was rare, recognisable by experts, and belonged to one of the wealthy nineteenth-century families who had made a fortune out of diamond mining. Our family. Ironic, that we came from a wealthy background. No wonder Dad had a chip on his shoulder.

"So did you ask what he thinks it's worth?"

"He's still waiting for confirmation, so we mustn't get too excited. It could be a copy. A good one, but still not the real thing."

"So it is worth something? He gave you an idea?"

Sally smiled. The suspense was killing me, my legs wouldn't stay still.

"He did, but I don't know if I should tell you."

"Of course you should! Sally—"

"You should definitely sit down."

I sat down.

"If it's the real thing . . . sixty or seventy thousand pounds."

For a moment, I couldn't speak. I thought I'd misheard. Eventually, I said: "How much?" She repeated herself, and I let out a huge whoop of joy, grabbed her and whirled her around the kitchen until she wriggled free.

"Whoa, Ricky, hold fire," she said, laughing. "We don't have confirmation yet."

"But he's pretty sure? They are diamonds, anyway?"

"He's pretty certain, and yes, the stones are real. It's worth something, no doubt about it."

To me, it was a huge amount, much more than I'd imagined, even in my wildest dreams.

Of course, straight away I started imagining all the things we (you) could do with the money. My imagination ran wild. But Sally pulled me back. She was insistent that I shouldn't tell you until we knew for sure, and of course she was right. So I waited. It was a few weeks before it was confirmed, and by then I'd managed to persuade myself that the news was going to be disappointing. It was going to be a copy: a good one, but not valuable in a life-changing way.

But one day a letter came for Sally, and she opened it without thinking. Luke was out feeding the animals and I was at the kitchen table surrounded by school books. Sally dropped into the chair in front of me with a strange look on her face. She handed me the letter. The brooch was genuine, and worth a fortune. Seventy thousand pounds, Leo. A fortune to us, anyway.

By then you were in the middle of studying for GCSEs. Sally and Luke decided I shouldn't tell you until you finished your exams, so you wouldn't get distracted. We hid the brooch away in a corner of the safe and I did my best not to think about it. I, too, was in the lead-up to exams, and I needed to do well, for my own self-esteem if nothing else.

I was a bit flummoxed by the news about the brooch, if I'm honest, Leo. People like us don't know what to do with that kind of money. But anyway, it comforted me to know that you and Mum would have more than enough to escape from Dad, and I managed to put the knowledge in a box in a corner of my mind until you'd finished your exams. It was hard, though.

Yet somehow, in June when you'd done your exams, it never seemed the right moment to tell you. I talked to Sally and Luke, and they were worried if I wrote it in a letter, Dad might somehow intercept it, which would have been disastrous. I had visions of him appearing at school and threatening everyone until I gave in and handed over the brooch. That kind of money changes everything. Obviously I couldn't sell it — it was Mum's, and yours — but I started to think maybe I could borrow some money against it and somehow get it to you. I don't know, I had all sorts of weird ideas, then.

CHAPTER TWENTY-ONE

Leonora

She has read the books, practised the papers and done her homework diligently, even in the subjects she finds tedious, like History and French. When exam time comes, she turns over each paper, tense with anticipation. The relief when she finds familiar questions sends tingles down her spine. The answers flow, she finishes on time and experiences an unexpected feeling of quiet satisfaction at the end. She says nothing to her classmates. They whinge and groan and anticipate failure.

But though she's always done well in class tests, she's never before pulled it off like this. Seven beautiful red, shiny As and two navy blue Bs — the best GCSE results in the school. Kelly, happy with a mixture of Cs and Ds and one triumphant B for English, hugs her and declares how proud she is of her friend. Her generosity almost reduces Leonora to tears. Miss Archer says: "Well done, Leonora. You're on the way to university!" Leonora feels an odd mix of embarrassment and pride and hopes none of the other kids have heard.

She and Kelly go down to the canal to see their friends and tell them the news. As they walk along the towpath, the summer air warm on the skin of her arms, Leonora feels almost happy. Her foot is on the first step of the stairway to a better life. The first part of her plan is in place.

* * *

"Mr Bates? Do come in, I'm sorry to have kept you." Miss Archer's voice oozes charm as she ushers Leonora's dad into the room. Leonora, sitting waiting, stares stonily ahead.

"Leonora," he says, settling into the armchair next to her in front of Miss Archer's desk. "Dad," she mutters, not looking. She catches a whiff of his musky smell and shifts her chair a fraction, away from him.

Miss Archer looks from one to the other, one eyebrow raised. The air in the room almost thrums with tension. Miss Archer clears her throat and opens a folder from a small pile in front of her. Leonora's name is on the cover.

"Well, Mr Bates. Firstly I'd like to congratulate you on your daughter's success. She's worked hard and got the results to prove it. I'm sure you're extremely proud of her."

The plastic chair creaks as he crosses his legs. He nods, his face impassive. Miss Archer pauses to put on a pair of reading glasses and looks over them at Leonora's dad as if waiting for more, then clears her throat again. Leonora wonders if she's nervous. Her father's mood is not friendly.

Miss Archer studies the folder for a moment. "You should be. She's done so well — the best GCSE results in the school. She has a great future ahead of her. I don't think I'm being disloyal to say that it's a challenge for bright pupils here, with the catchment we have, but Leonora's shown us that hard work reaps rewards. We're looking forward to having her in our top A-level group."

"She won't be staying." His voice is low, and gruff, and dangerous.

"I beg your pardon?" Miss Archer's eyebrows disappear into her hairline. Leonora, rigid with dread, wills her to be strong.

"She won't be staying on. She has work to do at home." As Miss Archer continues to gaze at her father's brooding face, Leonora begins to worry she might take it too far. She picks at the sleeve of her jumper, where the yarn is coming loose.

"Her mother's sick. She's needed at home."

"I'm sorry to hear that," Miss Archer says, removing her glasses and gesturing with them as she speaks. "But Leonora is one of the brightest pupils we have — probably the brightest. It would be a terrible waste of her intelligence if she left her education now. We would very much support a university application at the next stage."

"That's not going to happen." His foot begins to tap on the floor. It makes a hollow sound on the faded parquet. Puffs of soft turquoise rise from the floor, fading at his knees.

Miss Archer folds her glasses carefully, places them on the desk, and stands up. Leonora holds her breath. Miss Archer turns to a cabinet behind her and pours herself a glass of water. Pale pink sprinkles in the air. She takes a long draught and turns back to her desk. Tap, tap, turquoise. When Leonora is tense like this, the colours are especially vivid, distracting. She uses them to calm herself.

Miss Archer sits again, leans back in her chair.

"Mr Bates," she says firmly. "I sympathise with your situation, of course. But your daughter has a bright future. She could go far. With the right support she will get to university and ultimately have a good career. Her prospects are good — there are so many opportunities out there for a bright girl—"

"Waste of time."

Leonora risks a quick look at her father's face. He's staring at Miss Archer with a look of pure contempt. She can't believe Miss Archer is being so patient with him. But the teacher keeps her voice level and says: "Excuse me?"

"It's a waste of time educating the girl." Though she's heard this before, Leonora flinches. Her belly twists with loathing, but she keeps her eyes down. The cuff of her jumper continues to unravel as she picks at it. The tapping grows louder, like a bomb ticking, its billowing turquoise growing more intense with every second.

"There's plenty for her to do at home. She's needed there. Then she'll get married and have kids, that's what she'll be doing. That's what girls do. It's all she's good for."

"Is this what Mrs Bates wants for Leonora? Surely . . ."

"Mrs Bates wants what I want." As her father's tone becomes increasingly belligerent, Leonora wants nothing more than to leave.

Miss Archer gives it one last try. "And what about what your daughter wants, Mr Bates? Surely you want her to be happy?"

The tapping stops abruptly. "My daughter will do what she's told. Now if there's nothing else . . ." Her father rises from his seat, towering over Miss Archer, who stands hurriedly behind the desk. As her father strides out into the corridor, Leonora turns and whispers, holding back the tears with a huge effort: "Thank you for trying."

Afterwards she feels calm, almost euphoric. Her father's response has ruled out the tiny possibility that she might be able to stay on at school with his consent. So the decision is made: she has to leave home now.

She's known for a long time that she needs to get away from him. But she must also stay on at school. It's part of her plan, and without it the plan won't work. She already knows how she'll bring it about.

First, she needs to talk to her mum.

She picks her moment with care. Her mum has got worse again since her hospital stay, drinking solidly from lunchtime onwards, almost every day. In the mornings, she gets up to make breakfast, then goes back to bed as soon as her husband has left. What time she then emerges varies according to her hangover from the previous night, but it's usually around eleven. Today is no exception.

It's almost the end of the school holidays, with only two days to go before the autumn term begins. Leonora has to do this now. She waits for her mum to dress and come downstairs.

"Mum — I need to talk to you," she says. "Come and sit down. Here's your tea."

"I'm tired, Leonora, I didn't sleep well. What is it?" Her mum sounds irritable, but later in the day she'll be even less receptive.

Leonora slides the mug of tea across the table. She chooses her words carefully. "You remember I got good grades?" Her mother nods. "Well, I'm going to stay on at school, do my A levels. I want to go to university."

Her mum shakes her head, her neck drooping. She is a drab, grey version of herself, defeated by the circumstance of her marriage. "Your dad won't let you. I can't do anything about it, I'm sorry."

Leonora takes a deep breath. "I know, Mum. That's why I'm going to leave home."

Her mum covers her face with her hands and for a moment Leonora wavers. She won't be able to bear it if she cries.

She keeps her voice steady with an effort. "I've got somewhere to go that is safe, where the people are kind. I can't . . . I can't live with him anymore, it's destroying me. I'm going to go in the next few days. I just wanted to warn you, so you can prepare yourself. I won't tell you where I'm going, so you don't have to lie to Dad, but it's all settled. I have to do this."

"But you're too young, you're still a child! And Dad will go mad — he'll come and find you, drag you back. You know what he's like."

"Mum. I've got to go. I want to stay at school, he can't stop me. Any other father would be happy I want to get a decent education. Oh, Mum. Why do you stay with him? Why don't you leave?"

"I can't. He controls everything." Her face crumples. She pulls a tissue from her pocket, wiping the tears from her eyes, pulling hard at the delicate skin. Leonora looks away.

"He won't allow it, you know," her mum says. "If you're going to Kelly's—"

"I'm not going to Kelly's. You can tell him that. He mustn't bother them. I'm not going to cause trouble for anyone, if I can help it. I know I'm a minor but I'll call the police if I have to, I'll tell them he's violent — they already know what he did to you. I can't stay here, Mum. I have to give myself the chance to have a good life, away from here, to use my brain. He wants me to stay here, to cook and clean and be his— be a drudge, and I'm sorry, Mum, I just can't do it."

Tears fill her mother's eyes, already made huge by the purple smudges beneath them. Lines of unhappiness are etched into the faded skin around her mouth and on her brow. At her temples her hair is coarse and grey, like brush-strokes in oil.

"It's my fault, Leo. I'm sorry, I haven't been a good mother to you. It's just — so hard . . . you know, with him. You know what he's like, and I'm not strong enough . . ." She hasn't called her daughter 'Leo' since she was tiny. Leonora almost falters, her throat tightening around a great lump of sadness.

She reaches for her mother's hand across the table, struggling to stem her own tears. "Mum, it's not you. You know I think you should leave him, and if you do, I'll try to help you. I will still come and see you, when he's at work. But I can't stay here if he won't let me go to school."

Her mum nods, her lip quivering. "I know."

She holds Leonora's hand tight across the table.

CHAPTER TWENTY-TWO

Leonora

She takes a single suitcase, a battered one from under her parents' bed. A few clothes — she doesn't possess many, anyway, her books, her ancient teddy bear, the box of letters from Ricky. She opens the drawer that contains the scissors, the razors and the knives and looks at them for a moment, then throws them into a plastic bag, runs downstairs and dumps it in the dustbin.

She takes a last look around her bedroom. There's nothing here for her, no happy memories, no childish objects to tear herself from, no family photos or posters to take with her. Just shabby walls and furniture, a threadbare carpet on the floor. She won't miss it.

At the front door, her mother stands waiting, her face stricken. She looks small and thin. Hopelessness casts a pall in the air around her. She wraps her bony arms around her daughter. Leonora holds her for a moment, then pulls away. There's already a whiff of alcohol in the air.

"I'll be all right, Mum," she says. "Try to look after yourself. I'll come and see you, soon. When he's not here."

Her mother nods, biting her lip. "Leonora—"

"Don't, Mum." She opens the door, walks down the front path. She doesn't look back.

* * *

The sense of freedom is overwhelming. Straight away, this feels like home — this cramped box with its fold-down beds and cubby holes and tin mugs. The gentle drift of the water rocking her to sleep, the green views from the curved metal window of her tiny room, the smell of the grass and the fields beyond. For the first time in her life she can breathe properly.

"You can come and live here, you know, with us," Maria had said. "If he won't let you stay at school. We'll stay the winter with you, for as long as you want. There's not much room, but we'll make it work."

When she'd started to object, barely believing it was possible, thinking it was asking too much of her friends, Maria said: "Look, you're a bright girl, you're prepared to work hard, we know you can do it. It would be a crying shame if you left school now. We'd love to help you and it's no trouble for us. It's less than two years. Think about it."

"But my dad . . . I'm still a child. Won't you get into trouble?"

"We're not proposing to kidnap you, just to give you a place to study in. We'll deal with your dad, if we have to. Don't you worry."

She told nobody, not Kelly, not even Ricky, in case it didn't happen. She could hardly believe her luck. That someone should care enough about her to want to help was incredible — and to help in such a major, life-changing manner seemed simply too good to be true. But it was true, and it happened, and now she's here it's wonderful.

The first day, she puts her meagre possessions into the tiny single room next to the shower room, sitting on the bed for a few seconds to prove to herself that it's real.

But she knows it's not long before her father will be home, and she needs to warn Kelly and her family that he might be on the rampage that night, or the following one. The last thing she wants is for them to suffer her father's rage.

She runs all the way there, her heart thumping with joy and fear, scarcely believing what she's done. When Kelly opens the door, she blurts out, unable to hold it in any longer, "I've done it — I've left home!"

Every day she approaches her walk to school with caution, joining groups of other people where she can, hiding her face under a hat or a hood, knowing it will be fruitless if he sees her. Her joy at being free is tempered by fear of her father's looming figure at the school gates, his heavy step on the deck of the narrowboat at night.

Miss Archer, delighted to have her best pupil back, asks no questions, to Leonora's relief. Perhaps Miss Archer thinks her father's had a change of heart, been persuaded by her mother. Whatever the reason, she accepts her into her English A-level class with a warm welcome.

She lies in wait for Fred the postman, now her friend and confidant, to tell him where she is. He's bemused but unsurprised. Perhaps he saw the bruises and came to his own conclusions about her family life. He seems happy to walk the extra distance to the canal to deliver her letters from Ricky.

She writes straight away. This year is crucial for him, with his final year exams and the looming prospect of discussing his plans with his father.

She can hardly bear to think of her father's fury when Ricky tells him he's not coming back. She fears that her brother might not be strong enough to resist, especially a physical onslaught — even though he's probably taller since she last saw him three years ago, the idea of him squaring up to their father is terrifying.

The storm brewing about her own defection will be nothing compared with the one Ricky will have to face.

* * *

118

Wow Leo, I'm so proud of you! You said you'd do it if you had to, and you did, brave sister. I'm not sure I'd have had the strength to stand up to him. I hope that by the time you get this, you're still there and he hasn't come charging round to get you. You stay strong, girl!

I haven't got long today as I'm about to go to class — Maths revision session, oh the joy. It's going well, though, and I'm fairly confident I'll get the grades. Fingers crossed! So happy for your news, look after yourself. R x

* * *

A dark shape separates from the tree as she walks along the towpath, the brown smudges of his footsteps a warning signal. Her heart starts to thump and she stops and turns, ready to run. But he says, his voice calm, menacing: "Leonora. If you run away now, I'll find you. You won't escape a second time."

She turns back, her heart beating out of her chest, lifting her chin. He takes a couple of steps towards her.

"Stop, Dad. Don't come any nearer." Her voice shakes but she doesn't care. "I swear, I'll tell the police if you touch me. I mean it."

For a moment she thinks he's going to lunge at her and she prepares to flee, but he stops and stands, glowering. "You really are a piece of work, ordering me around," he says, his finger stabbing the air. "You come home now, or else."

"Or else what, Dad?" Hot tears cloud her eyes, unbidden, the words tumbling out, as loud as she dares. "Or else what?"

A look of surprise flits across his face and she steels herself. The fingers on his right hand are already curled into a fist. She knows she's pushing him, but she will not give in.

"I'm not coming back, Dad. I'm going to finish at school, get my exams and go to university. You can't stop me."

"I bloody well can." An angry flush is creeping up his cheeks. "You're my daughter and you'll do as I say." He makes a swift movement towards her and she's away, off up the bank above the towpath, grabbing at the long grass as it steepens.

"Everything all right?" says a voice.

She's never been so happy to see Pete. He's standing at the top of the bank, holding a supermarket bag full of shopping, the ring in his beard glinting. She scrambles up to him. "My dad," she says in a low voice. Pete nods, puts the shopping down and steps forward.

Her father, now at a disadvantage at the bottom of the slope, stops, uncertain. "You stay out of this," he says with a gesture at Pete. "Leonora, you come with me."

"I'm not coming, Dad. I told you." She stands next to Pete, who squares his shoulders and rolls up his sleeves, revealing a snake tattoo on his right arm. Her father hesitates, scowling up at them.

"I think she's pretty clear about that, don't you?" Pete says in his deepest voice. Her dad's face contorts with rage.

"You haven't heard the end of this, girl," he shouts, pointing his finger like a weapon at her head. "You'll be seeing me again, very soon."

CHAPTER TWENTY-THREE

Leonora

The weeks that follow are the happiest of Leonora's life. Her routine on the narrowboat settles into a comfortable rhythm in the lead-up to Christmas. Despite the lack of space, the sheer homeliness of the place makes it the perfect bolthole for Leonora. She loves waking up in the mornings to the gentle rocking sensation as Pete and Maria move about making breakfast, and though the mornings are dark and the evenings becoming darker, she walks to school and back again filled with energy.

It helps that Pete disappears off to Wales for days at a time. They're renovating the cottage stage by stage in the winter months and his absence gives them all a little more space. Maria stays with Leonora, assuring her that she'd rather stay here than deal with the dust and the noise of Pete with his drill and his hammer.

Leonora falls into a routine. Each day, when she arrives back from school, she studies for a couple of hours while Maria prepares supper. They light the stove and the warmth dries their newly washed clothes. They snuggle up with blankets and cushions when it gets really cold. Maria is calm and easy-going, with a playful sense of humour and a deep love of plants and animals. She's sensitive to Leonora's moods, which veer from a state of almost-happiness to one of deep guilt and hopelessness.

At weekends Leonora allows herself time off studying. On Saturdays she works at the farm shop, and sometimes on Sundays Kelly comes over and they hang out together playing cards or listening to music. She brings cake, sometimes home-made bread from her mother. Leonora is still too nervous to visit the family in case her father somehow finds out.

Being in the sixth form is almost a pleasant experience. The teachers treat the sixth-formers as adults and have more time for each person. The subjects are more challenging, too. At last Leonora begins to feel she's using her brain, not just learning through repetition. English continues to be her best subject, and she reads voraciously — Jane Austen, Dickens, Trollope alongside Isabel Allende, Gabriel García Márquez and Hemingway.

There are extra freedoms this year. They can visit the shops at lunchtime, go home early if there's a free period, and they have their own common room, away from the noise of the younger pupils. They can spend all their free time in the library, if they choose, and it becomes like Leonora's third home. She misses Kelly, but she finds to her surprise that most of the students who have stayed on are bright, interesting and ambitious, like her. On the whole, she likes them, though she doesn't have time for socialising with them. At the beginning of term they included her in their invitations to a party or to the pub, but by half-term they've stopped asking. Leonora prefers it that way.

She can't help worrying about her mother. Guilt stabs at her whenever she thinks of her, alone all day, dreading the sound of her husband's key in the lock. Living in fear, powerless to leave, dulling her pain with drink. Giving in, giving up, losing her health and her mind, killing herself slowly.

When she allows herself to think like this, usually at night when she's alone, hope deserts Leonora. There are no relatives to contact, no friends they can rely on, no money, and her mum has neither the will nor the strength to help herself.

On her first visit back home her mum barely recognises her. She's comatose on the sofa when Leonora arrives, an empty bottle of vodka on the floor beside her. Leonora tidies up, cleans the kitchen, puts some washing on. She prepares a sandwich for her mum, wakes her with a glass of water and leaves.

At supper Leonora can barely eat, weighed down by the tragedy of the scene at home. Maria sits next to her on the narrow bench under the window, puts her arm around her and Leonora sobs her heart out for the first time since she left home.

Maria says nothing, waits for the storm to settle, then gets a notebook and pen. They write down everything that could be done for Leonora's mum — all the possible scenarios, everything they can think of, anyone they could contact for help. Afterwards they choose the three actions that seem the most practical and workable. They're going to ask Mrs Clark from next door to take Leonora's mum to the doctor. She is kind at heart: perhaps she'll be willing to help. Maria will contact a charity for abused women and see if there's any financial or practical help they can offer, and Leonora will visit the Citizen's Advice office after school and ask them what help her mother might be able to get locally.

With Maria's support, there may be something Leonora can do to improve her mum's situation. The weight lifts a little from her chest.

When she's not worrying about her mum, she worries about Ricky. The moment of truth is approaching rapidly. November will be his last full month at school, and he has the ordeal of the final prize-giving to get through before Christmas. Their father will travel to South Africa for the first time since Ricky started school there, to attend the ceremony and accompany his son home. If he comes home.

* * *

To my best brother Ricky,

Did you get your exam results yet? I'm sure you've done well. The sixth form at school is much better — we get treated as people now, rather than idiots. The work is hard — much harder than before, but better, more interesting. I do at least two hours' homework every night, but I don't mind, it's all for a good reason.

I love living on the narrowboat. Maria and Pete are great, so easy-going. They never argue and they talk to each other like best friends, all the time. We trip over each other a lot, because it's so small and cramped, but we just laugh. It's so different from home. I don't want to call that place home any more. It never felt like I belonged there, not really.

I visit Mum every week, in the afternoons, before Dad gets home. She's drinking, a lot, and doesn't eat much, so she's getting very thin, and doesn't look well. I think she's given up. The good news is that we (me and Maria) have sorted out a helper to come in twice a week. She cleans up, cooks for her and makes sure she showers and gets dressed. Without the helper, she stays in bed all day. I don't know what Dad thinks, or if he even knows about the help. If he finds out, he should be glad. Not that I'd get any thanks from him.

It's odd that Dad hasn't come looking for me again. Perhaps he's expunged me from his life (good word?) and doesn't care what I do now. I really hope so.

But he does care what you do, Ricky, and I'm worried. Are you going to stay out there in December? Because if you come back, even for a holiday, he's not going to let you go again. You'll end up doing what he wants, because you won't be able to get away like I did. You're the one he's focused on. Stay in South Africa if that's what you want. Don't worry about me and Mum, we'll manage. And as soon as I can I'll come and see you, if I have to save every penny. Have you got the brooch somewhere safe?

Did I tell you I've got a Saturday job in the farm shop? The money's not great, but they're nice, and I get discounted and out-of-date food (that is perfectly all right), which is great because it's a small way to pay Maria and Pete back for what they've done for me. I give Mum some decent food when I can. And I'll be able to work there full-time in the holidays to cover for the other staff. With my new paper round as well, I'm managing to save a little bit. Miss Archer says I'll qualify for a full grant at university, as there's no family income to support me.

Write soon!

Love,

Your best sister,

Leo xx

* * *

Dear Best Sister,

Have you studied Robert Burns? He wrote an apology to a mouse, because he'd upset its nest while ploughing a field. It's called, imaginatively, 'To a Mouse'.

> But Mousie, thou art no thy-lane [you aren't alone]
> In proving foresight may be vain:
> The best laid schemes o' mice an' men
> Gang aft agley, [often go awry]
> An' lea'e us nought but grief an' pain,
> For promis'd joy.

I know you think I need a plan, and I agree. I promise I'll be prepared. My plan will have two elements: one: Tell him what I'm going to do, and two: RUN!

But seriously, I will think about what's going to happen. I have decided — properly decided — that I want to work with animals, and to stay here. I have the support of Luke and Sally, and of my tutor, who's advising me on courses I can do to become a ranger. I've already applied for a couple of them. In the short term I'm going to work with Luke full-time, in return for my keep, looking after the nature reserve at the school. It's all settled and there's not much Dad can do about it. I'm eighteen now and he can't force me.

I did get my exam results. I got two As and a B! All Dad could say was "What happened with the B?" Literally, that's all he said. No congratulations, no pat on the back (metaphorically, as he was writing), no praise for working hard. Typical. I'm happy, though. It's enough to get me the qualifications I need, and enough for an employer to know

I'm not stupid. I'm going to get a prize at Speech Day for rifle shooting, and probably one for my work on the estate — though I'm not telling Dad in advance, there's no point.

The real reason he's coming to Speech Day is to make sure I go home afterwards. Not sure I can stop him buying a plane ticket for me, but it can't be helped — I'm not going to tell him before he gets here, that's for sure.

Anyway, this camping holiday in the mountains with Dad: I'm dreading it. I can't think of anything worse, him pretending to be a father to me, being all chummy. And he knows nothing about camping, or being in the bush, or the animals. He's expecting me to arrange it all for as little money as possible. Still, maybe there's the tiniest chance that I can get him interested in the wildlife and he'll begin to see why I want to stay. I doubt it, but you never know.

Don't worry, I'll think of something. And when the fuss has died down and I've got enough money, I'll pay for you to come over. The fund is growing!

Keep fighting, Leo — you're a star.
Your best brother, Ricky x

P.S. When you see Mum, give her my love and tell her I'm thinking of her (I'm not sure she sees my letters, or maybe she doesn't read them). Well done for organising the help. X

* * *

December is only days away and Leonora's sense of dread about her father's visit to South Africa gets worse every day.

These days her mum's mind often wanders. She lives in an increasingly isolated world, and sometimes it's hard to get her to focus on anything for more than a few moments. But today she seems a little brighter than usual, a little more willing to talk. Music from her old Roberts radio plays in the background as they sit at the kitchen table.

"Mum, what do you think's going to happen when Dad goes out to South Africa?"

"What do you mean?"

"I mean — is Dad really expecting Ricky to come back with him?"

The surprise in her mum's eyes tells her the answer. "Of course he is; that's the point, isn't it? Apart from going to Speech Day."

"But what if Ricky doesn't want to? Come back, I mean."

"He is coming back — he'll go to university next year, like your father wants." Her mum frowns at her across the kitchen table. "Why, has Ricky said something to you?"

"No, I just — well, he's an adult now, he can do what he likes, can't he?"

"Not where your dad's concerned. He's set on university and a top job for his son, whatever Ricky wants."

"But that's my point, Mum. Ricky doesn't have to do what Dad wants."

Her mum shrugs and gets up from her chair with an effort, closing the discussion. She flicks the kettle on and opens the cupboard above, where she keeps the vodka.

CHAPTER TWENTY-FOUR

Ricky

Dad arrived the night before Speech Day and stayed at Luke's. I didn't want him to, but Luke said it was fine, it was only one night, and they'd feel wrong if they didn't invite him. I was worried about how he would behave, and I didn't want him invading this, my special place, where I was so happy. But it was only one night, and then we'd be off to the mountains, so I swallowed my concerns.

He arrived in the afternoon. Barely acknowledging me, he shook hands with Luke and Sally, nodded to the children and grumbled at the dogs. I'd barely slept the night before and was tense with nerves. Speech Day with my father there was a bad enough prospect, but then I had to endure his company on a camping trip, when I was going to drop the bombshell that I wasn't going back. I was not looking forward to it.

I showed him round, introduced him to the animals. He responded with a series of grunts, barely concealing his contempt. "It's not right," he said. "Animals in the house, spreading germs. Still, some people live like that." I had to stop myself retorting that living like this was heaven compared with living in his grim household. Supper was unusually quiet, his mood affecting even the children, who seemed scared and intimidated by him. Luke and Sally did their best to engage him in conversation, but he didn't even have the manners to try. Even before we'd all finished, he rose from the table and announced he was going to bed.

I was angry and embarrassed, but Luke clapped me on the back and said quietly: "Don't let it get to you. It'll be okay." I was grateful to him but I didn't believe him.

Speech Day went by in a whirl. Dad spoke to nobody apart from the head, and he was curt even with him. He didn't thank him, or my teachers, or acknowledge what they'd done for me. Luckily I'd written a note to each personally, telling them how grateful I was for their support.

When I collected my prizes, he managed only a grudging nod of his head in acknowledgement. I was paralysed with shame and hatred for him. I couldn't wait to get out of there.

* * *

The Land Rover dropped us a mile or so from the entrance to Giant's Castle Reserve. It's the nearest reserve to the school, and it didn't take long to get there. I reckoned as Dad wanted to do everything the cheapest way possible, the best thing would be to hitch-hike, which I'd done a couple of times before.

I soon realised that Dad was useless. He had never done anything like this before — not hitch-hiking, camping, or cooking over a real fire. It seemed to me he'd never even climbed a hill before, let alone gone trekking in the mountains. So, for once, I was in charge. I rather enjoyed it.

The hitching was easy. There is only one main road that goes by the school and the man in the Land Rover on his way north took us most of the way. We didn't want to go right to the entrance anyway — our plan was to avoid the fee and sneak in where we wouldn't be noticed. That all worked well and soon we were on foot, heading right into the remotest area of the reserve.

The Drakensberg area is stunning, Leo. I hope I can show you one day. The mountain range is huge, with some of the highest peaks in South Africa and the most spectacular views. There are remote valleys, unspoiled forests and huge rock formations. You can walk for days without seeing a single person, though you will see plenty of animals, birds and insects. I'd been there many times before with Luke, so I knew what to expect and I was looking forward to exploring a different area.

Dad tried to pretend he wasn't a complete novice. Luckily Luke had been able to lend us most of the kit — a tent, cooking equipment, sleeping bags and so on, and also some hiking boots for Dad. Although I was carrying almost everything on my back I had to slow my pace for him to keep up, and it took longer than I thought to reach the area I was aiming for.

Each evening I did everything. I decided where we would stop, put up the tent, set the fire, cooked, cleaned up. I wasn't expecting much from him, admittedly, but he really didn't have a clue. Even if he had, I don't suppose he'd have helped.

We didn't talk much. He was too unfit to talk as well as walk, which suited me fine. When we stopped, I was busy sorting everything out — which was a good excuse, and he seemed content just to lie about and watch. It didn't take me long to wonder how long I was going to last.

The truth was, I was pretty certain our trip would be cut short. If I was going to tell him my plans, the fallout from that would be enough to put paid to any further time together. So it was up to me to pick my moment, knowing that we'd probably be heading back as soon as the bomb blew.

And yet, despite everything he'd done and everything he'd said, a small part of me hoped there was still a chance he would understand. I wanted him to realise how beautiful South Africa was and how it felt to be surrounded by wildlife.

If he could just see how knowledgeable I was, how important this was to me, perhaps he would relent and give me his blessing to stay on.

What a fool I was.

On the third morning I woke early. While Dad was still asleep, I took my backpack and the gun and walked for an hour or so into the bush, happy to be away from the dark cloud that seemed to surround him. A couple of Cape vultures wheeled above me in a clear pale-blue sky, and I watched out for snakes as I walked. I was hoping to spot some eland, the large spiral-horned antelope that have inhabited the area for millennia, but all I saw was a couple of dassies, the small rodents that live in crevices in the rocks. I sat on a rock for a while and took in the spectacular views, breathing in the clean air. It was good to be alone.

Being with Dad had always felt like an effort. But now, knowing what I knew, it was excruciating to spend time with him, and I could barely look him in the eye. I could see nothing in his character that was good, or even tolerable, and his behaviour towards Mum and you had crystallised my view. I used to feel guilty that I hated him, but now I felt cold, hard contempt.

I decided then to tell him my plans straight away. Somehow I had to find the strength. I felt I couldn't last another twenty-four hours, and the further we got into the reserve, the longer it would take to get out. There would be no way he could find his own way back, so I would be forced to spend at least another three days with him, even if I did the deed right then. I steeled myself and headed back to camp, fearful but full of resolve.

When I got back to the camp, he was still sleeping, the rasp of his snoring disturbing the quiet air of the morning. I started the camping gas, put some water on to boil, and clattered about a bit until he appeared, his eyes puffy with sleep.

"Coffee?" I said, holding a mug out to him.

He took it with a grunt and sat down. I glanced at his face, trying to gauge his mood, but it didn't help. Whatever his state of mind now, there was no doubt it would soon be worse.

"Dad?"

He grunted without looking at me, sipping his coffee noisily. He wasn't going to make this easy.

"I've decided what I want to do after school." That made him look up, his eyes narrowing, but I looked away. I rushed on before my courage left me. "Dad, I'm going to stay here and study to be a ranger. I want to look after wildlife here in South Africa. Luke's going to help."

His response was predictable, word for word. "Like hell you are," he said, putting his mug down. His voice was gruff, threatening, as the anger rose. "You'll do as I say. You're coming back with me and going to university in the UK. No arguments."

"No, Dad. I'm not doing that," I said, my body poised for a sudden move away from him. "I've found what I want to do. I love this environment, all the wildlife here, working on the reserve. Can't you see? It's perfect for me. This—" I took in the expanse of the horizon with my arms, "This is going to be my career. I'm not coming back with you."

At that, he jumped up, finger pointing, jaw jutting, an angry flush spreading upwards from his neck. But I was ready and the pan of hot water was between us, so he had to get round it to get at me. I was on my feet in a moment, facing him, and I was taller than him — only by a fraction, but it felt good. Though I was quaking with fear, I managed to resist recoiling and running.

"You fucking little shit," he yelled, stepping around the stove, his finger now inches from my face. "After everything I've given you. All that swanky education has given you ideas, has it? How dare you! You're just like your sister, a waste of space! You're coming back with me if I have to drag you there."

By then, I was shaking. But oddly, it didn't feel like fear. A stronger swell of emotion was forcing me to stand my ground. It burst from me, like the moment I'd heard about Mum. "I'm not going, Dad!" I yelled, spitting the words into his astonished face. "You don't give a shit about me, or Mum, or Leo, you only care about yourself! You've never done anything for anyone else. I know what you did to Mum — you're a coward and a bastard! You treat Mum like a slave, and she's broken because of you! Do you hear me? Broken! She drinks to escape from the hell of living with you. You don't deserve a family, you're despicable . . . I hate you — we all do!"

With a terrifying roar, he struck out at me, his fists balled, his face contorted with rage. I raised my arm to protect my head and managed to deflect the first blow, though it had me stumbling backwards into the tent.

Before I knew it, I had the gun in my hand. With an instinct I'd learned from my training, I used it as a shield, countering the onslaught as best I could while his arms flailed around trying to get at my body. I held on, my entire body tensed against his.

For a moment, everything stopped. Our bodies were frozen in a tangle of arms and legs as each fought for supremacy. We were in perfect balance, our strength exactly equal, one cancelling out the other.

The sound of the gunshot smashed into the mountains, ricocheting off the rocky outcrops, piercing the deepest caves, screaming past the kudu and the jackals, the snakes and the lizards, reaching far into the heavens where the eagles paused for an instant before gliding on through the huge South African sky

I stood for a moment, reeling, the shot ringing painfully in my ears, my hands still grasping the gun.

The next minute, he was yelling at me.

"Fuck! Look what you've done, you stupid little shit! You've shot me! Fucking — do something!"

I stayed put. He was trying to remove his belt with one hand while stemming the flow with the other. His trousers were already dark with blood; it was flowing fast into the grass beneath him. I stared, fascinated, as it pooled. "Get me a towel, tighten this up. Help me!"

When I didn't move, he looked up at me. The red flush of anger had drained from his cheeks but his eyes were still flashing fury. "What are you doing? I'm serious, you'd better bloody help me now!"

"No," I said, my voice steady. "I'm not going to help you. You never did anything for us — not me, nor Mum, nor Leo. You don't deserve my help." I lowered the gun, turned and started to pack my bag.

"For fuck's sake!" he yelled, still struggling to tighten his belt around his leg. In the wrong place. He didn't even know how to do that properly. "I could die from this!"

"You might," I said, shouldering my bag and looking around. Low mountains encircled us, carpeted with high grasses that rustled in the gentle breeze. Rocky outcrops and clumps of bushes were the only other landmarks. "If you're lucky, someone might come along before you peg it, though I doubt it."

For a moment, he gazed at me with a look of utter astonishment. "You — you want me to die? I'm your father, for Christ's sake — what's wrong with you?" He tried to crawl towards me, but stopped with a groan, clutching at his leg. The patch of blood on the grass was growing rapidly. "Are you just going to stand there and watch?"

"I'm going to leave you. It's no less than you deserve."

He squeezed his eyes shut at that. "Please, Ricky, please, son, help me. Run and get help, at least. I'm in agony . . . I don't want to die like this . . ." His voice was already fading, his strength trickling away with the blood. For a moment I almost felt sorry for him.

My eyes filled with tears. Not from pity — even then I couldn't pity him. I mourned the father I never had, the pain he'd put us all through. The fact that he'd never called me Ricky before, or son. I wept for Mum and for you, Leo.

But when he saw my tears, his mouth twisted with scorn. "You always were a feeble little pussy," he said.

CHAPTER TWENTY-FIVE

Leonora

Every day Leonora's anxiety grows. She puts the music on loud in her cabin and lies on her back, watching the colours rise and merge, fall and sparkle with every note. It's a release, if only temporary.

Even if Ricky makes a good case for staying in South Africa, she can't imagine it will work, not in a million years. Every scenario she conjures up ends badly. Why did she encourage him to stay rather than come back for Christmas? At least at home she can help him. Out there, his friends gone, the school closed for the holiday, he'll be entirely on his own. She can only hope Luke and Sally can protect him.

If she were Ricky, she reasons, she'd wait until the last moment to deliver the blow. She'd get away from the school, avoid the humiliation of a scene in front of friends, and give their father as little time as possible before his flight leaves. But Ricky does things his own way and she has no way of knowing what's going on. She just has to wait.

And there's a further worry. With her dad away, her mum has abandoned all pretence of sobriety.

As Leonora approaches the house after school, Mrs Clark stops her at the gate, a sympathetic hand on her arm. "I'm sorry, Leonora, but your mum's in a bad way. This morning she keeled over on the front path, knocked herself out. Luckily the postman found her. He got her inside and came to fetch me."

She feels the blood drain from her cheeks. "Is she hurt?"

"She seems all right now. She's lying on the sofa in the sitting room. She wouldn't let me call the doctor until you got here. Nasty lump on the head and some bruising — luckily not more, but it was a miracle she didn't kill herself. She could have been there for hours if the postman hadn't come."

A sense of helplessness almost overwhelms Leonora. "Thank you so much for helping," she says, her voice shaking. "But — what can I do? Dad's away, and I can't . . . look, could you come in for a minute, do you think?" Mrs Clark nods and follows her in.

Her mum lies on her side, her head propped on a cushion, her bare legs drawn to her stomach. Her eyes are closed, her mouth drooping. She seems to be sleeping. She wears only a nightie and dressing gown and one slipper has fallen onto the floor beside her. A livid purple bruise is spreading across her forehead. Cuts and grazes pattern the arm that lies draped over the faded chintz. A reek of stale alcohol fills the cold air and a half-empty vodka bottle lies abandoned on the floor. Leonora picks it up. She strokes her mother's hair away from her forehead, listens to her breathing for a moment and fetches a blanket to cover her.

They creep out of the room and go to the kitchen.

"Mrs Clark, can you help me?" Leonora says, her voice breaking. "I don't know what to do. Should I call the doctor?"

"Well, she can't look after herself anymore. Your dad's not going to do it and you can't do it. Last time the doctor saw her, he said she must stop the drink or risk serious long-term damage. But she doesn't care. The minute we were out of the surgery, she was off to the shop for more. She needs help. Come on, let's call the surgery now."

After a brief examination the doctor calls an ambulance.

"It looks like she might have had a stroke," he says. "We'll do some tests and keep her in until we're sure, but if she carries on the way she's going, it doesn't look good. I'm sorry, but I believe, given the circumstances, it's time to consider some kind of residential care. When is your father back?"

Leonora, struggling to absorb the implications of this, says: "Two days' time."

The doctor looks from her to Mrs Clark and back again. "Are you able to contact him?"

Leonora shakes her head. "He's trekking in South Africa, with my brother."

"Well, not to worry. She'll be in hospital until at least then and she'll be well looked after." He looks around, taking in the shabby kitchen, the stained floor, the greasy curtains at the window, the sink full of grimy dishes. "And how will you cope, Leonora?"

"I'm not living at home anymore — I'm with friends. I'll be fine."

"Good. So I'll leave you to let your dad know what's happened. Please ask him to contact me on his return."

Leonora nods, already visualising the note she'll write and leave on the hall table. There's no way she is going to be there when he gets home.

* * *

In the middle of the night, the dove-grey thud of boots on the deck wakes her with a start. Adrenalin kick-starts her system and she's instantly awake and trembling. It must be her dad — he's come to get her. The boat tilts and sways against the bank and she hears the gentle yellow slop of water on its bows outside her bedroom window. Her eyes strain into an impenetrable blackness, unable to make out even the closest piece of furniture. She stumbles out of bed, tiptoes to the door, listens until her ears almost hurt.

It's two days now since he was supposed to arrive back but there's been no sign of him. Part of her is relieved, part panicked. Yesterday she couldn't resist going to the house to check. She went under cover of darkness, her hood pulled over her head, as far as Mrs Clark's house. But there was no sign of life at the Bates house: no lights, nothing to indicate he had returned, with or without Ricky.

She's been waiting for something to happen, and now it has. She flinches at a strident rapping on the hatch, deep blue flares falling as her eyes strain through the darkness. Maria's feet pad in a haze of pale pink past her door. She creeps out after her. A light goes on, illuminating Maria, a blanket round her shoulders, standing by the steps to the hatch, gazing upwards. Leonora wishes Pete was here.

She grabs a coat and flings it on, then takes Maria's hand, trembling with cold and fear.

"Who's there?" Maria calls.

"Police. We need to talk to Leonora Bates."

Leonora breathes out. It's not her dad. But then she feels a slow ripple of fear along her spine. Something must have happened.

"I need some identification," Maria says firmly. "Can you pass it through the gap?"

A small slit has been carved at the bottom of the doors that open outwards at the top of the steps for letters to be delivered. A police warrant card in a black leather case is pushed through. Maria scrutinises it for a moment, seems satisfied, pushes it back. "Wait a moment."

She scrabbles with the padlock and bolts on the inside of the hatch. Torchlight streams down into the cabin as she opens the doors and a pair of large black boots appear at the top of the short flight of steps. Maria backs away to allow two uniformed policemen to enter. They look huge in the tiny kitchen space. One of them has to remove his hat and bend his neck to stand comfortably.

"Sorry to disturb you," the older of the two men says, glancing around. "I'm DI Metcalfe, this is DC North. We need to talk to Leonora Bates. Is that you?" He looks at Leonora, still clinging to Maria. She nods, biting her lip to stop it trembling.

"Perhaps we could sit down?" Maria indicates the narrow bench by the wall and they shuffle their way around the table with difficulty. She lights another lamp and fills the kettle. The red clink of tin mugs as she prepares tea comforts Leonora as she perches opposite the two men.

DI Metcalfe shifts his weight. His legs are impeded by the table post so he's forced to sit at an awkward angle, his shoulder against his colleague's. Maria sits, taking Leonora's hand again. She grasps it as if she'll never let it go.

"I'm afraid we have bad news." There's a sharp intake of breath — sea green — and she realises it's her own. "We've been to see your mum, in hospital. She told us you were living away from home. We've been round the houses a bit, trying to find you, I have to say." He looks around the small space, as if assessing it as a hiding place.

Leonora says nothing. A vision of Ricky, cold and dead, fills her terrified imagination. She begins to tremble and as if in sympathy, the kettle rattles and steams. Maria rises to fill the teapot. Nobody speaks as she brings the tray to the table and fills the mugs, adding milk for herself and Leonora.

"We've had a call from the British Consulate in South Africa," DI Metcalfe says. Leonora's hand flies to her mouth: *oh, Ricky*. Maria puts an arm around her.

"They were contacted by the police in a district named, let's see . . ." He takes out a notebook and flips a few pages until he finds what he's looking for. "KwaZulu-Natal." He spells it out slowly, enunciating each syllable with precision. "I believe your dad and brother have been taking a holiday in the mountains there?"

Leonora nods, shivering so hard her teeth chatter.

"It seems they went to a nature reserve, a place called Giant's Castle. They appear to have got in without registering at the gate, so nobody knew they were there. That's why it took some time for the alarm to be raised. When they did send out a search party, I'm afraid, well — they found your father. They were too late, though. He was already dead. I'm so sorry."

She can't say anything. She stares at the DI, his words hanging empty in her ears.

"H . . . how?" she whispers, her mind spinning.

"Gunshot wound to the leg." He glances at his colleague, who keeps a grim gaze on Leonora's face. "He bled to death, I'm afraid."

The words sink in slowly, like the drip, drip of water from a tap. There's a ringing in her ears. The rest of her seems paralysed with shock.

Dad's dead. Those words should give her some relief, but something's wrong. Something's missing. She opens her mouth, searching, but nothing seems to transfer from her brain. Maria's arm tightens around her waist. She says the words Leonora is looking for.

"But . . . what about Ricky? Where's Leonora's brother?"

* * *

Everything's black again. The only sounds are the ochre-tinted slap of water against the sides of the boat, the occasional deep blue bleat of a sheep in the field nearby. She lies with Maria in the double bed, cocooned in her arms, eyes wide open.

Ricky is lost, disappeared, gone. And he's suspected of murder, wanted by the police.

She repeats to herself, over and over again: "What am I going to do?"

CHAPTER TWENTY-SIX

Leonora

The days go by in a haze of numbness.

She's dimly aware of Pete's arrival on the boat, of Maria's arm around her, of the warmth of the cabin and food she can't eat. She lies silent on her bed, watching the reflection of the water ripple across the wooden ceiling. Her mind feels blank, empty, her emotions on hold. There's no question of going to school. She forgets to worry about social services. They could do anything with her and she wouldn't care.

When Kelly comes, her eyes are full of tears. She climbs onto the tiny bed with Leonora. They lie in each other's arms, and Leonora feels the comfort of a true friend.

She rises only to see her mum. Maria drives her to the hospital in Pete's beaten-up van, goes in with her and waits patiently until she's ready to come home.

Every morning, in that dim, blissful moment between sleep and wakefulness, she forgets that Ricky's gone. When realisation comes a heartbeat later, she's left gasping. She stands naked in the tiny bathroom, waiting for the cold to seep into her bones because it's a different pain from the one in her heart.

Her mind is like a whirlpool, tossing questions around, sucking in stories of what happened out there in the mountains, spinning them until they break into tiny pieces, spewing them out again. Did Ricky tell their father what he wanted to do, was there a huge fight? Did the gun go off by accident, or was Ricky pushed so far he shot his own father? If Ricky is alive, where is he? Did he run away, was he taken, did he get lost? How will they find him, and if they do, will he go to prison for murder? Perhaps he's still out there, living in a cave somewhere, using his knowledge of bushcraft to keep himself alive. Perhaps he fell and lay injured for days, unable to move, and died a horrible, lonely death.

It's too much to bear.

Every day that passes without news of him she feels it more. Every instinct urges her to get out there, somehow, and search for him herself.

But she's only sixteen. Though she's strong enough to leave home, to face her father's wrath, this is so beyond her sphere of experience, she can't even see how to begin. She has rarely left the town she was born in, let alone travelled abroad. Even if she had the money to get there, she knows nothing about South Africa; how things work, where to start. Not even if it's safe. The scale of the task seems enormous, and nothing she's learned in her short life has prepared her for it.

The man from the Foreign and Commonwealth Office, a young man in a pinstriped suit, with the kind of hair that never moves, calls by as Leonora lies dazed with shock on her bed. He is reluctant to talk to Maria and Pete, though they try their best to get more details from him. He leaves a card and asks Leonora to call as soon as she is able. She listens to the conversation and watches him through her tiny window as he walks away.

She sits at the table, turning the card in her hands.

"We should call him," Maria says, as she clears the table of dishes, wiping the crumbs away carefully.

Leonora looks up, relief sweeping over her. "Would you help? I don't think I can do it by myself . . . sorry."

"Don't be sorry. Of course you can't do it by yourself. We'll help you in every way we can. You don't need to ask."

Tears prick at the rims of her eyes. She's cried so much in the last days, yet the tears still come. She wonders if they'll ever stop.

"Thank you."

It's all she can say. Maria and Pete didn't sign up for this when they invited her to stay and they don't deserve these complications in their simple lives, but they've been unwavering in their support. There will never be a way she can repay these kind, loving people.

* * *

At the house, time has stopped. The air stands still and stale, undisturbed since her mum left for the hospital. There are letters on the mat by the front door. Bills, flyers, a free newspaper. Maria gathers them up and puts them in her bag. "We can look at them later," she says.

The phone squats on the hall table, a small stool beside it.

"I'll make the call if you like," Maria says.

While Maria dials, Leonora walks up the stairs, tiptoeing for reasons she doesn't understand.

Ricky's room. She can smell him, feel him all around. The bed is bare. Dust coats the bookshelves, the chest of drawers in the corner. The wardrobe door hangs open — it never did shut properly — revealing a dark, half-empty space and some shirts on wire hangers, their cuffs and collars faded and frayed.

But he's still there, somehow, the essence of him. She breathes in deeply, her back against the wall. An old pair of trainers, too small for him now, lie discarded under the bed. A navy-blue dressing gown, the sleeves already too short on his last visit, hangs behind the door. She buries her face in the towelling, breathes in its faint odour. She remembers his tousled head in the mornings when he'd just woken up, his eyes puffy with sleep.

"He can't be dead," she whispers. "Please God, don't let him be dead."

Maria calls from the hallway. "Are you okay, Leo?"

"Coming," she says, unhooking the dressing gown from the door.

CHAPTER TWENTY-SEVEN

Leonora

They've come to London to meet the man from the Foreign and Commonwealth Office. It's the most imposing building Leonora has ever seen, with soaring arches, staring statues and carved figures above the entrance. Already shocked by the crowded pavements, the traffic noise and the sheer size of the city, she feels small and insignificant as she and Maria hurry up the wide front steps. The enormous front door opens into a massive, dusty space where a receptionist sits yawning. She hardly gives them a glance before waving them to a bench in the corner, but it's not long before a woman appears and they are ushered up a soaring marble staircase into the interior.

The young man with the solid hair looks uncomfortable, his shirt collar tight against the skin of his neck, where a rash of pink pimples rises towards his chin. As if sensing her gaze, he runs a finger round the inside of his collar, leaving tiny folds of skin that ease out slowly. She wonders why he doesn't just undo the top button. Nobody would notice, or care.

"Miss Bates," he says, pulling his chair closer to his desk and searching through the pile of papers in his in tray. "I'm sorry for your loss. Thank you for coming in today."

The journey was a struggle. Relentless rain battered the van on the way to the station and soaked them on the platform. Leonora was too fidgety to sit in the waiting room. The Underground was packed with travellers, damp and silent, and Maria and Leonora were forced to stand for eight long stops. Then they'd asked directions and got lost, arriving late for their appointment. By the time they eventually sat down in the young man's office, Leonora was ready to explode. Maria, sensing her state of mind, accepted with alacrity his offer of tea on behalf of them both.

Leonora can barely contain herself. She watches his hands flicking through the pile of papers, willing herself to keep quiet. Could he not have prepared himself? They were late, after all; he's had the time. She digs her fingernails into the palm of her hand and the sudden image of a blade cutting into her thigh flashes into her mind. She wishes she had a penknife in her bag — she could go to the Ladies' and calm herself with one quick, blissful cut. She folds her arms across her chest, curls her legs into a tangle and bites her lip until she feels the sweet warm blood on her tongue.

The tea arrives, on a tray carried by a smart woman in a sensible skirt. She pours from a china teapot and leaves them to add their own milk. Leonora, her eyes still on the slow progress through the pile of papers, burns her mouth with her first taste.

"Ah, here we are. Apologies, ladies."

* * *

The moment her foot hits the pavement, she starts to run. Her feet splash through endless puddles and rain plasters her hair to her face, but she can't stop. She's dimly aware of Maria calling her, but she needs to get away from that place; find somewhere, anywhere, where she can let go. Over the road there's a gate to a small park with a square of grass and tall trees overhanging muddy paths. She navigates the traffic amid bronze-blaring horns, and runs in, almost colliding into a man with an umbrella coming the other way. "Sorry," she mutters, and keeps running.

Under a large tree she stops, panting, raises her face to its high canopy. Huge spots of rain land on her cheeks, in her eyes, on her shoulders. Water runs down her neck, cold on her back. She wants to drown in it, let it take her, whisk her away to some distant ocean. She inhales until her lungs are ready to burst, clenches her fists and screams into the tree, a shriek of deep despair, her body shaking head to foot. The sound blooms scarlet into the air around her and she kicks and kicks at the sodden trunk until there's a silver crack of bone and the pain from her toes overtakes the pain in her heart.

The man with the rigid hair has given them nothing. No crumb of hope, no lead to follow, nowhere to go. It seems that nothing's being done to find her brother.

In South Africa, the mountain search, conducted by a team of rangers and police, was called off after only a week. A week! Leonora was horrified, but the young man said this was normal, as if British boys disappeared all the time in the mountains of KwaZulu-Natal. She ranted and yelled at him, but he said there was little he could do. If Ricky was going to be found in the mountains, it would have happened by then. Anyway, there was no money to continue. The police search was extended for a short while to a twenty-mile radius, but there was no sign of the boy. No sightings in cafés or hostels, no evidence from credit cards (he didn't have one) or cash machines: nothing. Posters have gone up in local towns and villages and the international police have been notified. As if that's going to help.

It seems the mountains have captured him, consumed him, claimed him as their own.

* * *

Her mum's eyes are closed, the skin on her cheeks drooping. The lines on her forehead give her a permanent frown, as if

147

she's fixed in a constant state of anxiety. The hand that lies on the turned-down sheet over her chest is bony and white, except for the purple trails of her veins. Her nails are broken and untrimmed.

"Mum?"

Her eyelids flicker and open a crack, so Leonora can see only half the faded grey of her mum's irises.

"Mum, how are you feeling today?"

The bony hand reaches out and grasps her own. A ghost of a smile flits across her mother's face.

"Leonora. Where's Ricky?" she whispers through dry lips, spittle gathering in the corners.

The void in Leonora's chest pulsates. "Mum, do you remember what we talked about? Dad died, in South Africa. Ricky disappeared. They still haven't found him. I will tell you as soon as they do." Every time, it hurts to say the words. Since he vanished, she's had to say them over and over, and the repetition does nothing to ease the pain.

With the news, six weeks ago, of Dad's death and Ricky's disappearance, Leonora's mum suffered a second stroke. Her right side is severely damaged, affecting her mobility. She can't move her right leg or arm, and her face is numb on that side, causing her to dribble and making eating difficult. Her mind, already addled by the drink, seems to be in a state of constant confusion. Moments of lucidity are few and far between.

Thankfully there was one moment, early on, when she was able to respond clearly. It was when she was asked what she wanted to happen to her husband's body. "Tell them to burn it," she said, her voice strong and clear. "And don't send it back. I don't want it." The policewoman who'd been dispatched to get her decision looked uncertain, glanced at Leonora, standing by the bedside.

Leonora said: "Mum, are you sure?"

"I've never been so sure of anything in my life." Her mother's voice was steady. "And no funeral. We can't afford it and he wasn't religious. Get rid of the ashes, I don't want 'em. I don't care." It was the longest speech she'd given since arriving at hospital and afterwards her head fell back onto the pillows, her eyes closed. The policewoman looked at Leonora, brows raised.

"She means it," Leonora said. "That's your answer." The woman noted the answer on a form and left.

* * *

As always, studying helps.

School is the only place she can ease the maelstrom of her mind, stop the whirlpool of questions from tormenting her. At least there she has something else to focus on, and there are even moments when she's able to quell the terrible, draining madness of not knowing. Those moments, though fleeting, keep her going. After a while they lengthen into minutes and hours, when she's studying for her exams, when she can force her mind onto something other than Ricky. She channels her frustration, her grief, all her nervous energy into studying. She stays up late into the night and rises early for her paper round. Maria and Pete watch her with anxious eyes. They make sure she eats, they keep her warm, they play gentle music.

At school, Miss Archer offers her help and support, but otherwise behaves no differently towards her. She seems to know that what Leonora needs isn't sympathy and a shoulder to cry on, but distraction and immersion in something other than her problems.

She no longer thinks about her life plan. But she follows it anyway. She needs it to keep herself from giving up, from giving in to despair. She must find a way through, to be there for Ricky if — when — the authorities find him.

The authorities. There are so many different offices, and job titles, and people involved that Leonora bundles them up into one all-encompassing term. Already it seems that bureaucracy has taken over. All urgency has passed, despite Leonora's dogged phone calls every week.

They haven't been back to London, to the man with the solid hair, since that first meeting. There seems little point when he can't do anything.

CHAPTER TWENTY-EIGHT

Ricky

For a while I could hear him screaming my name. But I never faltered, never looked back, and I was soon out of earshot.

I walked for a couple of hours, placing one foot in front of the other, focusing on that alone. I kept my mind off the scene I had just left, away from the consequences of what had happened. Perhaps I was in shock, but I was calm, almost euphoric.

When I stopped to drink, I lay on my back in the grass for a while, staring up at the sky, listening to the plaintive calls of the eagles soaring high in the sky, the breeze touching the bushes nearby.

The Drakensberg mountains are spectacular. With very few people around, creatures get on with their lives in peace there. You can see for miles, over valleys to hills and mountains. There are no pylons, no houses, no roads, no rubbish bins. Lying there in the grass I could feel the mystical, calming effect of nature all around me.

I must have dozed for a few minutes because when I opened my eyes, a family of dassies was feeding nearby. I watched them for a while, and when I moved, they scurried away into the tall grasses with trills of alarm.

When I roused myself, I focused on the practicalities of my situation. I hesitated for a moment over taking the gun, but decided it was better to leave it — I didn't need to draw attention to myself. I climbed up a rocky crag and hid it halfway up, beneath a pile of stones that had fallen into a dip in the land. It was hard to get to. I had to scramble along a steep incline to get there — I doubt anyone had ever trodden that path before. I hid it well and half-fell, half-climbed back down again.

In my money belt, I had my passport, my plane ticket and some cash, taken from Dad's wallet before I left. And of course, the brooch. When I'd packed up at the end of term, I'd figured that if I was forced to return to England, I'd better have it with me — and if I was going to stay in South Africa, I could simply return it to Luke for safekeeping, or sell it, if you wanted me to, Leo.

Setting off, I reckoned I had most of the afternoon and some early evening hours of daylight. I was pretty confident I'd get where I needed to be before dark. I needed only the sun to guide me. If I ran out of time, I would find a safe place to hide myself for the night and start again in the morning.

The calm I'd felt lying in the grass stayed with me as I walked, and I drank in the smells of the plants and animals on the gentle breeze that cooled the midday sun on the back of my neck. I felt a weight lifting from my shoulders. The burden of my father's expectations had gone, and it was as if I was tasting freedom for the first time in my life. At last I had mustered the courage to break away.

I felt nothing for him, no guilt, no sadness. I didn't think once about the kind of death he would be suffering, alone in the wilderness.

CHAPTER TWENTY-NINE

Leonora

The worst thing is not knowing. Not knowing what happened, not knowing where he is, if he's dead or alive. There could be a million explanations. It's as if a new part of her brain has developed, conjuring up every possible scenario, analysing, comparing, contrasting, unable to stop until something clicks into place and the mystery is solved.

Every week she calls to ask for news, allowing herself a tiny sliver of hope. As she waits to be connected, she imagines how it might be to hear he's been found. How the next ten minutes could transform her life, how she will react, who she will tell first. What it will be like to hear his voice, see his face.

With Maria and Pete, she makes another list, sitting around the table after supper, music splashing colours around her. She writes his name in big letters at the top of the page. The orange of the R is comforting, as if providing proof that Ricky is still here. This time, they focus on all the people and organisations that might be able to help find him. The police department in KwaZulu-Natal, the Missing Persons Bureau, the rangers who looked for Ricky when he first disappeared, local mountain rescue teams, hotels, lodges, campsites. The school, his friends, Luke and Sally, Interpol, the British Embassy in South Africa, the local bus company, the train company. The list covers any and every possibility.

They put them in order of priority and work out how to get contact numbers and addresses. They categorise the list into people they can call, people they can write to, and others they need to track down.

Though she knows it's likely to prove fruitless, it feels better to be doing something, not simply carrying on with her life, accepting what she's told every week. As always, it feels good to have a plan.

* * *

Two letters from South Africa arrive at the house. When she sees them, Leonora feels the fizz of fear in her belly.

The first, with a Savoy School stamp on it, is addressed to 'Mrs S Bates'. Leonora opens it, fingers trembling, the fragment of hope rising. But it's a note of condolence from the headmaster and a promise to 'help in every way we can' to find Ricky.

The second is addressed to her, and it's from Luke.

Dear Leonora,

Sally and I were devastated to hear about the tragic death of your father, not to mention Ricky's disappearance. It must have been such a shock to you and your mother, expecting Ricky back after his final year at school, only to hear of this tragedy, so far away from home. We can't begin to say how sorry we are. Our children are inconsolable.

Over the few years we've known your brother, he's become part of our family. We and the children love him dearly, and miss him very much. We can only hope that some strange circumstance has caused his disappearance and may equally deliver him back to us, and you, safely. What that circumstance might be we are at a loss to know, and I'm sure you've jumped through the same hoops as we have in trying to imagine what on earth has happened. I myself went out on the initial searches for Ricky — *I know the area well* — *and have returned every week to search. I have scoured a huge area and found no trace.*

What I can say, which may give us hope, is that Ricky is a great bushman. I know, because I taught him myself and we camped many times close to the place where he and your father were trekking. Left on his own in the mountains, he would be able to survive for a long time. If he was injured, he would have been found by now, and forgive me for writing the words, but there's no evidence — *none at all* — *to suggest he died. This gives us small hope* — *but hope it is, and hope we do.*

Leonora, I'm writing to you to offer my help if you need it. I know that your mother is not well, and that you're probably having to bear the burden of this tragic event. I also know that you and Ricky are close: he speaks of you with great fondness. You must be feeling helpless and by now quite possibly desperate — *but believe me, you have our support, and if you ever decide to come here, for whatever reason, you will be most welcome to stay with us for as long as you need.*

Ricky told us before your father arrived that he had decided to stay here and continue to work with animals. We were delighted to hear it. You probably already know that he was going to tell his father this while they were away, but we have no way of knowing if this happened or not.

Anyway, his possessions are still here. We will keep them in his room until he is found, but please let us know if you would like them sent back to you.

We will not give up hope, and neither should you. Ricky is out there somewhere and we will find him.

With all our love and best wishes to you and your mother,
Luke

* * *

Dear Luke and Sally,

Thank you for your letter, and for offering me a place to stay if I come over. As you mention, my mother is not well and I'm still at school so it's not likely I can come any time soon. But it's good to know that if and when I can travel, I can come to you. I know Ricky loved living with you and that you were always kind to him.

154

Thank you also, so much, for searching for Ricky. I know you've done your best and I could not do any more.

I don't know what else to do to try to find him, but I am still hoping that he is alive and well. Please let me know the minute you hear anything.

Love,

Leonora

P.S. Is my mother's brooch among his possessions? I know you were looking after it for him.

* * *

Dear Leonora,

I felt I had to write back to you straight away to say that Ricky took your mother's brooch from the safe before the Christmas break. I assumed he was going to return it to her, or to you. Just in case, I have checked thoroughly in his room, and double-checked the safe, but it's definitely not here.

We will of course contact you immediately if we hear any news about Ricky.

Much love,

Sally

CHAPTER THIRTY

Leonora

Leonora's mum can't walk or look after herself. The doctor's advice is to rehome her in a residential unit, where she can get round-the-clock care. This means a shared room in a shabby old people's residence run by the local council, but as things are there seems to be no choice. The decision is taken and on a freezing February day, when the air seems to settle in a cold sheen on her cheeks, Leonora accompanies her mum in an ambulance to her new home.

Her mother seems oblivious to her change in surroundings: exchanging a hospital bed for a similar one in a care home, nurses for carers. She accepts her new circumstances without comment or complaint. Even sharing a room with three others doesn't seem to bother her. It seems clean and orderly, though the faint odour of shepherd's pie mixed with disinfectant makes Leonora want to gag, and she opens the window by her mum's bed as soon as the carer has left.

* * *

Leonora has become an expert in dealing with paperwork. Her father's death has led to an explosion of forms to be completed, queries to be answered, bills to be paid. Her mum signs everything, asks nothing. Gradually the aftermath is dealt with.

Leonora is surprised to learn that the house her parents lived in all their married life was passed down by her maternal grandparents to her mother, the mortgage paid off long ago. Perhaps her mum didn't realise it, perhaps she forgot or maybe she assumed the house belonged to her husband once they were married — but the house has belonged to her all along. Leonora wonders if she knew, but decides against asking her. If her mother realises what it could have meant for all those years, it could upset her.

Leonora works slowly through the contents of her father's desk. At the back of the bottom drawer, hidden within a file of bills, she finds a folder marked 'Stocks and shares'. At first she has no idea what it means — the columns of names and numbers refuse to reveal their secrets. So she takes it back to the narrowboat with her and hands it to Maria.

To Leonora's surprise and fury, it appears that her father has been investing, a little at a time, for many years. In time, his investments have grown in value into what seems to be a considerable sum — no doubt unbeknown to her mum, who has brought up two children believing there was barely enough money to feed them.

Memories of musty second-hand clothes and meals of nothing but toast and butter come flooding back. On the rare occasions when the children plucked up the courage to ask for something, he would bellow: "Where's the money going to come from?" and they would be scared into silence. Yet all the time he was squirrelling it away. What he meant to do with it is a mystery, but he clearly had no intention of spending it on his family.

"I don't know how much there is, exactly, because we need to get a current value," Maria says, a pair of red reading glasses perched on the bridge of her nose. "But it could be quite a lot. We'll have to get your mum to sign a letter requesting the information. What is it, Leonora — this is good news, isn't it?"

Leonora can barely contain her anger. It's no wonder her mum turned to drink.

He was despicable and he deserved to die.

* * *

Leonora's mum asks after Ricky at every visit.

A surprising side-effect of her illness is that she's lost her taste for alcohol — or maybe she's simply forgotten about it. Whatever the reason, the damage to her health is done, and recovery of any meaningful kind seems unlikely. Unaware of her surroundings, she spends her days staring into the distance, dozing or sitting listlessly in a high-backed chair in the residents' lounge, the other occupants slumped in various stages of decay around her. Everywhere the air is saturated with the smell of cheap disinfectant and cooking oil.

Leonora takes glossy, garish magazines from Mrs Clark, plump grapes and moist fruitcake from Maria. But her mum smiles her crooked smile and puts them to one side without registering.

On her way out, Leonora glances back to see two silver-haired women moving in on her mother, their eyes focused on the tray where the food lies untouched.

She sticks to her routine. Work hard at school, do the homework to the best of her ability, keep on with the search for Ricky. Everything is done with dogged determination. If Ricky is still missing when she finishes school next year, she will use the money from the shares, if she can access it, to fund a trip to South Africa and a renewed search. Even if the money is tied up, she'll find a way — she has to.

In the summer holidays, she works full-time at the farm shop, selling meat and cheese, fruit and vegetables.

Jack appears, smiling, one day in the shop, back from agricultural college for the break and working on the farm until October. His hair, once halfway down his back, is short now, with unruly curls falling onto his forehead. His T-shirt stretches tight across broad shoulders. He's turned into a man.

"Thought I'd find you here," he says, taking an apple from her display and biting into it, the juice running down his chin.

"Jack — you're back!" Her first thought, to her shame, is that she'll have to leave her sanctuary on the narrowboat. The room she's taken over was his, before he left for college.

"Only for the holidays. I'm working here, in fact. You don't seem too happy to see me."

"Oh, I am. I mean — I just—"

"You just?" There's a smile around his eyes, though his face is serious. "Don't worry, bunny, I'm living here, in a barn. I like it, actually. You're safe where you are." The smile in his eyes fades. "I know you've had a tough time. I'm not going to make it any worse."

Each day, he seeks her out when he's finished work in the fields and they walk together down to the canal. Most evenings, when it's not raining, Pete sets up a table on the bank and the smell of barbecued fish drifts around them as they play ball games or sit on the edge of the canal, their feet dangling.

She finds herself drawn to Jack in unexpected ways. He's different from anyone she's ever known. While he's gregarious — he talks to everyone they meet on the canal, about anything: he's naturally curious about people and their lives — he keeps his feelings to himself. He's good-looking, with his dark eyes and flashing smile, he's tall and strong, and there's a certain mystique about him that Leonora finds intriguing. He seems to have a large group of friends, many of them girls, but none of them more important than any other. He seems content to spend time with her, though, to her surprise, and to understand when she doesn't want to talk about her family. She's happy to leave it like that.

There was a time when she and Jack became close. It was difficult not to, when she was living with his parents on the narrowboat in those weeks after she left school, before he went back to college. He was there every night for supper. They spent long evenings on the banks of the canal, talking, listening to Pete's guitar, sometimes just sitting in companionable silence, watching as the last glow of sunlight faded into the dusk.

One evening, he took her hand as they walked along the towpath. There was no one else around, no wind rustling the bushes beside them. Even the birds had fallen silent. Under a spreading tree, he turned her by the shoulders to face him and drew her close.

"I like being with you, Leo," he said. Lifting her chin, he gazed into her eyes, a slow smile on his lips. She could hardly breathe, her stomach in a knot as he gently dropped his head towards her face. She wanted so much for him to kiss her, but she couldn't do it. Turning her head, she drew away.

"I'm sorry," she said. "I like you too. A lot. But I'm — not ready for anything more. I don't know if I ever will be."

There was a brief pause while she hung her head, hoping she hadn't lost a friend. Then he drew her into a hug. "It's okay, Leo. I understand, and I'm not insulted. I'd rather have you as a friend than not at all."

She's still grateful to him for not letting it harm their friendship. After that night, they were as close as ever, if not more. But he never pushed her, never tried to force her into anything, and she loved him for that. Perhaps all men were not like her father, after all.

Boyfriends have never been a priority for her, because of her father. Her experience of growing up has been too painful, her childhood years too marred by fear and neglect, for her to harbour any desire for close relationships or children of her own.

Only Kelly and Jack's family know about her home life. With everyone else, whether through misplaced loyalty, shame or self-preservation, she keeps her problems to herself. To be seen as a victim is the last thing she wants. For Leonora, school is for learning, not for meeting boys. And though there are some boys in her year she can call friends, especially in the streamlined sixth form, mostly she finds their humour puerile, their physicality baffling.

Perhaps because he's older, though, Jack is different. The void in her life where Ricky should be feels a little less bleak when he is around. But no one will ever take his place.

CHAPTER THIRTY-ONE

Leonora

Missing, M: a dark, sludgy grey, like the bottom of a deep well.

Ricky is now officially a 'missing person' in South Africa. Leonora turns it over and over in her mind. He's missing, she's missing him, he's missed, she missed him.

What this actually means is hard to ascertain, and despite all her work, the endless letters and phone calls, she's no further ahead. So many disappointments. It seems like a never-ending spiral, going nowhere. There's not a single credible sighting, not a glimmer of hope to hang on to. It seems an eighteen-year-old white boy with a backpack can become invisible in a country like South Africa.

At the house — she doesn't call it 'home' anymore, her home is a narrowboat on the canal, where Maria and Pete are — she lies on her back in his bedroom, thinking of him, his photo in her hand. It was taken by Luke in South Africa and shows Ricky laughing into the camera, his eyes bright beneath the brim of his sun hat, posing with the family dogs. She keeps his picture with her always.

The pain of missing him is constant. Sometimes it's dulled by the distraction of studying, of friends, a good book, but it never goes away. There's an ever-present ache, deep inside her, that is slowly becoming part of her life. There are moments when it all seems hopeless, when the pain becomes needle-sharp, like the stab of a knife sliding into her gut, and she has to grit her teeth and tell herself, over and over, to keep believing.

A footstep on the deck, grey flashes before Leonora's eyes. Pete's away and this person is too heavy to be Maria.

A man's voice says: "Hello? Anyone home?"

She stands, opens the hatch. A large balding man, his coat flapping, looks down at her, his eyes narrowed against the wind. It's rare for strangers to come aboard and she feels vulnerable with nobody else around. Grabbing her jacket, she steps up onto the deck and stands with her back to the entrance, forcing him to move away from her, nearer to the edge. With a nervous glance at the water below, he clears his throat.

"Sorry to disturb you." He has the rounded vowels of a public-school education; his suit looks expensive. His shoes are polished to a high shine, though spattered with mud from the towpath. He looks awkward, out of place on the gaily painted narrowboat.

"I'm David Cassell, from the Foreign and Commonwealth Office in London," he says, holding out a large, well-manicured hand. "Are you Leonora Bates?"

"That's me," she says. His hand is cool and dry.

There have been too many disappointments for her to feel anything like hope, so she decides not to ask him in, yet.

"We tried to contact you, but there was no answer from the number we had. The authorities in South Africa have been in touch. There's been . . . a development in the case of your father and brother. Could we—?" He indicates the doors behind Leonora. Still wary, she stands aside and waits for him to negotiate the steps before following him down.

He can barely stand inside, his bulk making the furniture look even smaller. Leonora, keeping herself between him and the door, clears her books from the table and indicates to him to sit down, drawing up a chair opposite him.

"A development?" she echoes. A missing person, a development, a tragedy. Words to hide behind.

"I know this has been extremely difficult for you and your mother," he says, his hands folded on the table in front of him. "This is not going to help, I'm afraid. It appears that the investigation in South Africa was . . . mismanaged, somewhat, at the time of your father's death and your brother's disappearance."

Mismanaged. There he goes again.

"Mismanaged? What do you mean? Did they make a mistake?"

"It seems so. It was a difficult time, the police were distracted." He shakes his head. "It's hard for us to ascertain now exactly what happened. For whatever reason, it's become clear that the investigation failed in one key respect." He pauses, rubs his forehead, seems to be searching for the right words. "The time of your father's death was uncertain. It took a long time to find him, the weather didn't help, there'd been . . . some animal activity." He flashes a look of embarrassment at Leonora. She stares back without comment. If this is about her father, then she's not interested. This seems to make the man uncomfortable. He shifts in his seat and clears his throat again.

"Regarding your brother's disappearance at around the same time: it appears they checked with the airports in the area at the time, but they found nothing to indicate he'd travelled anywhere. Whether they checked the wrong days, or missed his name, I don't know. Whatever it was, if they had done their work properly, things could have turned out quite differently. I'm so sorry."

"Wait . . . what? What do you mean?" A tingling sensation at the back of her neck rises and spreads to her cheeks, her scalp.

"While the search parties were still out in the mountains, before they'd even found your father, your brother took a flight from Durban back to England. We've been looking in the wrong place."

CHAPTER THIRTY-TWO

Ricky

It was almost dark when I reached the road and I was lucky to catch a ride with a lorry on its way to Durban. The driver seemed happy to have company, but he didn't care if I spoke or not. He barely looked at my face — I kept my hat on, preferring to stay as anonymous as possible — and kept up a constant conversation as we travelled. The lights began to glow in towns and villages along the road as night fell. I listened for a while to his talk of his family, his leaky roof and the money it would cost to fix. He seemed happy with an occasional 'yes' or 'really?' and then, when it was dark, I drifted off to the murmur of his voice. He didn't seem to notice, or care, luckily for me.

Just outside Durban, he stopped to refuel and I roused myself, thanked him and departed on foot. I walked away from the road and spent an uncomfortable night in a thicket at the end of a dirt track, rising early and returning to the road to hitch a lift to the airport.

It wasn't difficult to change the flight, though I had to pay extra and wait a few hours for the plane.

Soon enough I was boarding, with little more than the clothes on my back, the brooch, and a few rand. I had no idea what was awaiting me, and no plans. My only priorities were to lie low and see what happened.

As the flight took off, I settled into my seat. I'd bought a newspaper at the airport, thinking vague thoughts of checking the news for reports on Dad, but also as an excuse to avoid conversation. But the man next to me fell asleep immediately and his wife in the next seat was absorbed in her book, so I was left alone.

I flicked through the pages of the newspaper, but I found nothing. I leaned my head back and allowed my mind to absorb what had just happened. I knew it was a terrible thing — but I felt no panic, no guilt. In fact, my emotions seemed to have gone to sleep.

I thought quite rationally about the scene. They — someone — would find my father, almost certainly dead, because it would take them a few days to find him. He would have bled to death from a gunshot wound to the leg, which would be pretty obvious — but it wouldn't be clear how it happened. A tragic accident — or a murder? Would they be able to tell which?

And I would be missing. Would that indicate guilt? I hoped they'd think I'd gone for help, but they'd surely know that would be fruitless, with those distances to travel. But would they know I was aware of that? They would imagine I panicked, lost my way, and they would search for me in the mountains. They wouldn't know I left him to die alone with no intention of finding assistance.

I could have stayed with him, I suppose, waited for him to die. But I reacted by instinct — I could no more stay with him than shoot myself in the leg in sympathy. What could I offer him, the man I hated? A hand to hold, a few words of comfort, while he breathed his last, poisonous breath? He didn't deserve even that. He never loved me, or you, or Mum. He was incapable of love. I had no compassion for him. He'd destroyed any feeling I might have had for him many years ago. And if, by some terrible stroke of fate, he lived, I had no doubt he would continue to ruin our lives, me, Mum, and you, Leo.

So if my going missing meant they suspected me of murder, then so be it.

Of course, I didn't want to be arrested, or go to prison, and I was going to do everything I could to avoid it. I thought it through, in those long hours in the dim light of the aircraft cabin, with people snoring all around me and the odd sense of detachment you get in a metal tube moving at speed, high in the sky.

My ambitions of staying in South Africa were in pieces now, but even that didn't bother me. I had some vague sense that I might be able to return one day, but the path I'd chosen had for the moment stopped my dreams in their tracks. Now I had to survive, as best I could, and at least for the moment, I had to hide.

I did think about you, Leo, of course I did. But I was eighteen and I had no idea what the repercussions would be. Accident or not, I had abandoned him and he knew it. I hadn't even pretended to go for help. I imagined them finding him close to death, leaning over to catch his last words, my name written down, the alarm called. Would they put out pictures of me? A search warrant and police at roadblocks, with checks at the ports and the airports? I had no idea how these things might work. Perhaps I had been quick enough, and they were out in the mountains still, calling for me, searchlights scouring the hillsides, the animals lying low in the bush until they left.

Maybe when I got to Heathrow the police would be waiting, and I'd be quietly taken to one side and led to a cell.

The last thing I wanted to do was to put you in danger. So, unsure of my crime and my fate, I decided not to contact you or Mum. It sounds cruel, now. You would hear soon enough about Dad, and I was pretty sure what your reaction would be. But when you heard I was missing, I knew you'd be frantic with worry.

Home would be too obvious, the first place they'd look. I figured that if I left it a good while — a few months, perhaps — then it would be safer and I could get a message to you that I was alive and here in England. I needed to know, first, what I was suspected of, whether the police were on to me, if I was a wanted man.

My only option, I figured, was to lie low, keep an eye on the news, wait until my position was clear.

So I walked onto the streets of London, where dark alleys, hidden doorways and litter-strewn underpasses became the corridors and rooms of my new home.

CHAPTER THIRTY-THREE

Leonora

While she believed Ricky was missing in South Africa, it felt like her worst nightmare. But somehow, she managed to come to an agreement with herself to deal with it after her A-level exams, to achieve what she needed to get a place at university, to follow the plan. Then she would focus on getting to South Africa and doing what she could to track him down. How exactly, she wasn't sure, but going there seemed to be the first, essential step.

But he came back.

Now there are new and different questions, many of them just as disturbing and terrifying as if he were still lost in the mountains of KwaZulu-Natal. Why did he come to England, instead of going back to Luke? Why did he leave immediately, contacting nobody, leaving everyone searching for him? Why didn't he get in touch? He must have known that Leonora would be devastated and would search frantically for him. But he didn't contact her — not even his sister, his closest friend and ally, who would always support him — and he still hasn't been in touch. None of it makes sense.

Something terrible must have happened.

She can't think about anything else. Maria and Pete listen with endless patience while she talks and wonders and speculates. She wanders along the towpath, where the warm air of spring has transformed the barren banks and the wild flowers grow strong and tall. Leonora, her mind whirring, is oblivious. She lies for hours on her narrow bed, listening to the yellow slip-slop of the water on the bows of the boat, watching the strum of Pete's guitar whirl and waft in swathes of colour on the ceiling.

Maria says: "Leonora, what about your exams? They're only a few weeks away. You have to decide whether to take them now or not. If you're not up to it now, you could wait and redo the year when you're feeling better. I'm sure they would agree to that."

Leonora picks at a ragged fingernail. "I know the exams are getting close," she says. "And I don't want to wait a year to do them. But if Ricky's here, in England, I've got to find him."

"Of course you do," Maria says. "And there are lots of things that can be done to find him." She takes Leonora by the hands. "Listen, if you're determined to take the exams this year, we'll keep searching for you while you do your revision, just until you've finished your exams. Then you'll have all the time in the world. We'll be happy to help, won't we, Pete? It'll give us something worthwhile to do. You've worked so hard and you're almost there. We want you to get these exams. You deserve to do well."

"We'll do everything we can," Pete says, the silver ring in his beard flashing as he nods.

So Leonora forces her mind back to her studies.

Pete and Maria register Ricky as missing, talk to the homeless charities, the border control at Heathrow, the airline he travelled with. They ask the police to inform the UK arm of Interpol, so they can liaise with the police in South Africa. They enlist the help of a printer, who, when he hears the story, offers to print posters and leaflets for nothing. Ricky's smiling face, under the headline *Local Boy Missing,* gazes out from trees and municipal noticeboards, in the library and the church hall. They even take them up to London and post as many as they can on fences, trees, and gates.

They make notes of everything they've done and everyone they've spoken to, and almost every day they walk up to the Bates house to make calls and check for messages. Though they've never met him, they couldn't do more for their own brother than they do for Leonora's.

The exams arrive in a rush of nerves and last-minute preparation. Somehow, Leonora gets through them and to her relief there are few surprises. When they are over, she's numb with exhaustion. She walks the three miles from school to the care home and holds her mum's hand while she dozes.

Then she goes back to the narrowboat and sleeps for hours, only waking up when the smell of the evening barbecue drifts through her open window.

CHAPTER THIRTY-FOUR

Leonora

If you don't want to be found, even in a developed country like Britain, you can disappear, and even the most determined person would struggle to track you down. Leonora learns this early on.

She soon realises how little she knows. However well-read she might be, however aware of the world, nothing has prepared her for a task like this. It is over a year since he stepped off that plane, the last time he was seen. He could be anywhere by now and anything could have happened.

As soon as the exams are over, she goes up to the house and sets to. She flings all the windows open, allowing the summer air to flow into every room. Sunlight flows into the dark, dusty corners of her father's study. She clears the surfaces, boxes up his soldiers, his books and his African artefacts and puts them in the garage. With some difficulty, she moves his toad-like desk to the window, where she can see into the garden. The desk looks smaller there, less forbidding, and she likes that the bright sunlight will fade the leather top and scald the wood.

She empties the drawers and puts the contents into a pile in the corner. In a junk shop she finds an old, bent flip chart.

She straightens it up, attaches a new pad of white paper, sets it in the middle of the room. This is to be the nerve centre of her search for Ricky.

At first, she focuses on the work that Maria and Pete have done, following up on every contact, reminding people that her brother is still missing, drawing up lists of organisations, actions, ideas, dates. This is like police work, she thinks. Solid, meticulous, patient.

But it's a daunting task. Every phone call she makes seems to be complicated. It's the wrong number, she needs a different office, or the person she needs isn't there. She keeps a note of everything she does. She writes letters, longhand. There is no typewriter in the house, let alone a computer. She writes to the school in South Africa, to Luke, requesting addresses of Ricky's friends, his teachers, so that she can write directly to them. In case they won't release the addresses, she writes lists of questions and encloses them with the letters, so they can pass them on and write back to her. She encloses stamped addressed envelopes to encourage them to reply. It is laborious, thankless work.

Apart from the study and the kitchen, she leaves the rest as it has always been, though she knows that it will probably be down to her to decide what to do with it. Her mother is incapable of organising anything, even the release of the money from her husband's nest egg to fund the continued search for Ricky.

Pete helped Leonora find a lawyer to see what could be done, but the advice was not encouraging. To deal with the house and the money on her mother's behalf, Leonora would have to obtain power of attorney — and even if she did that, it's unlikely the money would be released with Ricky still missing. The lawyer suggested she wait until her mother dies, or alternatively for seven years, after which she could declare her brother dead. She left the meeting with tears in her eyes.

She can't bear to stay at the house on her own. Her father is too present, there are too many reminders. They lurk in unexpected places — at the bottom of a chipped mug in the kitchen, in the dip of the sofa where her mum would lie.

Maria and Pete invite her to stay on the narrowboat for as long as she likes. She does her best to pay her way, to help them to look after it. Her job at the farm shop earns her enough to pay a small contribution and she brings back end-of-line and out-of-date produce when she can. The rest goes on the campaign to find Ricky. It leaves her nothing for herself, but she is used to that. She has to do everything she can to find him, and these months are dedicated to that.

She's still close to Kelly and her family. Her visits there are a relief after the frustrations of the search. Kelly has a regular boyfriend, a quiet, unassuming lad called Matthew, who works in the local Lloyds Bank. It is expected by all the family that they will soon be married.

Leonora is struck by the contrast between her own life and Kelly's — one so complex and full of sadness, the other on a straight path to fulfilment.

* * *

She's pondering her list of actions on the flip chart, wondering where to go next, when the shrill cry of the phone breaks the silence. Silver lines float from wall to bookcase, fading as they fall to the floor. She watches them for a moment, transfixed, before stirring herself to answer.

"Leonora?" The soft Scottish burr is familiar. The staff at the nursing home where her mum lives are friends now, after so many months of visiting.

"Hi, Louise."

"I was wondering if you're coming today? Your mum didn't eat her breakfast, or lunch, and we thought she might be better if you came . . ." Her voice fades with the last few words and Leonora knows this is bad news. The nurses have a way of speaking in euphemisms that at first had Leonora confused. 'She's been a little unsettled' means her mum has been up all night, while 'she's bright as a button today' could indicate she's said a few spontaneous words to her carer.

"I'll come now," Leonora says. "Be there in fifteen minutes."

Her mother's thin body causes barely a rumple in the bedclothes, her skin grey against the white of the pillow. Her eyes are closed when Leonora sits in the rickety chair beside her bed.

There are places for four in this room, though one bed has been empty for a week or so, stripped of its covers, its former occupant cleared away neatly, soon forgotten. The smell is stifling. Leonora cracks open a window, at risk of being told not to by the other occupants of the dim room. Today, only two beds are occupied, one emanating a loud red snore from a tangle of sheets, and her mother's. The other occupant has no doubt been cajoled into going to the communal lounge. In that soulless room overlooking the car park, where the TV seems to be the only living thing, they sit for most of the day in various states of crookedness and sentience.

"Mum, it's me," Leonora says, taking the desiccated hand lying motionless on her mother's chest. It feels cold and lifeless. For a moment Leonora holds her breath, watching her mother's chest for movement as she's done many times before. But the sunken eyes twitch open and a flicker of recognition passes across her mum's face. "Hello, Leo," she mouths. It's barely a whisper.

"Mum, you must eat." Leonora lifts the steel cover from the plate that lies on the stained bed table. The food is grey and congealed and Leonora resists an urge to gag. "I'm going to get you some bread and jam, and a cup of tea." Bread and strawberry jam — her mum's favourite. Not so nutritious, but soft and filling — and usually available from the tiny kitchen at the end of the corridor.

When she returns, balancing a mug of tea and a plate of buttered bread on a tray alongside two half-finished pots of jam, her mother appears to be asleep. As she places the tray on the bed table, a nurse appears and beckons Leonora into the corridor.

"I'm so glad you're here," she says. "If you can get her to eat anything, you're doing better than we are. She's very frail, and she's losing weight. We're beginning to worry about her. She keeps talking about Ricky." Leonora nods, biting her lip. "She says she's going to see him very soon. Any news?"

"Nothing, I'm afraid. What can we do?" Leonora glances towards the bed where her mother lies motionless.

"We're already giving her high-nutrition drinks," the nurse says. "She doesn't want to get out of bed, or watch TV, or talk to anyone. I'm afraid, when they get like this . . ." She puts a hand on Leonora's arm. "We're worried she's given up."

When Leonora goes back to her mum's bed, she sits and strokes her forehead gently, hoping she will wake and eat, but she sleeps on. Gazing at the ravaged face, she remembers how her mother used to look. When Leonora was small, she was beautiful. Life has not been kind to her.

Three days later, she arrives at the house to find a message on the machine to call the care home. She knows before she dials what has happened. Her mother has not reached her fifty-second birthday, and Leonora is now an orphan.

At the funeral, attended only by Leonora, Maria, Pete, Jack and Mrs Clark, she weeps for a life not lived, joy unknown, love denied.

CHAPTER THIRTY-FIVE

Ricky

It was terrible at first, of course it was — I wasn't expecting it to be easy. But I was eighteen, just out of an elite boarding school in South Africa, and though I knew about wildlife and survival in the bush, I had no concept of how hard life on the streets of London could be. It's a miracle that I survived.

I got off the plane in the middle of a British winter wearing shorts, walking boots and a T-shirt. I was freezing cold. After wandering around the airport for a bit, I found a bus that went into London and jumped off somewhere near the centre. I had no idea where, I'd never been there before. It was still quite early in the morning, but there were people everywhere, so many, rushing and running, ignoring the young, tanned boy in shorts standing in shock on the cold pavement. There was so much noise — huge buses growling their way slowly along the roads, black cabs honking at each other, pedestrian crossings bleeping. Even before I went away, I never experienced anything like it. It was overwhelming. And the smells! I had never known such a mixture — stale cooking fat from the tatty restaurants lining the street, diesel fumes from vehicles of all shapes and sizes, dust, rain, coffee, cigarette smoke — I felt dizzy with it all.

I walked around for a while, trying to familiarise myself with my new surroundings, learn where I was. I searched out the quiet places, the back streets, the little squares where you could sit and watch people go by. In a café I ordered a coffee and considered my options. I had changed my South African money at the airport, and I had around twenty pounds to my name. I had nowhere to stay and was pretty sure that my only option for the moment was to sleep on the streets, so I needed to buy warm clothes — at least some trousers and a jumper. Then, I thought, I would have to find work, and London would be the easiest place to stay anonymous. There were more nationalities here than I'd seen in my whole life, and I was hopeful that I could find some kind of menial job where they paid cash and asked no questions.

I chanced across a charity shop, where I bought some well-worn jeans, a threadbare jumper and a long shabby coat for less than five pounds. A big chunk of my money — but I looked more anonymous and suitably down-at-heel to fit in with the other rough sleepers. And I had half a chance of surviving the night.

I don't think I had ever experienced cold until that night, not really. It probably wasn't even that cold, although it was late December. But I was used to the sunny days of South Africa, and there, though the nights were sometimes cool, you barely needed a jumper except in the mountains.

I found a supermarket and bought some frugal rations, enough to keep me going for the rest of the day. I spent most of the evening in a café, eking out a single cup of coffee for as long as I could until the room emptied out and the man behind the counter started giving me looks. Then I went back out into the cold and walked to a quiet area where I'd found a little square flanked by hedges. I was hoping to find a bench to spend the night.

But all the benches were taken, their occupants huddled together over bottles of cider, or piles of belongings left to reserve the space. Their glances were hostile — they saw at once that I was competing for their sleeping spot. So I carried on. I walked for a long time, exploring the dank backstreets, the alleys and shortcuts of old London, testing the gates of closed parks and gardens, looking for somewhere, anywhere that looked at least halfway safe and dry. I was exhausted and inexperienced. And not a little scared.

In the early hours of the morning I went round the back of a row of small shops, in a dark alley that smelled of urine and rotten cabbage, and huddled up behind some bins.

It wasn't the worst place I would sleep over the next weeks and months, but it was pretty bad.

I knew I wouldn't last long if I didn't find out how it worked. Living rough in London, that is. After that first horrible night, when I had nowhere to wash, when I pissed in a drain in the corner of the alley, when I woke up smelling of rotten cabbage and shivering so hard I couldn't speak, I almost gave up and went to the police station, if only to sit in the warmth for a while.

I was vulnerable and I knew it. A young man alone, barely able to protect himself, more at home in the bush of South Africa than the concrete and tarmac of a big city. I was planning to live among the poor, the addicted, the rejected, in the darkest corners of the metropolis. And that wasn't all that made me a target. I was acutely aware of the brooch, burning a hole in my gut from its pouch in my money belt. If someone wanted to take it from me, I didn't have a chance. It meant I had to be doubly careful to avoid danger.

Emerging from my sordid alley, I dragged myself down the streets, back to the square where the benches were occupied the previous night. All the people had gone, except one, who was lying under a filthy blanket, a woolly hat pulled down over his eyes. He smelled very bad, of unwashed clothes and stale alcohol. I didn't want to alarm him, but I didn't have many options. I shook his shoulder and said: "Hey. Hey, can you help me?"

One hand appeared, a woollen glove covering all but the tips of his fingers, and lifted the hat an inch or two. A pair of eyes blazed from beneath. I had woken him and he was annoyed. "What?" His tone was not friendly.

"I need help," I said. "I have nowhere to sleep, and no money. Where can I get help?"

With a groan, the man eased his feet to the ground and the rest of his body to a sitting position. He pulled his coat, once a stylish herringbone, now torn and misshapen, around his legs. He fixed me with a suspicious gaze. "You shouldn't be on the streets," he said, his voice gruff, unfriendly. "Go home to your mum." He started to gather his meagre possessions from around him. A supermarket bag full of dirty clothes, a book, ripped and bent, a piece of plastic sheeting he'd been lying on.

"I can't. I — I don't have any family." It was easier to lie than explain, Leo. But he wasn't fooled.

"In trouble with the police, are you? Drugs, is it? Forget it, who cares." He stopped pulling his things together and stared at me, a belligerent glare from beneath the black rim of his hat. "You won't last five minutes here, little boy." I squared my shoulders, stared back at him. I had learned to stand my ground, thanks to the bullies in boarding school, and I needed him to help me.

He looked away, coughed: a painful, rasping sound that came from deep in his chest. Then he sighed and his frown softened. I realised with a shock he was young, not much older than me. I wondered what his story was.

"Okay, here's my good deed for the day," he said, his voice gruff with phlegm. "Go to St Luke's Church — it's about three streets down, on the left." He waved vaguely towards the gate. "He'll be there about ten o'clock. If not, wait. He'll help you." He stood, picked up his things, and started to shuffle off.

"Wait — who? What's his name?"

"Ben. Just say I sent you. Marky sent you."

I watched as he walked on unsteady legs towards the gate, his shoulders drooping.

* * *

I never saw Marky again, but I had much to thank him for. I found the church and sat on the step, shivering, for what seemed like hours. By then it had started to rain and I was regretting not spending some of my meagre cash on a hat and a scarf. Gloves seemed like a good idea, too — my hands had turned red, then white with cold and I had to put them into my armpits to get any kind of warmth into them.

I waited because I had no other plan.

At last a man's voice said: "Woah, I nearly trod on you. You must be freezing to death out here. Come in, come in and get warm." A slim figure in a black raincoat, its hood raised against the relentless downpour, wrestled with a large key in the lock of the church door. Eventually he won the battle and pushed it open, beckoning to me to hurry in.

Inside I stood dripping on the discoloured tiles of an old church floor, looking inwards and upwards towards stained-glass windows and rows of dark wooden pews. It was warm, warmer than I expected for a large space, and I peeled off my coat and hung it on the end of a bench, where it dripped with a regular beat onto the floor. The man had gone straight through the church to the nave, disappearing from view. After a few moments I was beginning to wonder if he was coming back when he suddenly appeared from behind me with a dry blanket under his arm.

"Here, stick this round your shoulders," he said. "And come with me."

I followed him into a small room off the side of the church, where a table covered with papers and books acted as a desk. Opposite it was an armchair, its upholstery ripped and stained, and he indicated for me to sit down, taking the chair from behind the desk and sitting down in front of me.

"That's better," he said. "Let me introduce myself. I'm Ben, and I'm the vicar here."

I was surprised. Without his coat, he looked like a student, his jeans frayed at the hem, his trainers old and worn. His jumper had holes in the elbows and an old tartan scarf was wrapped around his neck. He was unshaven, his hair long and unkempt. He smiled, guessing my thoughts. "I know I don't look like your typical vicar, but we come in all shapes and sizes now, you know. We need to blend into society to make a difference, otherwise people don't accept us."

"I'm . . . Oliver," I said, hoping he hadn't noticed the hesitation. I'd decided to use my middle name, but it didn't come naturally yet.

"Good, well that's the formalities over then. What are you doing here, Oliver, and how can I help you?"

"Marky sent me. He said you could help."

His eyebrows rose, but he said nothing.

"I've got nowhere to stay and no money," I said. "No family. I slept rough last night, but . . ." My words faded in my throat and I looked away. There was nothing else I could say, without him wanting to know more, and for some reason I didn't want to lie to him.

But he made no sign of being curious about my situation, though it must have been obvious I was a novice at this, that I'd come from a better place.

"That's not good," he said, shaking his head. "Well, you've come to the right person." He stood up and went over to the table, picked up a sheaf of papers and started flicking through them. "No, no, full, no. London is full, it seems." I must have made a sudden movement, or perhaps my despair was obvious, because he dropped the papers, came back over to me and clapped me on the shoulder. "No need to worry, Oliver, I'm good with a challenge. You can stay with me until we figure out what to do with you. You can't sleep out in that weather, anyway." His arm swept in a circle towards the door and I became aware of the rain drumming on the roof. He was right: sleeping in that would be impossible.

"Right! Have you eaten today?"

I shook my head, suddenly aware of the void in my stomach. I started to salivate at the thought of food.

"Come on, then," he said.

CHAPTER THIRTY-SIX

Ricky

I stayed with Ben for almost two weeks, in his tiny basement flat around the corner from the church, sleeping on the sofa. It was luxury compared with the sordid alley of my first night in London.

I was grateful for his generosity but I knew I couldn't rely on his charity for long. He had very little money: it was obvious from his possessions, which were few, and he lived frugally. I offered to help in the church, but there were other people to do that, so I cleaned and tidied the flat while he was out.

But I was eating his food, using his electricity, and I had no way of paying him back, so I left. He gave me a list of hostels, suggested places where I could get a cheap meal, told me how to register as unemployed. I think he knew I wasn't going to do that. He also gave me some advice on places where I might find temporary work, paid cash. Uncertain, low pay, but under the radar.

He must have suspected I was in trouble with the police, probably because I said nothing about my life or why I'd ended up on the street at my tender age. I will always be grateful to him for not asking. And for giving me twenty pounds from his own wallet. He made me promise to go back, any time, if I was in need of help. I promised, but I didn't mean it. He didn't need me hanging around, costing him money.

For the first couple of nights after leaving Ben's flat, I went to the hostels and managed to find a bed for the night. But I knew that wouldn't last. I needed money, and for most of them, identification. I couldn't risk showing them my passport. So, in a run-down part of Notting Hill, I went from seedy shop to tatty pub, asking for work: labouring jobs, cleaning, anything to earn a few pounds to buy food. In a pub I worked a couple of shifts changing barrels, cleaning the floors, and after a few days of working like this, they let me sleep in a tiny cupboard of a room upstairs.

The owner was a man called Ronnie — a small-time criminal with tattoos and a temper. He was probably around fifty, though he looked older. He never smiled — his default expression was sour, as if someone had put a rotten egg under his nose — and when he was angry, his cheeks turned purple and his eyes popped.

Under the counter he dealt cannabis and other substances to the local community. He seemed to know everyone who frequented the pub, and they knew him. They would sidle up to the bar, mutter something to him and he'd pour a drink without a word. When they paid, a small packet of something would accompany the change. It would be pocketed swiftly, with a nod.

There were some interesting characters in that pub. Rastafarians with the longest dreadlocks I'd ever seen, their striped woolly hats balanced on top of the thick ponytail of tangled dreads. They were generally quiet and friendly, but they didn't hang around. There were a few old blokes who were regulars. They'd get their half of bitter and sit on the bench seats that ran down the sides of the front room, muttering to themselves or to each other. Their faces were puffy and red — they looked unwell and miserable. They came in at the same time every day and generally left after a number of beers, late in the evening, shuffling off into the dark, unsteady and alone. I sometimes wondered if I would end up like that, Leo. And I thought of Mum, and wondered how she was.

It was a pretty bad place to work, really. I didn't get much money and I never knew how many hours I would be needed. Ronnie decided on a whim, depending on what mood he was in. If he was in his foulest mood, I got more hours because he disappeared upstairs to his flat: a couple of filthy rooms with a TV and a mouldy sofa. In a less foul mood (you could never say that Ronnie was in a good mood), he would appear in the pub and help behind the bar, dealing his silent deals with a scowl. He never indulged in small talk, which suited me fine — the less curious he was about me, the better. The closest he got to a conversation would be after hours, when he'd bring out the whisky bottle and sit in the back corner with a couple of cronies. I'd hear the odd word and a guffaw every so often, but I kept my distance and my mouth shut. I didn't want to be associated with his drug dealing.

My job at the pub didn't last long, as it happened, because of his under-the-counter business.

Ronnie always had his eyes peeled for 'the filth,' as he called them, and he made sure I knew what to look out for, too, so I could warn him when they came into the pub. They were surprisingly easy to spot, and I wondered how the police ever managed to go undercover, they seemed so bad at it. It was a good lesson for me, though. I had to look out for myself, and was avoiding the police for my own reasons.

One lunchtime the pub was busier than usual and I was working hard at the bar. Ronnie's usual clientele were people who didn't like to be kept waiting, so I focused on taking the orders and pouring the drinks as fast as I could. I never stopped to chat anyway and tried not to make eye contact. I was learning fast how not to attract attention to myself. So when a couple of men came up to the bar and stared at me, alarm bells rang in my head.

They always looked the same. Jeans, trainers, T-shirts; usually black leather jackets. The haircut completed the look. Always too neat. And there was something about the way they walked, the arrogance in their stance, that gave them away. Yet they didn't know it.

I asked them what they'd like, and they ordered beer, both of them. I kept my head down and my eyes on the drinks, turning to the till as soon as they handed the cash across. I was hoping they'd move to a table but they stayed at the bar, watching me with a kind of intensity that made me uncomfortable. To my relief there was a lull in the stream of customers and I took the opportunity to go into the back room where Ronnie sat smoking at his desk. I told him the police were in the bar and he took a quick peek to see if I was right. As soon as he saw them, he stubbed out his cigarette, grabbed his jacket and exited via the back door, ordering me to get back to work.

But turning back to the bar I saw that in those few moments, one of the policemen had gone behind the bar and was rummaging around the cupboards. It was only a matter of time before he'd find the stash of drugs and I wasn't going to be there when he did.

I turned tail, dashing up to my room where I grabbed my few possessions. Moments later, I left by the same door as Ronnie.

* * *

Then began my second, longer stint living on the streets. I was better equipped this time round. The job in the pub, though short-lived, had taught me a lot, and I'd had the time to learn about the community in the area, to spot a policeman from behind, to see who was stealing or using drugs. I'd learned how to be invisible.

But I was still a rookie, and it was hard. It was even colder now than before, and though I had a little money from my job at the pub, it wasn't going to last for long. I knew I could get a bed in a hostel when the temperature dropped right down, but even on a normal winter's night the cold creeped into my bones, under my skin and into my mind. I became thin and bony, which didn't help when you were sleeping on the hard ground, and the skin on my lips and hands was cracked and sore. My hair grew long and I stopped shaving, even on the odd occasion when I had the chance, because with a beard I would be harder to recognise. I was probably unrecognisable within a month of living rough. Keeping clean was difficult, to say the least: I would try to wash in the public toilets, which were pretty grim themselves and never had hot water. My clothes became stiff with dirt and I had to get used to the idea that I smelled. In the worst moments I heard my father's voice, scoffing at me, telling me how useless I was, how he expected nothing more of me. Though I tried to block him out, he was always there.

I became on nodding terms with some of the other street people. We would exchange a word or two, sometimes chat. Often we'd sit together in silence. Each had a story to tell, though, and sometimes, on a good night, someone would open up, talk about what their life used to be — their family, their job, their home, all lost because of one thing or another. Often booze or drugs, sometimes just plain bad luck. Nobody chooses a life on the streets — not in London, anyway. I remember wondering if I should get out, wander the countryside where I'd feel more comfortable, where I could have wildlife and fresh air to sustain me. But I didn't do it. I was safer, more anonymous here, where nobody noticed me and nobody cared.

Those were dark days. I thought about you often, Leo, every day. But the longer I left it, the more I felt it would be stupid to contact you — the police would be watching you and I would be caught. I didn't want you to get involved, to get into trouble because of me.

There was no question in my mind that I was guilty. I'd left my father to die in the most callous way. Even if they believed the gun had gone off by accident — which they might not — I was convinced that because I'd disappeared, they would assume I'd committed a crime. If I was caught, my punishment would be many years in prison, and I deserved it. But I couldn't face it. Life on the streets was hard, but I was free. If boarding school had been bad, prison would be ten times worse, and the bullying I suffered from my schoolmates would seem like a tea party compared with the horrors I would endure.

Never once did I think of giving myself up.

I clung to the brooch as if my life depended on it. Despite my addled mind, I knew it could rescue me, and more, but it was yours, Leo, and I was determined to return it to you one day. Perhaps you could use it to help Mum, or improve your life, or perhaps you would want to keep it. Anyway, it wasn't mine, and I was steadfast in my determination. On the few occasions when I was able to have a proper shower, I took the money belt in with me, hung it somewhere away from the stream of water and strapped it on firmly under my jeans before I emerged. If I washed with other people around I kept it hidden as far as I could. The money belt, that also contained my now dog-eared and stained passport, became filthy and smelly and once or twice I washed it and put it back on wet. I couldn't afford to leave it anywhere and I had nowhere else to hide the brooch. Not safely, anyway.

There were occasions when I feared for my life, but I would never have given up the brooch. I'd already committed the worst crime, and I clung on to my pledge to you as if somehow it proved that I wasn't a bad person.

One miserable night when the rain had been pounding the streets for hours and I'd struggled to find somewhere dry to sleep, I woke in my narrow doorway to find someone rummaging in my pockets, pulling at my clothes. For a moment I froze with fear. Perhaps this saved me, because I opened my eyes just a crack without being detected while my heart pounded, urging me to lash out and run. I saw a dark face, half-hidden by a curtain of sodden hair dripping onto me as I lay, a hairy mouth muttering obscenities as the hands fluttered and pawed at my trousers. I knew if he felt the brooch in my money belt he would know instantly that I was hiding something. Luckily I was sleeping on my side, practically lying on the brooch, which was why he hadn't found it straight away. As he scrabbled in my jeans pocket, I grabbed his arm as hard as I could, digging my fingers into his flesh, at the same time winding my free hand into the trailing mat of hair. He squealed with surprise and pain as I pulled his head away from my body and stood up, holding him down by the hair so he was bent double. My heart was beating fast. I didn't know if he had a knife, but he was a big man and it was only the element of surprise that had given me the advantage.

"Get off me! Fuck you — get off!"

I said nothing, but dragged him down the street by the hair, our feet slipping and splashing in dark puddles on the gum-spattered paving stones. He put up very little resistance. We reached the corner and I pushed him hard, so he fell to the ground. For a moment we stared at each other. His eyes were crazed and pleading, flitting from my feet to my face. He was in even worse condition than I was and for a moment I felt a surge of compassion for this drenched, cold, desperate person.

But on the street, in the end, it's everyone for himself. I raced back to my doorway, gathered up my things and ran in the opposite direction, through the rain. I ran for what seemed like a very long time, until my chest hurt and my trousers were soaked to the knees. I didn't look back.

I got no more sleep that night.

CHAPTER THIRTY-SEVEN

Leonora

"But Leo . . ." Maria's earnest face, creased with concern, faces Leonora across the table. Raindrops drum lemon yellow on the roof above Leonora's head. She listens to the sound, watches the colour as it falls in clouds around her.

"I know." She picks with her thumb and forefinger at the piece of toast in front of her, reducing the corner to a pile of crumbs. "But I can't see the point, now. It doesn't matter anymore. Nothing can be more important than finding Ricky. I have to put that first."

Maria takes her hand, the one fidgeting with the toast.

"Of course it's important to find Ricky, we all know that. And nobody's expecting you to stop searching. But that doesn't mean giving up your dream, Leo! You got the best exam results the school has ever seen, in its entire history, and an unconditional place on the best journalism course there is. It's something to be really proud of. I know you can do this." She pauses and takes a deep breath. "You have a bright future, love, a fantastic opportunity. It's what you've always wanted. Ricky wouldn't want you to waste it. And I hate to say this, but what if you can't find him? In ten, twenty years' time, will you regret losing this chance?"

Maria gives her hand a little shake of encouragement, maybe hoping she'll raise her eyes from the table. But she can't. It all seems so hopeless now. Without Ricky, nothing seems worth doing. She has to keep looking for him, if there's even the smallest grain of hope.

"At least I will have tried," she mumbles at last.

Maria doesn't give up easily. "Listen to me, Leo. We've already done pretty much everything we can to find him, haven't we? We've registered his name everywhere, contacted everyone, chased and followed up until we've become a nuisance. I don't know what more you can do, especially if you're thinking you'll do it full time."

She has a point. It's a thankless task. And if there was anything more they could do, they would have done it already. But there must be some way forward, there has to be. She can't give up now.

"Go to university," Maria urges. "Follow your dream, Leo. Pete and I can carry on the search while you're away, and you can pick it up in the holidays if you want to." Leonora looks up then, sees the hope in Maria's eyes, her smile full of compassion. It hurts to look at her, so she gets up from the table, clears her plate and mug and goes to the sink to wash up. When she turns round, Maria is looking thoughtful. "Come and sit down again," she says. "I've got an idea."

Leonora sits, stares at her hands.

"Why don't you defer the place for a year, or even two?" Maria suggests. "Lots of people take a gap year. I'm sure they'll let you do it. Instead of travelling or doing charity work, you can keep on with the search for Ricky and at the same time earn some money to see you through university. Then, while you're studying, Pete and I will do whatever we can, I promise — and we'll let you know the minute we hear anything. How about that?"

She raises her gaze to Maria's face through a film of tears.

* * *

"Do you think I should go to South Africa?"

Leonora and Pete stand side by side in the tiny kitchenette, preparing vegetables that she's brought back from the farm shop. Rock music shivers in bright swathes of colour in Leonora's field of view. Somehow the colours never seem to interfere with what she's doing. Though it can be entrancing, her synaesthesia exists in the background of her consciousness like the other senses, without intruding.

A weak winter sun penetrates the misted windows of the narrowboat, casting dappled sunlight over the worktop. The weeks and months have passed more quickly than Leonora thought possible, and as Maria predicted, she's running out of ideas in the search for Ricky.

"That's a big question for a Sunday morning," Pete says. His long fingers, perfect for plucking guitar strings, peel and chop in time to the music.

"It's just . . . we don't know for certain that Ricky shot Dad."

"We don't. At the moment, nothing's clear at all. It's hard to find out what really happened at such a distance, that's for sure."

"If he did shoot him, it would explain why he disappeared, I suppose."

Pete nods. "It would. The police could be thinking that, anyway. Though it might easily have been an accident."

"But if it was an accident, why would Ricky just leave?" she asks for the thousandth time. "Doesn't that implicate him?" Pete, knowing it's a rhetorical question, nods and says nothing.

"I've been going through all the possibilities," she says. "Over and over again. Like — while they were out there in the bush, Ricky could have told Dad he wanted to stay in South Africa. They could have had a terrible row and wrestled with the gun, and it went off. Or Dad could have shot himself by accident, maybe. But then — why wouldn't Ricky have gone back to Luke and Sally's, to ask for their help? Or gone to find help at the reserve? And . . . if he did shoot him on purpose, wouldn't it be better to give himself up? He could talk to the police here. Dad was such a bastard, surely they would give him a lenient sentence, especially if it was an accident?"

"Leo, you're tying yourself in knots," Pete said. "And you're beginning to tangle me up, too. The way I see it, there's no point speculating. We have nothing to tell us why Ricky left — or if he was even there when your dad died. The authorities obviously have no idea what went on: they didn't even know for a year that Ricky had got on a plane. So I can't see how going to South Africa is going to help. It's expensive, and you don't know how things work there. Will it help to go out there? After all, we know that Ricky's here in this country, right now. I'm sure Luke and Sally have already done everything they can to find out what happened, and they'll keep going for as long as it takes. They love him like a son, don't they?" He clears the peelings into the bin and leans back on the counter to look at Leonora. "As we love you like a daughter."

"Oh, Pete," she says, giving him a hug, his long beard tickling her bare arm. Maria and Pete always use the present tense when they talk about Ricky, and she's touched by their compassion. "I love you both, too. I'm sure you're right. Thanks for being the voice of reason."

But as they prepare the rest of their dinner, she has that sinking feeling again. She's almost halfway through her gap year and she's getting nowhere fast. They're running out of ideas, and unless something happens soon, the rest of the year is going to be increasingly depressing.

* * *

In her dad's study, the piles of paper are growing. On the flip chart in the corner a list of missing persons charities, help-lines and government departments is written in large black letters. It's headed: *Regular Contacts*. Each name is followed by a series of dates, some spilling onto two lines. On the desk over by the window, piles of notebooks, manila files and newspaper cuttings jostle for space.

The phone trills its silver shafts of light. Leonora, making tea in the kitchen, replaces the kettle and tries to quell the inevitable rush of hope that today, at last, will be the day a miracle happens.

"Could I speak to Leonora Bates, please?" The woman's voice is soft and warm.

"Speaking."

"I'm calling from the *Stadbridge Standard*. I believe you applied for work experience?"

For a moment, her mind is blank. Then she remembers. In a fit of pent-up energy, she had written to the local newspapers, offering to work for nothing in return for some experience. She hadn't expected anything to come of it.

"Yes, I did."

"Would you like to come to see us? We've got so many people on holiday, we need someone urgently, for at least a month, possibly the whole of the summer. It'll be a bit of everything, but if you're interested in journalism, you'll get a good idea of how a newspaper works."

She replaces the handset with a rare rush of excitement. She's no further forward with the search for Ricky but this, at least for a few weeks, will provide a welcome distraction.

CHAPTER THIRTY-EIGHT

Leonora

'The *StadStan*', as it's known locally, covers the town of Stadbridge, a bus ride from Leonora's home. Its catchment extends a few miles into the surrounding area, encircling a handful of nondescript villages too small to support their own newspaper. The population is barely enough to support even this rather thin weekly publication, and the area's proximity to London means it includes many commuters who are more likely to buy the London *Evening Standard* or a national newspaper on their way to work than their local rag with its limited range of material.

But the paper has a loyal following of housewives, businesses and retired people, who rely on it for various reasons, and it manages to attract enough advertising to survive. A small team of journalists and sales staff works in a cramped room on a single floor of an old-fashioned seventies office block, the editor being the only person with the luxury of an office — though it bursts with filing cabinets and teetering piles of paper, and can hardly be called luxurious.

Leonora's job is to help everyone with anything, and she soon learns that tea and coffee play a big part in keeping people happy. She becomes familiar with the kettle, the photocopier and the local post office, and she carries out her work willingly and without complaint. It's not long, though, before more interesting things land on her temporary desk, which normally belongs to the most junior reporter, who is on holiday.

The chief reporter appears at her desk. "Come on, get your coat, we're going to get a story . . ." he says, and disappears towards the exit. She doesn't even know his name. She grabs her jacket, her notebook and pen and races after him.

In his car, he introduces himself as Matthew and gives her an outline of the story he's following. It's a typical small-town story: the local council has decided, with the help of a local children's charity, to plant an orchard in a neglected corner of the park. The first trees are being planted today. The Mayor will be there, as well as the head of the charity, and Matthew is hoping to get some comments from both. A photographer will get some official shots of the first tree and the story will go into this week's paper.

"It's not the most thrilling story," Matthew says. "But in a local newspaper, this is news. If you want to be a reporter, this is the sort of thing you'll need to get used to."

"I'm just grateful for the experience," she says. "The more I can learn, the better."

After the first week, Matthew gives her a story to write.

"Not bad," he says, checking her piece. "You've got the idea already. Just make sure the news is right up front, then expand on it later in the piece. A few tweaks on that first paragraph and you're there."

Her first ever news story is published in that week's paper, under Matthew's name. After that, he passes more writing to her and though she often needs to revise her work, he seems satisfied.

Once a month, the paper carries a feature on a local issue. When Leonora is asked to prepare a first draft, she's both nervous and thrilled. The theme is loneliness, and the aim is to promote the local council's drive to support the community, in particular pensioners who might be isolated and alone. With Matthew's help, Leonora records stories of long empty days, husbands and wives lost to death or divorce, illness or infirmity causing sadness and isolation. She works late into the evening to finish the piece — the longest she's written yet. When she's done, she knows it's the best she can do. The editor passes it, after minor edits, with a 'Well done — good piece', and she knows this is what she is meant to do.

It might even help her to find her brother.

* * *

"Where would you go if you didn't want to be found?"

She uses a small tape recorder, not too intrusive, so as not to make people nervous.

"A trainee, you say?" The woman sniffs and settles herself onto the low wall that encircles a small patch of grass beneath the dilapidated block of flats. She takes a long sip of her tea and draws the back of her hand across her mouth. Leonora notices the grime under her nails and the way her fingers tremble slightly. She looks tired and unwell, her hair hanging lank and greasy onto her thin shoulders. The cuffs of her oversized jumper are grey with dirt.

"I'm a trainee reporter, yes. I'm writing a feature about homelessness." Leonora sits next to her. The wall is cold on the backs of her thighs. She has learned to be patient dealing with these neglected, forgotten people. They have bigger things to worry about than she does. Their focus is on today: where will I get my next meal, where will I sleep tonight? She treats them with respect and on the whole they respond well.

"If I wanted to disappear? Easy, love. A big city. Best place to be if you want to be invisible. Find some other homeless guys and hook up with them. You have to be careful, mind. People prey on you if you don't know what you're doing. But mostly they'll help you if they can, find you a sofa to sleep on, a squat for the night. Tell you where the nearest hostel is."

"Okay. So, in the evenings, where would homeless people be likely to gather?"

"Depends. Parks, underpasses, underground stations, maybe. Doorways are safer if you want to sleep there, but you need somewhere to stash your stuff in the day if you don't want to carry it around with you. Cemeteries, church doorways. They're good too."

"And what about in the day? What do people do when they've got nowhere to go?"

The woman gives her a sideways glance. "If the weather's good, we hang about places like this. If not . . ." She shrugs. "Train station, McDonalds if they'll let you. Some go to the library. Not me, though. Stuffy old places." Her foot starts to jiggle and her eyes flit around the street as if she's expecting someone. Leonora wonders if she has a drug habit.

"Thank you, that's really useful. Just a couple more questions. Have you ever been in danger because of your situation?" The woman laughs, a cold, humourless sound. Leonora thought about taking this question out — now she wishes she had. It sounds thoughtless. "I'm sure it's not easy, sleeping rough. What sort of things do you have to look out for?"

The woman's fidgeting increases. She hunches over her knees. "I dunno. Usual stuff. Men thinking you're easy game, mostly. Pimps'll try and pick you up, then it's tough to get away. Easy to get hooked on drugs and booze. Makes it feel better for a while, but it's a bad idea, you get into all sorts of trouble. The young 'uns get pushed into running drugs. You have to look after yourself, eat, sleep, don't get sick." She sniffs and shifts away from Leonora. "Is that it?" she says. "Only I need to get on." Her eyes flit from side to side, as if she's watching for someone.

"That's it." Leonora stands to go. "Can I get you a coffee or something?"

The woman grunts, a soft violet shimmer, and shakes her head. She opens her lips in a grimace of a smile, revealing a crooked line of yellow teeth. "Need something stronger than that," she says, waving Leonora away. "You get on, love, you don't want to hang around these parts for too long."

As Leonora walks away, she passes two men heading towards the seated woman. They carry plastic shopping bags and the air is redolent with the acrid stench of stale beer.

Later that evening, as the summer sunlight fades from the tiny window in her cabin, she can't stop thinking about what the woman said.

If she wanted to disappear, she'd go to a big city.

CHAPTER THIRTY-NINE

Leonora

She's never been called in to the editor's office before. With a twinge of concern, she wonders what she might have done to be summoned. Has she done something wrong? In her entire time at the paper, she's barely seen him — he rarely comes as far as her cramped corner.

Matthew is already there when she knocks on the open door, a spatter of pink-tinged spots fading as she enters.

"Come in, Leonora," the editor says, manoeuvring around his desk to shake her hand. "Sit down. We've got some interesting news for you." He glances across at Matthew, who smiles at Leonora. It can't be too bad, then.

"The Chambers of Commerce — they're local business organisations — in our area have got together this year to run an award for local journalism," the editor says. "And guess what — you've won! Best newcomer category." He grins at her, waiting for her response. A phone trills its jade-green notes into the air on an empty desk nearby.

"But—" she says, confused. "I haven't entered anything . . ."

"I entered your series on local issues, Leonora," Matthew tells her, with a smile. "I thought it was excellent, and I was right. Well done, you. There's an award ceremony at the Town Hall next month. We'll get some good pictures and run a piece about you. It'll be great publicity for the paper."

She stammers out a 'thank you,' still not quite believing it, and goes back to her desk, their words of congratulation ringing in her ears.

That evening there's a small celebration on the narrowboat.

But her elation is short-lived. Later that night, the boat rocking gently against the bank of the canal beneath her, her mind turns to her family. Without her father around, her mum would have been proud, if she'd been well enough to understand. It would be good to think so, anyway. Ricky would have loved to hear of her success — they would have danced around the room together, holding hands, making ridiculous whoops of delight.

But their dad would have been scathing, destroying her moment in a heartbeat. Part of her always longed for his approval, and there was a time when she felt she could earn it.

There were moments, early on, when he was different. At times he was even playful, genial. But his mood would turn in a second.

The day she learned to swim was a huge moment for her. Once a week at school, the class would form a two-by-two crocodile and troop off to the local lido, where they shivered in the cold water as they practised their doggy paddle, their little arms held up with bright orange armbands, their legs beating a rhythm behind them. Leonora loved the water, the flashes of sunlight making patterns on the bottom of the pool, the feel of being supported, the way she could change direction with her legs. This day they were practising swimming with only one armband — they'd all been growing in confidence over the weeks and it was time to move up a level.

Without thinking, Leonora had discarded both armbands and swum an entire width before she'd even realised it. She got a special mention by the teacher and a medal — something nobody else had ever done. She'd run home after school, bursting with the news. Her mum and her brother were delighted for her, exclaiming over her achievement, and she'd felt warm with pride.

But when her father got home, it was a different story.

"A width?" he said, his voice heavy with contempt. "At your age, I was swimming miles! Proper strokes, not your baby dog-paddle. Why can't they teach swimming properly in this country? Where I come from, your parents throw you in and you swim or drown. That's the way to learn!"

"But Daddy," Leonora whispered, tears not far away. "I got a medal . . ."

She held the piece of cheap plastic up to show him.

"A medal? That's not a medal! It's a piece of plastic rubbish, that's what it is. When you've won a proper medal, for proper swimming in a competition, that's when you can be proud."

She'd spent the rest of the evening in the den, in tears, Ricky's arm around her.

Now she knows for sure that she would never have earned her father's pride, not in a million years. He would never have changed towards her, would always have treated her like a loser.

The second thing that happens, only a few days later, is even more astounding.

The start of the university year is looming. This has been what she's wanted for so long, but Leonora can't decide what to do. She hasn't found Ricky, hasn't a clue as to his whereabouts, even after a whole year of trying. It still feels wrong to carry on with her life, to put the search on hold, when Ricky is missing. She's not even sure it would be the best time for her to go to university, when she's still so obsessed with finding her brother.

But at the same time, the search is deeply frustrating. It's a treadmill of dashed hopes and bitter disappointments and she longs for a chance to take her mind off it.

She's sitting at her desk torturing herself with the same old questions when the phone on her desk starts to sing with a flutter of silver notes. Watching them fade, she answers without thinking.

"Leonora Bates."

"Good morning, Leonora. I'm calling from the *Tribune* newspaper in London. We wondered if you'd like to come for a chat over a cup of coffee."

"Excuse me?"

He repeats the statement, enunciating each word with precision.

Once she's understood what he's saying, she's so surprised, she almost drops the handset. She swings around in her chair and faces the bank of filing cabinets that flank her desk. Lowering her voice, she says: "Can I call you back, please? I can't talk right now. I'll call you back in five minutes."

* * *

On her way to London, she still isn't sure why she's going. She tries to prepare herself for anything. 'A chat' could mean just that. They could be wanting information from her, perhaps to do with her research for the series of articles in the *StadStan*. Could it be about Ricky? If so, then she will get the most she can out of the meeting: a news story or a feature in a national newspaper could make all the difference, though she will have to be careful. Or it could be the start of an interview process. She can hardly allow herself to think that could be possible.

She has with her a folder, stashed firmly under her arm as she sits staring out of the window at the passing countryside. She's on the slow train, which stops all too often at grey stations flanked by the backs of terraced houses, their gardens dotted with children's toys and garden sheds. But its wheels on the tracks, with their dark-red rumble of ever-decreasing swirls, have a calming effect and she's glad of the time to rehearse the answers to difficult questions.

The folder contains her CV, a picture of Ricky and a summary of what has happened. There are copies of her printed articles in the *StadStan*, a reference letter from Miss Stannard, the award certificate from the Chambers of Commerce and a cutting from the paper with a picture of Leonora, a nervous smile fixed on her face, shaking hands with a besuited businessman offering her the certificate. The photo belies her emotional state at the time: she had been proud, convinced there had been no other entrants (otherwise how come she had won?), embarrassed and delighted all at once.

He doesn't keep her waiting long. His name is Ben Freeman and he has a colleague with him, Jennifer Barker. They're both in their coats and barely stop to say hello before heading for the entrance.

"We'll go to the coffee shop next door," he says. "No privacy upstairs. We're packed in like a Tesco's warehouse in there."

Tongue-tied and anxious, she follows them like a schoolgirl following the teacher. Jennifer stands in the queue for coffees while Ben and Leonora find a table. She puts her folder on the table, then removes it again. It seems presumptuous, all of a sudden, even to have brought it with her.

"I'm going to get straight to the point," Ben says. "I know Jennifer agrees with me. We've seen your work, and we like it. We want to offer you a job. It's only an intern job, like an apprenticeship, really. Not well-paid, I'm afraid, but you'll learn a lot in a short time. You'll have to make coffee and tea, run errands, do unpaid overtime, keep your mouth shut and your eyes and ears open. But if you're as good as you seem, you'll soon get the hang of it. If you're interested and we like you, we're going to request you join our team."

On the train on the way back, she can't stop smiling.

* * *

After a short but agonising wait, her friend the postman delivers a white envelope to the narrowboat, with the paper's frank in the top right corner. With trembling fingers, she rips it open, reads: *We are delighted to offer you* . . . and almost faints with shock. It's there in black and white, what she's always wanted.

But it's a sweet agony she feels. Ricky's absence is like a blanket of cloud hanging over her, dark and oppressive, smothering her joy.

"What should I do?" she says to Maria, her belly clenching with the pain of his absence. "Here's my dream job, on a plate. I don't even have to go to university and study journalism, I can do it straight away — a proper job, earning money, in London, at a national newspaper!"

"It's fantastic." Maria gives her a hug.

"I could never have imagined something like this. But what do I do about Ricky? If I work full-time, I'll have even less chance to look for him than if I was a student. I can't defer a job at the *Tribune*. If I don't say yes, it'll be gone. I'll never get a chance like this again."

"You deserve this," Maria tells her. "It's a great problem to have. You can go to university and learn to be a journalist, or become a journalist three years earlier and start earning money straight away. I know what I would do."

"But what about Ricky?" she says again.

"Pete and I can carry on the search for Ricky. We'd be happy to," Maria reassures her. "And you know what? As a journalist in London, you'll learn ways to discover things you never would when you're studying. That's the job of a journalist, to search out stories, find the facts. And remember, it's possible he's been living in London all this time, so you could be nearer to him. Look, if you really want to get a degree, you can do it any time — why don't you talk to the university, see if you can defer again? Then, if the job doesn't work out, you can still go, and you'll already have some of the skills you need. You'll be ahead of the game."

"Oh, Maria," Leonora says, jumping up and throwing her arms around her neck. "I love you guys."

* * *

In the space of a few short weeks, she has to make many decisions. First of all, the family house. Because Ricky is missing, she can't sell it unless she declares him dead, which is unthinkable. She can't bring tenants in officially but she's going to need the money to get somewhere to live.

She mentions this to Mrs Clark, and gets an instant response.

"I can sort you out," Mrs Clark says. "Don't you worry, I have ways and means. I'll ask around."

Leonora can't believe how quickly Mrs Clark finds someone. Through the local church she hears of a family who needs a house to rent, and within days it's organised. The income won't be much — the house is too run-down — but it will help towards the cost of a room in London. They want to keep most of the furniture, which is a relief. There's far too much and it's too old and heavy for Leonora to take with her. Mrs Clark will even keep an eye on the place for her.

"You're my guardian angel," she says. "I don't know how I'll ever repay you."

"Go on with you," Mrs Clark says, smiling. "No need to repay me. Just let me know how you're getting on, come and see me sometimes. That'll be perfect."

Next, Leonora needs to find somewhere to live. This is daunting: she doesn't know London, doesn't know where to start. So on Maria's suggestion, she talks to the newspaper again, asks if they know anywhere she can stay, even temporarily, when she starts work. Jennifer asks around, and within a couple of days a girl called Claire, who works in the accounts department, telephones to say there's a room going spare in her flat in Notting Hill. "It's nothing special," she says. "But it's cheap and it's in a great spot."

Leonora says yes without even seeing it. She takes a day off work and travels up to London to meet Claire at the flat. By the time she leaves, it's all organised.

CHAPTER FORTY

Ricky

Shame, along with guilt, were my ghastly companions. They followed me everywhere, their weight on my shoulders, relentless.

In those long days spent walking the grey streets of London, shivering on park benches, or huddled in the dark in back alleys, I imagined Dad's dying hours and what I had done. The horror of it seeped into my mind, little by little, like a snake's venom creeping towards my brain, until my skull felt as if it would explode.

I was tortured by images of his body out there in the Drakensberg mountains, slowly being drained of life, blood staining the grass all around him, his face grimacing with pain. In some of my worst moments, I would see his dying face on a living person, glimpsed on a bus or under the hood of a passing man, and it would be skeletal, frozen in a howl of agony. When it first happened, I stopped in my tracks, screamed: "No, no!" and ran until my lungs burned and my legs became weak and buckled beneath me. People stared, then looked away, ushering their children in the other direction, alarmed by my filthy clothes, my manic behaviour. I did not blame them, or want them to care about me. I was losing my mind.

In that cruel place where you're always a trespasser, where you can't close the door against the world, sink into a chair, open a cupboard to reach for food when you're hungry, or climb with a sigh into a warm bed at night, it is easy to lose touch with sanity. For me, it wasn't just easy. Sanity ran away from me as fast as it could and I had no idea where it had gone.

I had no plan, Leo, I confess. You always wanted me to have a plan. But when you've lost your mind, you have trouble organising the next five minutes, let alone planning the rest of your life.

Of course there was always booze and drugs, and I did succumb for a while. But they cost money, and narcotics made me worse. I would lose days at a time, waking up to a kick from a couple of lads, who'd laugh and run away, or a shake from a policeman wanting to move me on. I could never remember how I got there, or who had given me the drugs. Every time my hand flew to my money belt to check on the brooch, and every time I berated myself for being such a fool.

Alcohol made me weep with self-pity. I must have been a pathetic sight: thin, filthy, covered in sores, stinking and muttering to myself, or shouting and waving at nothing. Sometimes a kind person from a charity would find me in some sordid corner and take pity on me, and I would get a night or two in a hostel. I was ashamed of myself, my mind and body sick with guilt and self-loathing.

I lived in the shadows for months, maybe a year. It could have been more, but I was oblivious to time. I had no idea what day of the week it was, let alone which month. I shuffled from food bank to soup kitchen to day centre. Sometimes I got a shower and clean clothes, but only when I was having a good day, and those were increasingly rare.

I thought about killing myself. But I wasn't organised enough to do it, and anyway I was already on the fast train to oblivion. I didn't need to make that decision. I'd hit rock bottom.

* * *

My father's voice followed me everywhere, my childhood coming back to me in daytime nightmares. How I tried to please him in the early days when, in my innocence, I admired him and wanted to be like him.

One incident kept coming back to me. I knew he wanted me to be good at football, so I would practise often in the back garden after school, kicking the ball to you for hours on end, trying out the tricks I'd seen other kids do. You were very patient and never complained, but if I'm honest you were better than I was from the first.

At first Dad encouraged me. He was pleased I was trying. When he got home from work and saw us in the garden, he would come outside, taking over from you without a word, leaving you trailing your feet back into the house, your head hanging. But he soon realised how hopeless I was. Even when he took the time to coach me, I pranced around like a newborn foal, unable to control my spindly legs. The ball went over the fence into next door's garden so many times, the neighbours got used to chucking it back.

"For God's sake, try, Richard!" Dad would say. And I did try, as hard as I could, in my desire to impress him.

On this particular day, I was pleased with my progress. We'd set up a makeshift goal using a garden fork and a broomstick, and with you as goalkeeper, I'd been doing rather well. My goal count was going up, so I was happy to demonstrate to Dad when he got home. But fate was not on my side. Perhaps I was too keen to please, or more likely, nervous about performing in front of him.

Anyway, I took aim with enthusiasm, and kicked hard at the ball. But I slipped awkwardly and the ball rolled away harmlessly into the flowerbed, leaving me in a heap on the grass.

"Jesus!" Dad said. "You really are useless, aren't you? Can't even strike the ball when it's stationary. I give up." And with that, he strode back into the house, frowning and muttering to himself.

I took our 'goal' down after that, and stopped playing football altogether.

* * *

Dragging myself out of a troubled sleep filled with sweats and hallucinations, I became conscious of the sound of voices. This in itself was not unusual. By that time I experienced voices in my head all the time, telling me how despicable I was, shouting my name, threatening me with all kinds of terrible punishments for what I'd done.

But these voices were different. They weren't shouting, for one thing, and they sounded concerned, almost friendly. Opening my eyes, I saw faces looming over me, huge and frightening. I scrambled backwards in fear, but there was a brick wall behind me and I was trapped. I had no recollection of where I was, but it was probably one of the many filthy alleys I frequented: big bins along the walls, rubbish scattered around, water dripping from gutters high above. I shielded my face with my arm and tried to hide, but there was a hand on my shoulder and a voice at my ear: "Oliver. Oliver — can you hear me? It's Ben. Come with me." I forced my mind to focus. I knew there was someone called Ben, and I should have known who he was, but I couldn't remember. I lowered my arm and stared into his anxious eyes.

"It's okay, Oliver, we're going to help you now. We're going to get you food and medicine. Can you walk?"

I don't remember even trying to stand, but strong arms lifted me up and supported me as I tried to get my legs to move. Then I saw the ambulance and my heart started to pound. I stopped, shook my head and wrestled my arms away. "No, I'm not going to prison!" I shouted, backing away. "You can't make me! Leave me alone!"

I don't know how long it took them to persuade me to step into the ambulance. I would only talk to Ben, and it took him a while to get through to me. I knew I needed to go, but there was something nagging at me and I couldn't leave until I'd got it sorted. Ben's hand was on my arm, his voice soft in my ear, when at last I remembered. I rummaged around at my waist to disentangle the filthy money belt with its precious contents. I handed it to him and whispered: "Please — keep this safe for me? It's important."

He nodded and took the belt from my hand. At last someone wanted to look after me.

CHAPTER FORTY-ONE

Ricky

My hospital stay lurks in my memory in a blur of bright lights, drips in my arm and people in white coats. Even now I don't know how long I was there. It was certainly weeks, if not months.

After they had cleaned me up and carried out tests on various parts of my body, it turned out I had contracted pneumonia. My lungs were filled with fluid, I weighed under eight stone and I had a severe skin condition called perniosis, caused by the cold and the damp.

I had been unaware of any of this, only imagining that it was the cold that made my chest hurt and caused the skin on my hands and face to blister and flake. I had no idea what someone my age should weigh, or look like, only that I had been hungry for a very long time. When I had been able to eat a proper meal, it was in a soup kitchen or a temporary shelter, and never more than once or twice a week. The rest of the time I managed on what scraps came my way, or portions of chips shared with other homeless people. I hadn't looked at myself in a mirror for a long time, and when I glimpsed myself in shop windows or reflected in the walls of bus shelters, I ignored what I saw.

Fortunately for me, the pneumonia and the skin condition were treatable. On a regime of medication and regular meals, I gradually regained some physical strength. In three or four weeks I was able to walk the length of the corridor to the toilets, albeit slowly, and my weight was beginning to increase. The cough that I'd hardly been aware of while living on the street — because everyone seemed to cough, there — was easing.

But my mind was still lost. Like a startled bird, it had flown away, up into a dark cloud, where it hid, trembling.

Though my body was gradually getting better, sleep eluded me. All night I lay with my eyes open, listening to the voices, right through to the early morning crash and clash of breakfast trolleys and the distant banter of the auxiliary nurses and cleaners.

But the morning light did nothing to stop the incessant chatter. There was nothing I could do to distract myself. I was unable to read. The words meant nothing, a jumble of shapes which swirled and whirled and fell off the page. I couldn't get them to keep still, however hard I tried. The television shows which kept some of the patients amused were no better for me. On the screen, people smiled and their lips moved and I heard nothing. Perhaps the sound was down, but even when it wasn't, all I heard was a cacophony of noise. I gave up trying to understand what people said to me, including the doctors and nurses.

The voices in my head were too loud. They had taken over.

The doctors moved me to a psychiatric ward. I didn't know where I was being taken, Leo. It was probably a good thing nobody told me — or possibly they did, but it didn't register in my empty head — because at nineteen, or twenty, or however old I was, I would have probably fought them. I would have done everything I could to escape.

I remember noticing that the patients were different there. Some were quiet and shuffled about, talking to nobody. Some, though, screamed in the night, which scared me — and some wouldn't stop talking, or shouting, or whispering. These were the most difficult for me, with my absent mind, to deal with. They were frightening, but worse, they interrupted my voices.

My voices didn't like to be interrupted. I listened to them all the time, though they were always malicious. I was powerless — they ruled my every thought, manipulated my every move. It was always just the two of them — both male, one deep and powerful, the other with a hard edge that cut through any extraneous sounds. They told me I was useless, pathetic, my life was worth nothing, why didn't I just end it all, then and there. Why did I bother to take the medication, why didn't I find a knife and slash my wrists, or jump from the roof. On and on. In the daytime it felt as if they were right behind me, following my slippered feet to the shower or the toilet, taunting me even when I was brushing my teeth. My teeth were probably the cleanest in the whole place, Leo, I brushed them so hard and for so long in an effort to muffle the voices. At night their taunts would resonate around the large hospital room like never-ending echoes in a valley.

Sometimes it became unbearable, and I would scream and shout and punch the wall beside my bed to drown out their endless diatribe. That wall had to withstand a lot of abuse.

When that happened a nurse would come, sometimes two or three, wrestle me back to my bed and administer something that silenced my tormentors for a while.

CHAPTER FORTY-TWO

Ricky

Ben said: "I've got good news for you. I've found you somewhere to live."

We were sitting on a bench outside the hospital, in a patch of garden where people well enough to leave their ward could smoke and take their visitors. It was summer now, and someone had tried hard to make the small area into a proper garden, with flowers and lawn and a cherry tree which offered some shade.

It had taken me many months to get to this point, I can't remember how many. Hundreds of tablets. Weeks of therapy. With the help of a team of psychotherapists and mental nurses, the voices began to fade, bit by bit. At last I realised that they were extensions of my own personality: I had created them. With that realisation came control, and when they finally left the room, there was space in my head for my mind to return from the black cloud where it had found refuge. I was still fragile, but I had my sanity back.

Throughout my recovery, Ben was often there. He brought wild flowers picked on his way there, or a packet of sweets, or a book he'd read and wanted to pass on, though he knew I couldn't read them. He just kept saying: "Keep them until you're better." He was always certain I would recover, even when I was so far down my tunnel I felt I would never climb out again.

So when he called in unexpectedly one day to find me on the third chapter of one of his books, he was delighted. He started making plans for my future. Plans, Leo! He must have known me better than I knew myself. It had not crossed my mind that one day soon I would have to leave the hospital and find a way to live without descending into the pit again.

A place to live. My first reaction was fear, I admit it. At that point I had not faced up to the rest of my life. I was hanging on to my fragile recovery, and that was enough for me, I thought. But of course I couldn't stay there for ever, and somehow I would have to find a way to survive without going back to the streets. It was terrifying, and I could feel the blood drain from my cheeks and my hands begin to sweat at his words.

"I — I can't," I said, shaking my head.

"Yes, you can, Oliver," Ben said. "I know it's challenging, but I can help you. You've recovered well, and I'll support you while you get back on your feet."

"No, it's not that, it's . . ."

"What is it?"

I knew I'd have to trust him, but I still couldn't bring myself to tell him the truth. "I — I'm not using my real name. There's a reason, but I can't tell you, I'm sorry. I have no ID . . ." I was acutely aware that my passport, revealing my true identity, was in my money belt along with the brooch. It had become as important to hide the passport as it was to hide the brooch. Even if Ben hadn't looked inside — which he probably hadn't, being him — the money belt clearly had something passport-shaped in it. So he must have known I was lying, and I felt disloyal and miserable. But I knew the hostels would need identity papers, at the very least, before they would allow me in.

But as I say, he knew me well, and he never judged me. "It's okay, Oliver," he said, his voice reassuring. "I understand. I'll vouch for you. Homeless people often have no ID. Don't worry, we can sort it out."

He explained that, by a rare stroke of luck, a place had come up in a hostel close to his church. There were four residents, all needing and receiving help to live in society, and he knew each one of them. He would help me get some identification and then I could apply for benefits, which would give me just about enough to live. I would have my own room, and there would be people to support me while I found my feet.

I had no option, really. My feet were the least of my worries. First I had to make sure my mind stayed put.

As he said, it was okay. Initially, of course, I felt panicky and on edge. But Ben stuck with me all the way. He was patient and kind and I will never be able to repay him for all the things he did for me. When he returned my money belt with its precious contents, I knew how lucky I was to have found him. I threw that filthy old money belt in the bin and got myself a new one, that I wore all the time. At night I slept with it under my pillow.

It took me a while to get to know my housemates but we got along okay and to my utter relief, the demon voices stayed away. My new friends, two girls and two boys, were a similar age to me. Each had their own issues: anorexia, anxiety, learning difficulties. The two lads had jobs: shift work, which meant they didn't get back until late most days. The girls were volunteering with Ben while building their confidence to find paid work.

I survived on benefits, helped by frequent therapy and Ben. My name was Oliver Gates.

The hostel was in North Kensington, in a run-down area that belies its name. But it was beautiful to me, after sleeping on the streets for so long. A room of my own, with a comfortable bed, a proper bathroom and a kitchen. It was sheer luxury.

I began to venture out, to walk around London again, but this time as a citizen of the city, not as a vagrant. This time I saw it differently, walking for miles into areas I'd never been before, getting to know it from a different perspective.

One day I made an important discovery. London had a zoo. Walking through Regent's Park one day, I heard the distant sound of exotic animals, and followed the calls. The entrance fee was too much for me, but I walked around the perimeter, breathing in magic smells that conjured up the grasslands and bush of Southern Africa again. I could even see the giraffes wandering through their enclosure from the tarmac pavement that ran alongside.

The first time I went in I was hooked. Though these were caged animals, many of them bred in captivity, they seemed on the whole healthy and happy. Though I felt for the roaming creatures, deprived of their huge expanses of land, I knew at once that this place was important. Without seeing these beautiful wild creatures in the flesh, how could you expect people to support them and look after their future? How, otherwise, would some children ever get to see the majesty of the King of the Jungle, the antics of a tribe of monkeys?

I began to spend as much time there as I could afford.

Feeding time was the highlight of the day for all the animals, and I got to know the routines of the keepers, moving from lion enclosure to penguin pools to the giraffe house to catch the moment when the fresh food would appear, to be snatched and savoured. I sought out the African animals: the rhinos, warthogs, lions, zebras, African hunting dogs and more. The smells and the sounds comforted me and despite the locks on the gates and the coolness of the air, if I closed my eyes I could almost imagine myself back in South Africa with Luke.

One day, towards closing time, I was sitting on a bench waiting for the wild dogs to appear when a keeper came and sat down next to me. I asked about the dogs and their breeding programme and he seemed impressed with my knowledge of their habits. I told him about my schooling in South Africa, and how I'd developed a love of wildlife while I was there.

"You should volunteer here," he said. "They're always looking for people to help. They'd be delighted to find someone with a bit of knowledge."

For a moment, I was speechless. It had not occurred to me that I could work with animals anywhere except in Africa. This could be the next best thing. I was stunned. Could I really volunteer? I couldn't think of any job in London that would suit me better.

I felt a thrill of excitement in my stomach. But then I remembered who — or rather, what — I was. I wasn't sure I was safe, even then. So I told him I'd think about it, and went home, my brain whirring.

Was it possible I could work there and not be found out?

For the whole of the period of my recovery, I had managed not to mention the terrible thing I'd done, not even to Ben. Somehow, despite the months when the voices urged me every day to confess, telling me that I'd never have a life, that I should be in prison — I managed to hold my secret close. I crushed it up into a tiny ball of horror, wrapped it in layers of fear and guilt and shoved it into the deepest, darkest corner of my mind.

In the hospital, when people asked me about my background, I fudged it. I said my parents were both dead, I'd lost touch with my sister, I had nothing and nobody. I think I was so ill, they didn't want to push me too hard, so I got away with it. Though it was always there, a burden I had to carry for the rest of my life, I managed to keep it secret.

Thinking back, that was probably what made me lose my mind.

I suppose I'd persuaded myself that I didn't deserve a decent life, after what I'd done. I certainly never imagined that I would make my way in society, have a normal life, with a job, a partner, children. But the idea of working with animals again seemed to open a window to my future, just a fraction.

As I travelled back to my temporary home that day, I felt a tingle of excitement in my belly, a feeling I hadn't experienced for years and never had expected to feel again. Perhaps I could create a life for myself. Perhaps I did deserve to be happy. Maybe, even, through working with animals, doing something I loved, I could forgive myself.

* * *

When I received the offer of an interview, I was terrified, Leo. I lost sleep running through endless awkward questions and concocting a range of credible answers to cover myself. I tried to meditate, did breathing exercises, everything I could to relax enough to get through an interview. I was convinced I would have a panic attack and screw it up.

But I needn't have worried. Because I'd worked on the reserve at the school, and was familiar with African animals, they barely asked me anything else. To my astonishment, the position was mine. There was no money, but I didn't care — I could manage. I would be working with animals again and I could hardly believe it. When I received the offer, which came by letter, I almost fainted. I read and re-read it until I knew every word.

To most people, my job at the zoo would have seemed menial, certainly mundane. I mucked out cages, swept and washed concrete enclosures, picked up litter, emptied rubbish bins. I measured out thirty or so different meals, three times a day, into feeding bowls, bins and boxes for the keepers to take to their animals. Giraffes, zebras, warthogs and other hoofed animals were my team's responsibility. I wasn't allowed near the animals without someone more senior than me, and then only to back them up, opening and closing gates, shovelling droppings and clearing the remains of the animals' food. I loved every minute of it.

The community of workers at the zoo took a while to accept me. I kept myself to myself, avoided eye contact and didn't socialise with them, which some of them found odd. When the more gregarious of them tried to find out more about me, I prevaricated, giving them vague answers or replying in monosyllables until they gave up. They probably thought I was stand-offish, but I was always polite and I worked as hard as anyone. I listened well and I never complained. After a while they got used to my ways. They called me 'Stormy' because I was so quiet. I rather liked it.

CHAPTER FORTY-THREE

Leonora

"See you later!"

Claire's cheerful voice dispels the last vestiges of sleep as Leonora struggles onto her elbows, blinking in the brightness of morning. She reaches over to the bedside table where a steaming mug of tea sits alongside her books. The yellow crunch of the front door confirms that her flatmate has left for work.

Claire is a great person to share with. She's the same age as Leonora, loves her job and enjoys a lively social life. She's clean, tidy and cheerful, and she provides endless cups of tea and coffee for Leonora as if it's her accepted role in life. Leonora can't believe her luck.

Situated at the less salubrious end of Notting Hill Gate, not far from the streets where cannabis is openly sold on street corners and you learn not to linger, the flat already feels like a home. It has two good-sized rooms: a bedroom and a sitting room — now Leonora's bedroom, a kitchen and a bathroom, and it has the great advantage of only being a short walk to the Underground. At the back, a shared garden is overlooked by a block of what looks like former council flats. Though unkempt, the garden is intended for the use of the residents of the homes on one side, including Claire and Leonora's flat, providing a quiet space to sit in the summer months. At night, Leonora can lie in bed and listen to the emerald-green whoosh and buzz of London's traffic.

At first Leonora manages with a mattress on the floor and a single chair, her clothes hanging on a steel rail on one side of the room. But it doesn't take long to find an unwanted bed, a small chest of drawers, rickety but serviceable, and a chair. The rail does a good enough job as a wardrobe for the moment. A couple of planks on bricks serve as a bookshelf, and gradually, with some posters and brightly coloured cushions, the room begins to feel like her own. There's no TV, but Leonora is used to that. She's happy with her books and a radio for company when Claire isn't there. When she thinks about her life, she can hardly believe she's here, living in London, with a great job and a decent place to live. She's almost happy, some days.

London is everything Leonora hoped it would be. Bursting with energy, sometimes terrifying, always active. A city of contrasts — new and old, beautiful and sordid, cultured and vulgar, generous and grasping. A place to disappear in, and to be seen. So different from the sombre streets of her home town, which is close enough to the capital to be in its shadow, too far for the magic to rub off.

At first, she felt she'd lived until that moment like a horse with blinkers, unable to see more than what was right before her, oblivious to the wonders beyond. The pace of life unnerved her — the rushing people, the endless traffic, the burgundy growl of taxis at every corner. The sights and sounds of the city left her breathless, and every day was a sensory overload. The first time she walked down Kensington High Street, the noise — car horns blaring, diesel engines roaring, the squeal of children, the rumble of a plane overhead — created a tapestry of colour so intense that she stood transfixed in the street for minutes before she could move on.

But as she became accustomed to the ebb and flow of city life, she was entranced by it. Every day seemed to bring a new experience, and with it inspiration, discovery, hope.

This is what she wanted more than anything: to slough off the past, to create a future in a new world. That's what the plan has always been about: the plan that drove her through school, that pushed her to the top of the class, that won her the best A levels the school had ever achieved. A place at university to study journalism and a job she loves in London.

But though she'd always longed to leave her home town and create a life very different from that of her parents, her dream always included Ricky. She never imagined life without him. He would always be there, beside her. When he was about to finish school and wanted to stay in South Africa, she started to envisage a life for herself there — after all, she could be a journalist anywhere in the English-speaking world. If he'd said he wanted to live in Australia, on the other side of the world, she would have gone there too.

To lose Ricky from her life is to lose the dream. It's as simple as that. Everything she has achieved since she was twelve, when he walked out of the front door on the first leg of his journey to South Africa, is worth nothing if she can't share it with her brother. She has followed her plan as if he were still there, and she follows it now because she can't believe he's not. But without him, there's no joy.

* * *

"Well good morning, lovely Leonora," Rob says, opening the glass door of the office as she approaches. His name starts with R: orange, like Ricky. It's a good sign. Because of it, or more likely from instinct, she trusts him. He bows and ushers her in with a flourish of his arm and a mock-serious look on his face.

"Good morning, Rob." She smiles at him, performs a wobbly curtsy. "How kind."

Her job as junior feature writer in the small team of friendly journalists provides her with an anchor, and while the work is often challenging, she thrives on the atmosphere. She's learning to hone her skills on the job, and she doesn't care that the hours are long and the deadlines tight. She loves the speed of it all, the interviewing, the research, the sense of satisfaction when a piece comes together. When her first article was published, she couldn't have been more proud.

Rob follows her to her desk, where she hangs her coat on a coat stand, her bag over the back of her chair. "Are you following me?" she says, sitting down and powering up her computer.

"Stalking, actually."

"Isn't that illegal?"

Rob is an English graduate with a love of Trollope and a passion for cinema. He goes every week, and sometimes, if it's a film she likes the sound of, she'll go with him.

"Probably. But as we're colleagues and friends, it would be hard to prove in a court of law. Unless I start following you home, or sending you millions of letters, or emails. And calling you a hundred times a day . . ."

"Okay, okay, I wasn't asking for a definition. Haven't you got something better to do than hang about my desk being irritating?"

He holds his hands up and backs away, smiling. "It's okay, I'm off. I know where I'm not wanted."

She smiles back and starts typing. It's going to take a lot of work to hit today's deadline.

When she leaves her desk at the end of the day, almost everyone has gone — only her team leader and her boss are still there, engrossed in conversation over mugs of coffee. She passes Rob's desk on her way out. His jacket, always thrown over the back of his chair when he's in, has gone, his desk neat and ordered in preparation for the next day's work.

As she walks towards the tube station, following a stream of other workers heading home, her thoughts are on Rob and his gentle, teasing manner. She knows he likes her, but like others before him, he's having to accept being her friend and no more. She has perfected the art of banter without flirtation, of affection without escalation, of friendship without sex.

There have been dates — she's twenty and living in London, after all — but these are fleeting relationships, gone before they've even arrived. She hasn't seen a single one of them twice. Her choice, not theirs. Cautious at all times, wary of drinking too much, staying too long, getting too close, she's an expert in avoiding intimacy.

Now, when she visits Kelly, happy with her husband and her new baby, or when she sees a couple smiling at each other, holding hands, she sometimes thinks about love. Perhaps for each of us there is only room for one truly special person. For some it's their mother, for others a husband or a girlfriend. For Leonora, it's always been Ricky.

Perhaps it's because he's gone that she feels like this. What's certain is that his absence has crowded everyone else out: her heart's simply too full of him, of loss and longing and love, for anyone else. No one else has a chance.

CHAPTER FORTY-FOUR

Leonora

At weekends, she wanders round London, getting to know its corners, its secret passageways and green spaces. She wanders through streets where gracious white terraces line the pavements and flowers drip from manicured window-boxes, only to find around the next corner a run of dilapidated council flats, brightly coloured clothing hanging from cramped balconies, music blaring in a cacophony of colours. She loves the contrast, the surprises, the never-ending blend of buildings and streets and people.

When she comes across homeless people, she stops to chat, to buy them a coffee or a sandwich. Sometimes she asks them where the shelters are and drops in to ask after Ricky. Everyone is kind, but nobody has seen him.

Sometimes she walks round Regent's Park and goes to the zoo.

Exotic sounds greet her, exploding in a myriad of hues and shapes, flashes and flurries before her. In the Africa area, she breathes in the strange scent of the creatures, watches her own private display of colourful calls and grunts, laughs at the antics of the monkeys. At feeding time, their keepers are always nearby, vigilant, dedicated, as Ricky would have been with the animals in the school's reserve.

The giraffes are still her favourites. She will never tire of these graceful animals, with their long, gangly legs, their impossible, soaring necks, their sloping backs. The youngsters josh with each other and run, their necks swaying in time with their huge strides. They seem to have the best house in the zoo, designed especially for them with its tall doors and high feeding points.

Sometimes, she imagines the animals back in their natural home, where birds call, snakes sunbathe in the grasslands, insects crawl and fly. Where food is all around them and they can search it out rather than waiting for a human to provide it. Where the ground underfoot is soft soil, not harsh concrete, where grass grows lush and life flourishes. Where the sun shines, the air is warm, the horizon vast. In the immense reserves of Africa, they can wander where they like, sleep where they choose. She wonders how these foreigners feel in the cold grey of a London afternoon, whether they know from ancient instinct that they're not in their natural habitat.

The solitary animals in their too-small cages disturb her. They pace, and shake their heads, and pace again.

* * *

At Christmastime, she stays with Maria and Pete in their remote Welsh cottage. The narrowboat is asleep in a boatyard, closed up for the winter, not to be woken until May.

At the cottage, hens run free, a handful of rare-breed sheep roam in an adjoining field, a cat sleeps by the stove. Although Leonora enjoys living in the city, it's a welcome contrast. Log fires and an old-fashioned kitchen range make the house warm and welcoming, and they spend the evenings reading, listening to music and playing cards. Jack is there too, on a break from his work on the farm. The sound of Pete's guitar wafts around the cottage, a shower of blues and greens flowing around Leonora.

They talk about Ricky. "We're no further forward," says Maria. "It's a long process, following everyone up. But we're not giving up."

"I'll never give up." Leonora sighs. "It's so frustrating. There must be something else we can do."

"We could start a campaign. It's risky, though." They all know what Pete means. If the police are still looking for Ricky in connection with their father's death, the campaign could harm him.

"I'm going to visit all the homeless shelters I can find," Leonora says. "I've already started. There are so many people living on the streets in London. It's tragic — so many sad stories. I hate to think of Ricky having to do that."

"We don't know he did," Pete reminds her, gently.

"That's the problem," Leonora says. "We know so little. Sometimes I wonder if we'll ever find out what happened to him."

Maria squeezes her hand. "We will, Leo, I'm sure of it."

In the news on the radio is a story of a dog, lost for two years, reunited with its owners after being found in a rescue centre. The owner's voice cracks with emotion as she describes the scene. Leonora wishes there were similar centres for people, where you could go to adopt or reconnect. But the places for people are temporary homes, a place for the night, or perhaps two. To eat warm soup and rest your head on a pillow. Their residents can only stay a short time — there are too many of them; they have to move on.

Every day, she sends a promise to Ricky: she'll never give up the search. In the silent conversation she has with him all the time, she reassures him that she knows he is alive, she's still waiting for him, she loves him and she will always support him, whatever happens.

She writes to him, every month, sometimes more, if there's something she needs to tell him. She keeps the letters, his name lonely on the envelope, in a box under the bed. It's getting full now.

* * *

Her mobile rings in a shower of jade-green circles. She scrabbles in her bag. It never seems to ring for long enough and she's always in a panic to answer it. She hates having to call back, particularly if it's an unknown number.

"Hello, Leonora Bates here."

A familiar voice says: "Leonora, it's Anthony." She recognises the voice immediately. The man from the Missing People charity.

With a silent sigh, because she no longer has that pinprick of hope that used to accompany their calls, she says: "Anthony. Good to hear from you. Any news?"

"Not news, exactly. But something you might find interesting." His delivery is flat and colourless. Leonora imagines that even if he had something world-changing to announce, he would sound the same.

"What's that, then?" she says, to hurry him along. He leaves long pauses on the phone, as if he's expecting more from the other end than he's getting. She quells the rising irritation.

"You know about DNA, don't you?"

"Of course."

"Well, this is all quite new, so forgive me if I don't explain it too well. And also, I apologise if this is a little upsetting — but it's important that you know." He clears his throat. That pause again.

"Please go on."

"It's possible that familial DNA — yours, for example — could help when a body is found but can't be identified. That means, if you give your DNA to the police, they can test it against all the unidentified male bodies found in the UK. Are you following me?"

"I'm following you."

"This development could give relatives — people like you — closure. If they find a match, at least you'd have certainty. It could help you move on." Pause. "Do you see what I'm getting at?"

"Yes, yes I do."

Pause. "Shall I give you the details?"

"Yes, please." There's a long pause this time, that stretches into the darkness in Leonora's heart.

"Are you still there, Leonora?"

I'm still here, and I'm still waiting for you, Ricky.

* * *

On his birthday, she lights a candle on the windowsill beside the photo of him and Luke.

In the cupboard in the narrow hallway she keeps two boxes, the only things she brought from the house. One contains a few belongings from Ricky's bedroom and the little bundle of the letters he sent her from South Africa. The other box is full of papers and files she found in her father's desk, which she has never fully examined.

She carries Ricky's box to her bedroom, puts it on the floor beside the bed and starts to look through his things.

One by one she places his possessions on the bed. A thin T-shirt, his favourite when he was thirteen, probably far too small for him now. Today is his twenty-second birthday and she wonders how he has changed. Is he still slender, his stomach concave, his shoulder blades sharp against the thin fabric of his shirt? Or has he broadened into a man, his arms hardened, his stride long and powerful, his chin shadowed with stubble? He might even have grown a beard. Especially if he's hiding from the police.

There's a *Guinness Book of Records*, a throwback to his childhood, that he could never bear to throw away. The words spring out from the pages in a clatter of colours, as bright as the pictures of record-breaking people and places, weird collections and creatures. There's a soldier from his father's collection, that he painted and gave to Ricky when he was tiny. A couple of books: *The Catcher in the Rye* and *Catch-22*, both well thumbed, the pages beginning to yellow. A notebook in which he'd started a diary. It stopped short on the day he was told he was being sent to boarding school. The

231

entries before that were heart-wrenching, written in his careful, rounded scrawl, recording only the good things. There were not many: a Saturday with Leonora, spent eating ice cream and cycling round the industrial estate, a rare visit to the cinema to see a James Bond film, a day when their father was in a good mood and played football with him. As always, thinking of Ricky brings a dull ache to Leonora's stomach. She lifts his dressing gown to her face, hoping to breathe in a last vestige of his essence. But there's nothing left of him, not even a trace.

Once again she feels desperation stab at her. Can he still be alive? She has imagined every possible reason for his disappearance, however unlikely, but none has given her any comfort. Nothing can explain how he vanished so completely, nor why he would choose not to contact her. Four years is a long time to torment yourself, to long for someone. These days, when she closes her eyes and remembers his face, it's the face in the photograph, not the face of a living person. When she first realised that, she wept.

With a sigh, she closes the diary and goes over to the window.

It's early May and dusk is late closing its soft curtain on the London skyline. She opens the window and looks out onto the patch of garden at the back, recently cleared and tidied by the residents in preparation for summer. A blackbird chortles a spray of vivid magenta bubbles from the great plane tree that casts a shadow over the floors below hers. Opposite, in the windows of the shabby ex-council flats that face hers, lights begin to glisten as the sun fades. In one, she can make out the shape of someone looking out onto the garden, motionless.

CHAPTER FORTY-FIVE

Ricky

Though I felt better, it took many months before I felt strong enough to start looking for you.

I was still wracked with guilt for so many reasons. I was mortified that I'd left you to deal with Dad by yourself, that you'd had to shoulder the burden of an alcoholic mother as well as a cruel father with nobody to support you. I felt guilty that I'd abandoned our father to die alone, however bad a father he was. It was terrible that you had a brother who was capable of such a thing. I'd disappeared, left you once again to fend for yourself, and on top of all that, I felt guilty about Mum, and Luke and Sally and the children — that I'd left them all with no explanation.

But time had passed and nobody had found me. Perhaps the police had given up, assuming I was somewhere in Africa still and had disappeared, never to be found. Now that I'd rid myself of the demons and my delirious imaginings, I dared to believe I was safe. By now they had almost certainly filed me as missing and moved on. I had a paid job now, at the zoo. So I felt just a little more secure, a little more able to search for you.

I decided that even if it meant the police tracked me down, I had to find you. I'd prepared my story for them, of course, just in case. The gun went off by accident, I went off to find help and got lost, I panicked in case they thought I'd killed him on purpose.

My painful journey to this point meant I'd heard nothing of you or Mum since that December when Dad arrived in South Africa. At that time you were living in the narrowboat with Maria and Pete, so my starting point was the canal.

The stretch where Maria and Pete would moor was busy with boats of all sizes and shapes, but theirs was nowhere to be seen. I asked a couple of owners if they'd seen them, but they shook their heads. They were just visiting, hadn't seen anyone like that. I remembered they went to Wales in winter. Perhaps they were there now. But where were you? I was running out of options.

It was incredibly hard to go back to the house, Leo. As I walked towards it I took deep, slow breaths and forced myself to relax. I didn't want to spoil our first meeting after all this time by having a panic attack.

It was evening when I approached and there were no lights in the windows, no sign of anybody. The front garden, though, was neat and cared for, which I took to be a good sign. Perhaps Mum had recovered once Dad had gone. I stood on the opposite side of the road for a while, hesitating, then took a deep breath and walked up the path to the front door, where I rang the bell. It was a different tone from the one I remembered: you would always say it was the colour of putty, that sound. This one was a 'ding-dong' that sounded too loud, too cheerful for our house. I wondered what colour that sound would be, for you.

There was no answer, but when I peered through the window at the side of the door I noticed a child's tricycle in the hallway, small yellow wellingtons standing under an unfamiliar table to one side. The old faded wallpaper had gone, replaced by bright white walls that transformed the dark entrance into a light-filled, welcoming space.

I turned and walked away. I know it sounds stupid but I felt a terrible shock when I realised you didn't live there any more. I should have known, of course. Why would you be there? It was always an unhappy house, and without Dad and me, you and Mum wouldn't want to stay. You hated it there — you would be long gone.

At the gate I hesitated. I'd come all this way and I didn't want to give up straight away. The clue to your whereabouts must be here. Someone must know where Mum had gone, at least.

Once again I steeled myself. I walked down the path to Mrs Clark's house next door. I hadn't known her well, but I know she was kind to you when Mum was unwell, so I felt sure she would know where you had gone. It was unlikely she would recognise me, I figured. My hair was still long, though in a pony-tail. I'd kept the beard, though now it was neatly trimmed, and I wore a black baseball cap. It would have been hard to recognise the little boy who went away to school at thirteen.

This time there were sounds from inside in response to the doorbell and within moments the door opened. I suspected that this too would end in disappointment. A man, perhaps in his thirties, tall and slender, stood in front of me, a question in his eyes. "Hello," he said.

"I'm sorry to bother you. I'm looking for Mrs Clark," I said, uncertain what my story was going to be.

"That would be my mother," the man said. "Can I ask what it's about?" Strains of music came from behind him, a pop song, soft and romantic.

"I — actually I'm looking for the family that used to live next door. The Bates family. I wondered if your mother knows where they've gone."

"I'm sure she would have done, but she died, about a year ago."

"I'm sorry. It doesn't matter. Sorry to bother you." I turned to go, embarrassed, not wanting to risk getting into a conversation about who I was.

"Wait . . . Dad might know," he said. "Hold on a second, he's in the kitchen. I'd get him for you, but he's not good on his feet. Let me ask him."

I stood, tense and awkward, for a few moments. The music stopped and I could hear the low tones of a conversation from beyond the hallway, then footsteps as he returned to the door.

"Dad says Mr Bates died, four, five years ago, in South Africa. Mrs Bates passed away not long after. She's buried at St Peter's Church, round the corner. He thinks the boy — Richard, was it? — went missing in Africa about the time his dad died, it was all very sad. The house stood empty for a while, then the young family moved in — Mum knew them. They're still there. Are you okay?" He stepped towards me, concern furrowing his forehead.

His words had sent shock waves from my stomach to the top of my head. I stumbled, putting my hand out to steady myself against the porch. But I shook my head and managed to recover myself. He backed away.

"I'm okay," I said. "What about the sister, Leonora? Does he know where she went?"

"She left home before she'd even finished school, went to live with some people on the canal. My mother saw her every so often after that, but then she must have moved away. Sorry, that's all we know."

* * *

I don't know what I was expecting, Leo, when I went there. But I clearly hadn't prepared myself properly. As I walked away, something broke inside me, tears pouring down my cheeks. Grief, disappointment and guilt wrestled for domination in my heart. Mum had died. She died without knowing if I was alive or dead. And you Leo, just a child, you had to deal with it on your own.

It must have been horrible for you. No child should have to deal with that. As far as I knew, we had no other relatives and no money to ease the burden. In my belt I carried the only valuable thing our mother had to her name, and your legacy. I am sure it would have made a huge difference to you when Dad died. Perhaps it would even have paid for Mum's care.

It was dark when I left our street, but I made my way to the churchyard nonetheless, thinking I could at least visit Mum's grave. When I got there, though, the darkness was complete. There were trees everywhere and the gravestones were almost invisible in the blackness. I would have to find somewhere to stay if I was to pay my respects. For a moment I considered sleeping there, but I had promised myself that I would never sleep rough again, so the thought was only fleeting and I made my way towards the town centre to look for somewhere to stay. I soon found a modest B&B where I spent the night in a clean, comfortable bed.

In the daylight the cemetery was transformed. Paved paths ran between the lines of gravestones — shrubs and flowers lined the walls around the church. I looked everywhere for Mum's grave, without success, and I was beginning to wonder if I'd been given the wrong information when I spotted a 'Garden of Remembrance,' a memorial to those who had been cremated.

Through a gateway I found a small area with a couple of benches, where stones of varying sizes were laid side by side in neat rows. Fresh flowers adorned a number of them and others had wilting posies in small vases. In the back row, I found a small stone, standing straight, with the words: *Sandra Bates, Rest in Peace*, and the dates. Nothing more. There were no flowers, only weeds growing around it. I cleared them away with my bare hands. Seeing her name there, alone and neglected, brought tears to my eyes again and I wept uncontrollably. Mum's life had not been happy, at least not while we knew her, and she had died too soon. There was nobody to support her, to stop the downward spiral into addiction, and we were too young to understand or to help. At least now, I thought, her torment was over.

At that moment, I was glad I'd left my father to die in agony.

CHAPTER FORTY-SIX

Ricky

The news of Mum's death had a profound effect on me. I was expecting to find her an alcoholic, perhaps now recovering after Dad's demise. But it hadn't occurred to me that she might die while I was away. How wrong I was. I guess I was still fragile after my breakdown, because all the old feelings of guilt and self-loathing returned, magnified by a black curtain of grief. I fell back into a spiral of self-hate and unresolved anger.

Luckily this time I had the animals.

I spent all my time at the zoo, even when I wasn't supposed to be working. I got close to my African charges. I started to understand their habits, helping them to eat, play and feed their young. The wild dogs became a particular favourite, and now I was one of their team. They're beautiful creatures, so communicative, full of energy and alert. I watched how they worked together, the complexities of the group, their body language. They got used to me sitting close to them and they would approach me with curiosity, without fear, making little whimpering noises to greet me.

After a while, seeing me so often at the dogs' enclosure, the keepers asked me if I'd like to help monitor their behaviour officially, to take notes and report to the research-ers. Over time, I became involved in a major project to study pack coordination. While I focused on my work, my mind was able to rest from its darkest struggles. Gradually my grief became somehow separate from my self-hatred, and I felt myself recovering slowly.

But after this setback I couldn't bring myself to look for you again, Leo. That's probably hard to understand, and I'm sorry if it hurts you. It's difficult to explain how low my self-esteem was, how worthless I felt. But I was terrified of what I would have to tell you when I found you.

I imagined the scene a million times. You would open the door, not recognising me. You would ask politely if you could help me. I would smile and say: "Hello, Leo." You would gasp, your face would go pale, your hand would fly to your mouth. We'd smile, and hug each other tight, making up for all those lost years. You'd invite me in and we'd sit side by side, as we always used to do in the den. We'd talk about how we'd been, where we were living, what we were doing. What happened since we last saw each other, and then, when I told you about Dad—

I couldn't bear to think what your reaction might be.

So I left it, and left it. It was as if I needed to hang on to that fantasy, where we came together and loved each other like we used to, and I never needed to tell you what I'd done. I wanted to live with that happy fairy story for a while, before facing up to the terrible truth.

And then one day I saw you.

It was at the zoo. You were standing in the giraffe house, leaning on the rail, watching an animal feed. There was a dreamy expression on your face, as if you were thinking of something else, imagining other worlds, while the velvet lips and black tongue of the giraffe curled and pulled at her hay.

I was outside in the enclosure, tidying up while the ani-mals fed. Glancing through the tall doors of the giraffe house, I saw visitors in the viewing gallery and thought nothing of it. But something made me look again. It might have been that expression on your face. It was like the one when you saw your colours, when music played or there was a noise outside, or when you were reading as a little girl. It was as if you saw things that nobody else did — and it was true, you did see more than we did, you perceived a world of colour where we saw nothing.

One minute I was looking at a stranger, a young woman I'd never seen before, a visitor watching a giraffe at its meal. The next, I froze. In an instant, my stomach turned over, my legs no longer supported me. I sank back against the fence, grasping at a post to keep myself from falling. I couldn't believe what I was seeing.

You were some distance away and I had to be sure, so I backed away, through the gate. I ran around the enclosure and peered through a rectangle of glass in the swing doors, only to see you walking the other way. I tore back through the giraffe house, retracing my steps until you were in view again. Being careful not to be seen, I watched from behind a fence as you paused, entranced by the sight of a group of giraffes towering above you, still feeding from a net full of hay. You always did love giraffes, Leo — you used to say they were green, because of your colours.

The Leonora I remembered was a girl with a riot of dark curls, pale skin and a steely look in her eyes. When she frowned it was as if someone had dimmed the lights, and when she smiled, anything was possible. This Leonora was a woman, the unmistakeable traces of human experience in her eyes and in the tilt of her lips. But it was definitely you. Your face was thinner and you'd lost that softness of youth around the cheeks, but there was no mistaking the depth in your eyes, the angle of your chin. Your hair was scraped back into a thick ponytail, a few curls escaping onto your neck and cheek. You looked — self-contained.

You glanced towards me and I stepped back into the shadow. I don't know what I would have done had you looked straight at me — I probably would have run. Anyway, you didn't, which was a good thing. My body was bursting with adrenaline, my breath coming in short gasps, and for a moment I thought I was having a full-blown panic attack. I bent double, focusing on my breathing. When I straightened up and stepped back to look, you'd gone, leaving me with only the giraffes for company.

I ran after you, unsure what I'd do if I caught up with you, instinctively wanting to stay close. But you'd gone, disappeared into the clumps of families milling around the pathways, and though I ran to nearby enclosures hoping you'd paused to look, there was no sign of you. It was as if you hadn't been there.

But you had been there. You were alive, grown-up — you'd survived. You were in London, perhaps even living here. A strange warmth washed over me as I stood, panting, my eyes still straining to see you. My sister — my odd, wonderful sister — was here.

I knew that one day I would have to pluck up the courage to find you, to tell you everything. But I didn't have any idea how to do it.

CHAPTER FORTY-SEVEN

Ricky

Much of Ben's time at the church was spent helping homeless people in the area. He would welcome them in, like he did me, talk to them, try to find them places to stay and give them support and advice. At first, when I went in to help, it felt very strange, me only just off the streets, acting as if I knew what I was talking about. But often these people were desperate, as I'd been, and I soon realised my experience was valuable and I could help.

On my days off from the zoo, Ben sometimes took me out with him, visiting. He knew people everywhere, in all the dark corners and alleyways, the overcrowded flats and dingy basements. His huge network of friends and acquaintances, many of whom he'd helped, was his source of information. From them we learned who needed support, who was being thrown out of their lodgings, who was missing, lost on the streets. These people wouldn't go to the police. They were scared of authority, of being sent away.

Some of the buildings I became familiar with were full to bursting with families. Many were immigrants living in the country illegally, without visas or permissions. Sometimes the conditions they suffered were terrible. Old people living in damp basements, freezing cold, with mould crawling up the walls, toilets blocked, broken heating systems. Families with young children crammed into crumbling rooms, sleeping five to a bed, flakes of plaster falling from the ceiling onto their heads like confetti. Unscrupulous landlords turned a blind eye to their safety, failing to repair anything: roofs, plumbing, heating, crumbling stairs and balconies, only turning up to demand their money.

We didn't judge, we didn't question, we just tried to help. We'd return from these trips sometimes uplifted, often downhearted. Back in his office Ben would exhaust himself filling in endless forms, spending hours on the phone cajoling, pleading for help and support for those forgotten people. I never forgot how lucky I was to find him.

* * *

I was roused from my bed after a long shift at the zoo when one of the girls knocked on my door.

"Oliver — Ben needs us!" she said, out of breath, as if she'd been running. "Something's happened. There's been a fire, he's helping the survivors. Everybody's at the church. Can you come?"

As we hurried to the church, I learned what had happened. One of the buildings nearby, a typical ex-council block, had caught fire on the top two floors. I'd been there many times with Ben. It was filled to bursting with unknown numbers of displaced people, so a fire there would be disastrous.

The flames had spread so rapidly that those floors had been destroyed in moments, the levels below filled with acrid, choking smoke. The occupants on the lower levels had tried to help, but they'd been beaten back by smoke and fumes. Many people were missing, many had been taken away by ambulance suffering from terrible burns or smoke inhalation. No one was allowed back in while the firefighters finished their work, so Ben had opened up the church to the survivors, offering a roof over their heads and helping them find somewhere to go.

When I walked in, I saw the woman straight away. She was sitting on her own on one of those fold-up wooden chairs in a corner of the church, a dark scarf around her head, her skirts long around her ankles. Tears streamed down her cheeks in a never-ending flow, dripping from her chin onto her lap, trickling into her mouth. She dabbed at her face with a balled-up tissue, but the tears kept on coming. I poured her some tea and took the mug over to her, skirting round a family resting on a blanket on the floor.

She looked up at me, the anguish in her eyes almost unbearable. I crouched down and put the mug next to her. She tried to smile at me through the tears and took my hand in hers. She was younger than I'd first thought.

"Thank you," she said. "You are a kind boy." Her accent was heavy with the guttural sounds of the Middle East.

"How can I help you?" I said, fearing there was little I could do to ease her pain. Her grip on my hand tightened.

"My brother," she whispered. "He went back in — to help the other people. Please — can you help me find him?"

"I will try," I said. Her eyes were huge and dark, shining with tears. I almost wept with her, she was such a picture of misery. "What is his name?"

"Anwar. Anwar Abboud. Thank you, thank you. He is brave, too brave."

"I will add his name to our list. If we hear anything, I will let you know as soon as possible. I am sorry I can't do more."

"You are a good person, thank you."

"Do you have somewhere to go? Someone in your family who can help you?"

"I have cousins. I can go there. But I can't leave until I find my brother. He means everything to me."

"I understand. We will try our best."

She released my hand and I felt her gaze follow me as I went back to the desk, where we were collecting the names of the occupants of the building, marking them as survivors or missing. I added his name to the 'missing' list.

By the time I got back to the flat it was late and I was shattered. I'd spent hours trying to find somewhere to sleep for more than thirty people, talking to the local council, charities, hostels, relatives and friends. I'd helped set up an appeal for the survivors, mobilised the local soup kitchen to provide for those still in the church, and run errands for Ben. I had never done that kind of work before, and it was hard, but we had made some progress and I was glad I'd been able to help.

The emotional strain of the day had taken its toll, so I drank some water and fell into bed, ready for sleep. But my mind would not let go, and sleep would not come. I thought of all those families crammed into small spaces because they couldn't afford anything better. How they'd lost everything, all their meagre possessions. I thought of the people who'd died in the fire. What a terrible death that must be, and how painful for their families to imagine their torture.

Most of all, I kept seeing the stricken face of the woman in the scarf, the tears flowing endlessly down her cheeks. On her own, her home destroyed. Without her brother, who meant everything to her.

And then I got to thinking about people you love, and losing them, and the pain of being alone in the world. How it was for me, and how it must have been for you.

That's when I knew I had to find you, Leo.

But making the decision to see you was just the first step. I trembled at the thought, and I almost changed my mind a hundred times. But you deserved to know the truth, Leo. So I needed to work out what I was going to say, how I was going to explain all those lost years without losing you all over again.

I was terrified of your reaction. I was pretty sure you weren't sorry Dad was dead — but knowing I abandoned him to die alone? Nobody needs to know their brother is so heartless, and I shrank at the thought of telling you.

It seemed impossible that you would want to know me.

The only person I could talk to was Ben. Only he would understand. I'd never opened up to him about Dad, or what happened out there in South Africa — not because he would judge me, he wasn't like that, and he'd seen too many bad things to be shocked. I trusted him with my life. But deep down I felt the burden of my actions was mine alone. It wasn't right to share that burden with anyone, even Ben.

But now I was at a turning point. I wanted so much to see you, Leo, but I didn't know how to do it. Lack of sleep and stress made me desperate. I went back to the church.

"What's wrong?" Ben said, when he saw my face. "Is there bad news?"

I shook my head. "I'm just . . . I couldn't sleep."

"That's not surprising, after yesterday. Do you want to tell me?"

We went and sat in his office and talked. Somehow it all poured out. About you, and Dad and Mum, and the school in South Africa. How close you and I were, how much we suffered when I was sent away, how Mum's drinking got worse and Dad got more difficult.

I told him my father had been shot in an accident and I'd left him to die.

Ben was wonderful. He barely reacted to my story. He didn't move, or comment, just listened until I got to the end. I cried, then, and he made me a mug of coffee and sat with me until I stopped. I explained how I'd come back to England in a daze, unsure what to do and where to go, thinking the police were after me. Told him how grateful I was to him for all he'd done for me, and how sorry I was not to have told him the truth all this time.

I wept again, Leo, from self-pity, because I'd missed all that time with you.

Ben sat and listened and nodded. And when I finished he said: "Go and find your sister, Oliver— Ricky. You need her, and she needs you."

CHAPTER FORTY-EIGHT

Leonora

Arriving at her door laden with bags of food, Leonora finds a policeman on the steps outside. She knows he's a policeman, though he's not in uniform. There's a look about them that she's grown familiar with.

"Can I help you?" She puts the bags down and massages her fingers, the skin puckered and white where the plastic of the handles has dug in.

"Ah, yes, I hope so. I'm looking for a Leonora Bates?" He says her name with exaggerated enunciation, as if it's foreign or she's hard of hearing.

"That's me."

"I'm Detective Inspector Sam Gerrard." He flips open a warrant card. She glances at it — she's seen so many now, she can tell it's genuine by the case alone.

She extracts her keys from her pocket and opens the door. "Is it quick, or do I need to put the kettle on?"

"It would be best if we could do this inside," he says, picking up her bags. "I'll take these up for you."

She nods and leads the way up. Every time there seems to be someone new on the missing persons team. The missing are clearly not a priority.

They sit at the kitchen table. The mug she's given him, a curl of steam rising from the black coffee within, has *I'd rather be alone* printed in red on the outside. He raises an eyebrow.

She studies his face. Intelligent grey eyes gaze back at her. Hair neat and thick, with flecks of white at the temples. His clothes, while conservative, are clean and pressed. He seems different from the usual downbeat officers on the missing persons trail.

"I won't keep you long," he says. "I'm the investigating officer for the fire that happened last month in a block of flats in North Kensington. Are you aware of it?"

Surprised, because she was expecting to talk about Ricky, she shakes her head. "What happened?"

"A block of ex-council flats caught fire — we think it was a gas leak. But the building went up like a bonfire. A number of people died — there were lots of casualties, we don't yet know how many. The problem is, it was crammed full of unregistered people, some of them possibly living here illegally, so we have no way of knowing how many people were in the building at the time."

"I'm confused. What has this got to do with me?"

"We're still trying to identify some of the bodies. As you can imagine, it's not easy."

"Horrible."

"Indeed. It's a long, slow process. We've identified a number but we have a way to go. Most of them didn't even have dental records. We're using DNA matching — you're aware of this, I understand?"

"Well, yes, I am. My brother—"

"Is missing, I know. We found your DNA on file. That's why I'm here."

Leonora swallows. A hard lump forms beneath her rib cage. Something's wrong here, it must be.

"What do you mean?"

"In one of the flats, partially burnt out, we found filial DNA. DNA that matches yours."

She flinches as if she's been slapped. Her hand flies to her mouth, knocking over the mug of tea, which smashes to pieces on the floor in a burst of apricot spirals. The hot liquid splashes onto her legs and she cries out, not with pain from the burn, but with shock at his words.

He mops up the mess with a cloth, patiently picking out the pieces of broken china and placing them in the bin under the sink. Speechless, she stares without seeing. In her head she hears her own voice, over and over: *oh my god, oh my god, oh my god.*

Order restored, he sits down.

"I don't understand," she says. "Are you saying . . . you found my brother? Is he alive?"

"Please sit down, Leonora. Is it okay to call you Leonora? Are your legs burnt?"

She ignores his questions, but sits. "Is he alive?" The lump in her throat hardens. An invisible rope twists, tightening every moment.

"I'm sorry. We don't know. The good news is, we didn't find any remains in the flat. He may have been out at the time, or escaped down the stairs, or across the roof. But — we still have a number of unidentified remains, some of them male. Some of them were . . . almost completely destroyed." He looks down at his hands as she stares, her eyes widening.

"Wait. What does that mean? You will never be able to identify them?"

"We're still looking at dental records. But many of these people, particularly the illegal immigrants, have never been to a dentist here. It's possible, with a couple of them, that we won't have enough evidence to identify them."

Oh god, oh god, oh god.

"There are also two people still in hospital. One is in an induced coma, and we have been able to identify her. The other, who we can't identify, seems to be suffering with amnesia — temporary or otherwise, they can't tell yet. He appears to have forgotten his name."

"Have you checked his DNA?"

"As far as we know, he's committed no crime. We can't request DNA unless he's a suspect."

She stares at him in disbelief. "You haven't checked?"

He shakes his head. "No. We can't, unless he volunteers. We've had no reason to ask, until now."

She jumps up again, goes to the window, staring unseeing at the flats across the garden. "Are you sure? About the DNA in the flat — are you absolutely sure it's a match with mine?"

"As sure as science can be — and that's quite near certain. It's a fifty per cent match. Which means a brother or a sister."

"Where is he? Which hospital?" She turns, ready to go. He stays put, and she curbs the urge to shout.

"There is another possibility," he says. "I must ask . . . is there any chance there might be another sibling, one you don't know about?"

She gulps. "No. No! I — I don't think so. My parents are both dead. I found nothing in their things to suppose—"

"It's a possibility you should keep in mind."

It's so out of the question she can't even contemplate it. But she's not going to explain why. "Okay. I'd like to go to the hospital now."

"I'll take you there. It's not far. But please . . ." There's something in his voice that makes her pause.

"Yes?"

"You must prepare yourself on the way. This man — he's suffered some quite bad burns. And — I'm sorry, but the chances of him being your brother are, to say the least, slim. There were a lot of people in that building and we may never track them all down."

She hesitates for a moment, then takes a long breath. There are too many questions to unscramble the mess in her head right now.

"It's okay," she says. "I've had too many disappointments and shocks in my life not to have grown my own defence system. I'll cope."

When they arrive at the hospital a nurse at the desk looks up as they approach. It's outside visiting hours and the ward is quiet. He flips open his warrant card and she nods. "Is it the burn victims you're after? There's only one left now, the woman, the one in a coma."

CHAPTER FORTY-NINE

Leonora

"What do you mean?" Her voice is brittle, too loud. The nurse flashes a startled look at her.

DI Gerrard puts a gentle hand on Leonora's arm. "When was this, please? Was he discharged?"

The nurse switches her gaze from Leonora to the policeman.

"Let me check for you." She flips through a pile of papers on the desk beside her and pulls out a couple of sheets, held together with a paperclip.

"He left this morning, about ten o'clock — discharged himself. He didn't wait for the doctor, just got dressed and went. He needed further treatment, but we can't stop someone who decides to leave."

Leonora can't believe it. This person could be Ricky — it could really be him! — and now he's gone, before she's even had the chance to see him. Cruel fate, testing her once again.

"Was anyone with him?" Gerrard says.

"No. He had no visitors, apart from the police. And nobody saw him go, as far as I can tell. I wasn't on duty, but that's all it says in the notes."

"No idea where he's gone?"

The nurse shakes her head. "No, sorry."

"What kind of treatment does he need?"

She refers to the notes again. "Well, his burns aren't healed yet, so there's a risk of infection, and he's still on painkillers. And then there's the amnesia—"

"Was he being treated for that?"

"No, but he was under observation. He was supposed to be seeing a specialist, but that hadn't been organised yet."

Gerrard raises his eyebrows at Leonora.

"What did he look like? What age, what colour were his eyes?"

The nurse looks disconcerted. "Quite young, I'd say, twenties maybe. White. His face was quite badly burnt. I couldn't tell you what colour his eyes were . . ." She looks from Gerrard to Leonora questioningly.

DI Gerrard pulls a card from his pocket and hands it to the nurse. "Here's my number. Please call if he returns. It's important."

He guides Leonora by the elbow out of the ward. At the entrance to the hospital they pause while Leonora leans against the wall, inhaling great gulps of air.

"Are you all right?" he says.

When she can talk again, she says: "I thought I'd got over getting too excited about every possibility."

"It's disappointing. But it was always a long shot. He may have nothing to do with your brother."

"Perhaps it wasn't genuine."

"The amnesia? Quite possibly not. He may have been there illegally. He may not have wanted to talk to the police. Who knows? People who are scared behave in strange ways."

"Will you try to find him?"

"Yes, though I'm not holding out too much hope, I'm afraid. People who don't want to be found can disappear in London. It's hard to track them down."

"But the fact he needs treatment — will that help? Will you check the doctors' surgeries, the hospitals?" She can't bear the idea that they might give up. She has to know — even if it's bad news for her.

"There's only a slim chance he'll risk it, now he's discharged himself. But he may have nowhere to live, so we'll put out an alert. As far as we know, he's done nothing wrong, so we can't do much more. There's a limit to our resources. Here, I'll give you a lift back."

"No, it's okay, I'll walk. I need some air."

"Listen, I know it's frustrating," he says. "But even if we can't find this guy, the DNA match could have nothing to do with him. All it means is that your brother was here in London, either living in that building or visiting someone there. All the more reason to keep searching for him."

Walking away from the hospital, she feels a wave of despair wash over her. The world seems to go on outside her head, while inside everything is suspended in limbo, a no-man's land where nothing moves.

So the DNA might or might not belong to the man from the hospital. Who doesn't want to be found. It might be Ricky's, or it might not be. It could even belong to some long-lost sibling that she's never even heard of. How would she feel, if it does? She has no idea, but it would mean she's no further ahead in finding Ricky.

One step forward, two steps back.

She walks for a long time, not noticing where she's going, until her head hurts and her shoes start to pinch. When she stops to get her bearings, she realises her feet have led her to Regent's Park. The sounds of the zoo explode in curves of pink and yellow ahead of her.

It's late afternoon, and people are leaving as she buys her ticket. It's a good time of day to see the animals. They're more relaxed with fewer people around and she doesn't have to contend with the crowds. Some of the animals feed quietly in their pens while others have retreated into their sleeping areas. Still others are more lively at this time of day — when dusk approaches they wake up, keeping the hours they would keep in the wild.

Everywhere, the keepers are tidying up: collecting litter, sweeping animal pens, preparing to close the indoor exhibits. Every so often she comes across them, clad in their green London Zoo T-shirts, talking to their animals.

At the giraffe house she walks up the slope and steps inside to watch a female feed. She loves her luscious eyes, shiny and black as billiard balls; her dark, prehensile tongue that curls around her food like the tail of a monkey. She lingers a while, watching her, then goes outside again to watch the rest of her family, marvelling at the arches of their patterned necks, their strange, delicate legs.

Finding an empty bench, she sits for a while, listening to the sounds, bursting with colour. Monkeys whoop and howl in showers of ochre and cyan; birds screech in purple flashes and chirrup in clouds of pink; grunts and growls from unseen animals add rainbow colours to the cacophony. The noise of the zoo soothes her as she watches the vibrant ebb and flow that no one else can see.

Then, as they start to round up the late stayers, she walks the long way round to the exit. A knot of keepers, chatting close to the gate, glances at her as she leaves. One waves a friendly hand.

* * *

Claire's still not home when she gets back — she's with her boyfriend. She spends more and more time with him now, and Leonora barely sees her. She misses her. At times like this it's good to have someone around, especially someone like Claire with her cheerful view of the world.

Leonora slumps at the kitchen table, where DI Gerrard's mug still stands, its contents settling into a murky brown syrup. There are stains under her elbows and her jeans are stiff with dried tea, but she doesn't care.

The events of today have paralysed her brain, or perhaps she's too tired to untangle the facts from the emotions. An ominous band of pain begins to spread from above her eyes.

She goes to the window and stares across the London roofscape, wondering where the building was where Ricky's DNA was found. If it turns out he died in the fire, it would be the ultimate blow — she would know for certain that despite all she's faced in her life, despite every rocky, malevolent mountain she's stumbled up to get this far, fate is not on her side.

* * *

Scenario 1
Ricky lived in the block of flats where the fire was. His is one of the unidentified bodies. Possibility of identification via dental records/trace DNA. Or belongings in burnt-out flat (unlikely)? Action: police.

Scenario 2
The mystery man in the hospital was Ricky. He genuinely suffers from amnesia (good reason why he hasn't contacted me) and has disappeared. He may turn up at a doctor's surgery or a hospital, a refuge or on the streets. Action: Go back to the hospital to find out everything about mystery man. Police to alert all the possible places.

Scenario 3
Ricky was living at the flats — he escaped unscathed and without identification. He doesn't want to be found (why?). Action: Check with landlords/other residents? Are the police doing this?

Scenario 4
Ricky visited the flats but wasn't living there. So he's alive and possibly in London but doesn't want to be found (why again?). Action: L to find out what exactly they tested for DNA — hair/toothbrush/blood/other bodily fluids/clothing. Did it indicate he lived there?

Scenario 5
The DNA didn't belong to Ricky, but to some unknown sibling. Action: L to check birth records. UNLIKELY.

At this point, she pauses, her head spinning. If it's an unknown sibling, how on earth will she find them? She can't even think about that, and anyway it's so unlikely she won't waste her time on it. She has to focus on Ricky.

Assuming he's alive, why doesn't Ricky want to be found?

Why, indeed? She has considered many theories, some wild, some unthinkable. None of them help. This list of possibilities is going to be objective, based on the idea that it was his DNA they found in the burnt-out building.

1. He has amnesia (real, or maybe not?) and is living as someone else.

2. The police are after him. But why wouldn't he look for me?

3. He thinks I'm dead. Why would he think that?

4. He can't find me. Possible, but not likely. If he went back home, asked the neighbours, went to the farm shop or to Kelly's house, someone would be able to tell him where I've gone. The police??

5. Something terrible happened that he can't bear to admit, even to me.

She looks at the list for a long time. The only one that seems plausible is the last.

CHAPTER FIFTY

Leonora

"You okay?" Rob's voice is blurred by the emerald-green splashes of traffic passing by.

"Yes, why wouldn't I be?" she says.

There's a pause at the other end, the silence broken only by the sound of a distant siren, jade sprinkles fading.

"Sorry. I didn't mean it like that," she says. "I was miles away."

"Just . . . the fire. Your brother. You know."

She hadn't wanted to tell anyone about Ricky. But because of the DNA, and the fire, she was distracted, late for work, and Rob noticed she was upset. She could see the hurt in his eyes when she prevaricated, reluctant to tell him the whole story. It's just the way Rob is. It's not that he wants to uncover people's deepest secrets. He takes a genuine interest in people. He wants to know what is important to them, how they spend their time, what they've experienced. How they feel about events, people, politics. She can see this whenever they're in company. He draws stories out of people by being himself, asking the right questions, and they warm to him because of it.

So she told him everything. Most of it, anyway. Not the full extent of her parents' shortcomings, only that she had an unhappy childhood and her parents were now dead. But she told him how Ricky disappeared, her search for him from the age of sixteen, the shock of finding that he'd come back to England. And the filial DNA. Rob, astounded by the story, offered to help in any way he could.

"I'm okay. Okay but confused. Sometimes it seems like fate's against me, like I'm not supposed to find Ricky. I know that sounds nuts, but that's how it feels."

"So what's next?"

"In the search? Well, I suppose I have to assume the DNA belongs to Ricky. Unless my parents hid a brother or a sister from us all through our childhood. Which seems unlikely. Although with everything that's happened in my life, anything is possible."

"Are the police still looking for the owner of the DNA?"

"In all the usual places, though I'm not sure how thoroughly. The building's been evacuated, even though some of the flats were undamaged. I suppose it's unsafe now. I thought I might try to find some of the survivors — see if they could tell me anything. A long shot, though. If it's him, and he's been hiding for so long, he's probably not even using his own name."

"I'll help. But how will we find the survivors?"

She resists the urge to demur, unsure she wants his help. "The police are trying to identify everyone who lived there. Some of them were living there illegally, and might even be in the country illegally, so it's not going to be easy. I'm going to call the detective who told me about the DNA. Let's hope he'll help."

* * *

When she calls, DI Gerrard is unavailable. She leaves a message.

Today is her day off, and she's spending it looking for Ricky. She's found her way to the burnt-out building, where the pavement is still cordoned off, police tape protecting the front door and the steps to the basement. A notice says, in big letters: *Danger: Keep Out*. The lower floors seem untouched by the flames, at least on the outside, and the houses on either side are undamaged, though a thin film of ash coats the leaves of their front hedges.

It's early evening, warm and sunny, and the sound of music floats down to her from the upper windows of the house next door, creating a soft pattern of greens and yellows, in contrast with the grim exterior of the place she's heading for. She stands on tiptoe to peer through the window of the ground-floor flat, curious to see if its occupants have moved out, but there's too much reflection on the window.

She's still standing there, looking upwards, wondering which flat held the vital DNA, when a woman approaches, a shopping bag in one hand. She's black, with corkscrew hair pulled back into a pile of shiny curls on the top of her head. She pauses beside Leonora, says: "Terrible fire, did you hear about it?"

"Awful," she says. "Are you local?"

"I live a couple of doors down, dear. We were lucky they came so quickly, the firemen. It could have been much worse." She shakes her head. "Those poor people, a terrible way to die."

Leonora bites her lip. It could turn out that Ricky was one of them. "Did you know any of the people in the building?"

"A few of them, but only by sight. There was lots of coming and going, always different people. Lord knows how many were living there."

The woman has a kind, open face. She seems genuinely sad for the victims. Leonora takes a deep breath. "I'm sorry — do you mind if I ask you something?"

"Not at all, darlin'," the woman says with a smile. "Ask away, I'm not in a hurry."

"The thing is, my brother's been missing for a long time. He might have been living here, in this building, and I don't know if he's dead or alive . . ." The woman's hand flutters to her face in horror. She drops her shopping bag and grasps Leonora's arm.

260

"Oh my dear," she says. "Oh, my Lord. What a terrible thing. You poor girl, that's just dreadful."

"Thank you. But I wanted to ask, did you ever see a young man, he'd be early twenties — white skin, dark hair, coming and going?" Even to Leonora, who has a vague image of how Ricky would look now, this sounds like every other young man in London.

"Well, yes, I did, but there were quite a few who looked like that."

"Do you have any idea where they are now? I know it's not likely, but I really need to find him."

"Well, I know some of them went to the local church. You could ask there."

* * *

A banner outside the church declares: *Remember: no one stands alone.* The initial R shines out like an orange beacon in Leonora's eye.

Something's going on inside: she can see movement through the open doorway. As she approaches, a woman arrives, laden with shopping. She stands back to allow her through, peering into the gloomy space, allowing her eyes to adjust after the brightness of the sunlight behind her.

She steps inside and pauses, taking in the scene. A space has been opened up at the back of the church where she stands, pews moved to one side to accommodate some tables and groups of fold-up chairs. Families sit or lie on blankets on the stone floor, mugs in their hands, talking in low voices. Children cling to their mothers or lie with their heads on their parents' laps. By the wall is a line of tables, one where a woman helps to serve hot drinks from a steaming urn; another, where the first woman is unpacking her shopping, laid out with biscuits and sandwiches. At a third table two people sit at computer screens, the table-top covered with notebooks and papers. A young man talks into a mobile, his voice low and tense, his face turned away. His low murmuring has an orange tinge. It reminds her again of Ricky.

She stands, hesitating, unsure who to talk to.

"Can I help you?"

She turns to find a man smiling at her. He has long hair and a tartan scarf around his neck, and he holds a clipboard in one hand.

"I — I'm not sure," she says. "Are you helping the survivors of the fire?"

"We are indeed," he replies, his hand outstretched. "I'm Ben. Are you looking for someone?"

"Yes, though I'm not sure he was involved in the fire," she says, shaking his hand. It's firm and dry, and somehow comforting. He has a direct way of looking into her eyes.

"Let's sit down, see if we can help." Ben leads her towards the table and the young man on the phone stands and walks away. The girl at the other computer looks up and smiles as Ben sets down some fold-up chairs.

"It's a bit complicated," Leonora says, taking a deep breath. Though she's only just met him, she feels she can trust this man. "Here's the simple version: my brother went missing, years ago, and I've been trying to find him. I put my DNA on a missing persons register. They found matching DNA in the building where the fire was."

"I don't know too much about DNA — what does that mean, exactly?"

"I'm not sure. The police came to see me. They haven't identified the people who . . . died," she pauses to swallow a lump in her throat, "and — you probably know all this — they don't know who was living in the building at the time, officially or not. He could just have visited someone who lived there. Nothing's very clear. But it does seem to be his DNA . . . or at least, it's very unlikely to be someone else's."

Ben raises his eyebrows, lets out a long breath and reaches across the table for a sheaf of paper. "You've come to the right place. We're compiling a list of people who survived, as well as those we think are missing. What's your brother's name?"

"His name's Ricky. Ricky Bates. I have a photo, though it was taken a few years ago." She fumbles in her pocket for the now-faded photo of Ricky, retrieved from its frame. Though she protects it in a plastic bag, it's creased and dog-eared and it's hard to see the real Ricky. He's smiling into the camera, but the sun casts strong shadows around him and on his eyes beneath his hat.

Ben has a list of names in front of him, but he barely glances at it. "Bates . . . no, I don't think so. He hasn't registered here, anyway. Listen, that means nothing."

Though she's used to disappointment, she still finds it hard to hide. He takes the picture from her hands and holds it at arm's length, narrowing his eyes in the dim light of the church. "No, I don't recognise him." He gives her a long, intense look, a smile hovering on his lips as he hands the photo back. "Listen, why don't you leave your details with Oliver when he's finished?" He indicates the young man who walked away with his phone. He's still deep in conversation, leaning against the stone wall, his voice breathing a soft golden shimmer into the air around him.

Ben touches her shoulder gently. "Listen, every day there's some good news to keep us going. You'll find him, I'm sure of it."

"Thank you," she says, with an effort to smile. "I will."

As she stands, the young man by the wall finishes the call and turns round. Their eyes meet.

For a moment she's unable to move. It's as if her heart empties out and fills again, and when it fills, everything is different. She gazes, disbelieving, thinking she's finally lost her mind, she's hallucinating. He stands, transfixed. Then, slowly, his eyes fill with tears. In the dim light of the church her heart swells, and swells again. She steps towards him.

Ricky and Leo, Leo and Ricky. Since she can remember, they've known each other better than anyone else in the world. It's the same for him, she can see it in his eyes.

And she knows that what he's about to tell her will be hard, and brutal, and heartbreaking.

CHAPTER FIFTY-ONE

Ricky

So here I am, Leo, sitting at your kitchen table.

You sit opposite me, your eyes wide, your hands shaking a little as you push a strand of hair from your face. You look the same, but not the same. I can see how life has drawn itself into your features, leaving you with beautiful, sad eyes and a mouth that rarely tips up into a smile. There's the beginning of a line of anxiety between your eyebrows — it makes you look quite serious. You probably are serious, after all you've been through. Your movements are spare, your hands often in your lap as you listen patiently. Patience was never your strong point, but you keep your eyes on my face and say nothing while I speak. You look fragile, but you still have that strength from deep inside. It shows in the set of your shoulders, the power of your gaze. You're still Leo, my sister.

When you recognised me, all the colour drained from your face. For a moment I thought you were going to faint. I said: "Hello, Leo." My voice cracked, tears sprang to my eyes. All I could hear was a soft buzzing in my ears. And then, just when I could bear it no longer, you stepped towards me. You said: "Ricky. It's you," and you opened your arms. We sobbed and sobbed, there in the church, holding each other as if we'd never let go.

* * *

There you have it, Leo. My story of the lost years. Not quite the way I expected my life to go, perhaps. But then, while Dad was alive, I had very few expectations, because being his son was always a battle.

"I'm sorry, Leo," I say.

There are so many things to be sorry for, I could be saying it for years. It will never be enough.

"Don't be sorry. We're together now."

"I'm sorry for so many things. But I'm not sorry that he died. He was a cruel, heartless man who ruined lives. Mum's, your childhood, mine as well. The gun went off by accident, but he deserved to die."

"You mustn't blame yourself."

"I've blamed myself for years. If I'd wanted to save him, I could have. I could have tied a tourniquet, to give him time. If I'd raced for help and got him to hospital, he'd have survived. When I left him . . . in that moment, he knew I wanted him to die. He was your father too, Leo. It was a terrible thing to do." I hang my head in shame.

You walk round the table and put your arms around me from behind, and I rest my head on your chest.

"Ricky, listen. The gun went off by accident. It was an accident! And as for leaving him to die, the police said when they found him, he'd been dead for hours. The bullet hit an artery. He'd have passed out soon after you left, and bled to death in minutes. You could have run as fast as a — wildebeest — to get help and he would still have died."

That makes me smile, that you know about wildebeest.

"I've been so angry, Leo. If he hadn't insisted on coming over to fetch me home, things could have been so different. I could have stayed in South Africa, lived with Luke and Sally and learned to be a ranger. We could have sold the brooch and lived well out there on the money, you, me, and even Mum. We could have put her in rehab — she might still be alive, and you would have been spared all that heartache."

You sit down again and lean forward, your face close to mine. "Listen to me. We can't think about that now. We've both survived, haven't we? Our lives haven't turned out so badly. Against all the odds, you've found your dream job — and you're young enough to go back to Africa and become a ranger for real, if you want to. You don't need to worry about the police anymore. Dad died in an accident. There's no evidence to the contrary — it's your word against a dead man's."

It's true. If all this hadn't happened, I wouldn't have got the job at the zoo, or met Ben. And somehow everything I learned on the street, in the worst times, seems valuable now, a part of me. As if I needed all that hardship, the blackest days, to become the person I am.

And now I've found you again, Leo, I feel as if I have everything I've ever wanted.

* * *

When you heard about the brooch, your face was a picture. I had to tell you three times what they'd valued it at. I was so glad that I'd hung on to it for you, that I could give it back. It was always intended for you.

I explained as best I could about the background, and the stones, and why it is so valuable. You sat and stared at it for a long time and I could almost see the workings of your brain as you absorbed the implications of owning something so precious. Then you said: "If only we'd known."

"What difference would it have made?"

"Mum and I could have left."

I said: "But Mum wouldn't have left — you know that, in your heart. She would have stayed, and carried on drinking. She'd given up hope."

"You're probably right. She was a lost cause." You sighed, a look of utter sadness sweeping across your face.

"But you, Leo, look what you've achieved! Despite everything. You were always so determined to do well — and you did it. I always knew you would."

You didn't need the brooch to make something of your life. Nonetheless, it's some kind of compensation for you, Leo, for what he did to you.

You never knew that I'd found out and you never will. I said nothing when I realised what was going on — I was too shocked — and I knew you wouldn't have wanted me to know. You were like that, you protected me always, and you were so proud of being the strong one. So I kept quiet, filed it away in my memory where it crouched, weighing me down like a stone. Not to be ignored — not at all — but to be dealt with later.

It was that Christmas, when I came home from school for the first and only time. I couldn't sleep. Every night I found it hard to settle down. I always had this feeling of dread at home, as if something needed to be done about our parents but I was powerless to do it. It kept me awake that night.

I got up to go to the bathroom. It must have been around midnight and the house was silent. Everyone was asleep so I was careful not to make a noise. I didn't put on any lights. The landing was dim and shadowy, but I could see well enough by the light of the street lamp that cast a glow through the window at the top of the stairs.

As I emerged from the bathroom he was coming out of your bedroom. I shrank into the shadows as he creeped along the landing in stockinged feet, so he didn't see or hear me. I must have stood there for a good ten minutes before I dared to move — it felt like an eternity. I tiptoed back to my bedroom and sank onto my bed, my arms clasped around my knees, shaking.

Because when he came out of your bedroom, Leo, he was fully clothed, but he was zipping up his flies.

* * *

I'm glad you've found Rob. You need someone. You only ever had me before, and then not for long. He clearly cares for you, and I can tell he understands you. He makes you laugh, and for that I like him. There's never been much laughter in your life.

All through school your friends were getting boyfriends, having fun, beginning to understand about relationships, emotions. Love. But not you. There was too much to contend with at home. And you had me, for the first few years at least, and I was enough for you.

I hoped for a while that you and Jack would get together. You lived with his parents and they seemed a lovely, caring family, from what you said in your letters. It did seem like the perfect match. But then I disappeared, and you had the empty space that I should have filled, and the emptiness took up all the room in your heart for a long time. I'm so sorry for that, Leo. I will always regret that. But if it works out with Rob (R is for orange — a good portent, surely?), I can see a future for you at last, where you can create something new for yourself. You so deserve that, my dear sister.

CHAPTER FIFTY-TWO

Ricky

It was after that first Christmas holiday that I decided to kill him.

It started in my head the night I saw Dad coming out of your bedroom. I wasn't wrong to suspect him: I listened out, and there were other times that holiday. I had no doubt it would carry on, too, with me away and Mum incapable of helping. It could go on for years, for all I knew, and for all I could do about it.

I'm sure you wished him dead, Leo, many times. But for me it was no idle thought.

When I got back to school, my anger began to grow. It festered and ballooned until I could barely think of anything else. At shooting practice, every time I took a shot at a target, I imagined I was shooting at him. His head, to kill him outright. His body, to cause him the kind of pain he inflicted on you. His leg, so that he would bleed to death, and I could take my time to tell him what a bastard he was. I was full of anger at him, and my anger ate away at my insides. When I imagined shooting him at a practice session, it helped relieve the pressure, but I would come away exhausted.

Maybe it was normal for a teenager to feel such fury. Testosterone in action, so to speak. I hated Dad all the more for causing it. Without it, though, perhaps I would never have been so good at shooting. It focused me, gave me a reason to shoot straight, and though it was only ever in my head — I never confided in anyone about it — it became a part of me. I had a deadly skill and I intended to use it.

The bullies sensed the change in me. They even gave up using my nickname and just called me Bates. They were right to. I'd grown tall and muscled with all the training. I swam every day and my shoulders broadened — my arms were strong and sinewy. I was learning new skills all the time with Luke. I could build a fence, hold down an injured kudu, capture a venomous snake without fear.

So, this was my plan. It was a plan to beat all other plans, and I knew it would change my life, and yours, and that of both our parents. Once it was fully formed in my mind, I felt better. I was able to package it up and put it by for the right time. I got on with my life.

Then, when I finished school, it all fell into place. Dad wanted to come out to South Africa and was insisting on a camping trip to the mountains, full of remote valleys and hidden dangers. Where better for me to put my plan into action? He didn't bat an eyelid when I brought the gun on the trip — he believed my story about dangerous animals and snakes, because he knew by then that I could handle a gun as well as anybody. He was even proud that his son, the wimp, had at last proved he could do something manly. His pride made me sick.

It wasn't the perfect plan and I suffered the consequences — but it worked.

* * *

Twisting myself free from my father's grasp, I raised the gun.

On the trampled grass of our campsite, I held my position, my feet in perfect balance, forcing myself to breathe, as

270

I'd been taught. A look of incredulity passed across his face, rapidly replaced with a twisted smile.

"What do you think you're doing now?" he said. "Going to shoot your own father, are you? You couldn't kill a rat in a hole!"

"Get back." I was calm now, my voice low and firm. "I mean it. Don't take a single step closer. The gun's armed. I will shoot if you threaten me."

He laughed. He actually threw his head back and laughed, a full-throated belly laugh that didn't reach his eyes. When they focused on me again, they were burning with contempt.

"Well, I'll be damned. Look at my big man-son. Bet you've never shot that thing at a live target — you're too soft, like a girl. You've always been pathetic. Give it to me — now!" He lunged forward, his face contorted with rage.

I pulled the trigger.

The shot rang out into what seemed like a total silence, echoing endlessly around the mountains. It felt like the loudest noise I'd ever heard. For a moment I was stunned, my head pounding. I stumbled, fearing my eardrums were burst. In shooting practice, we had always worn ear defenders, and though I'd fired this gun many times without them, the noise it made on that day, in that place, resonated like the greatest crack of thunder in a tropical storm. In a strange moment of calm, I thought of you, Leo. I wondered what colour that sound would be. Surely the purest, most brilliant colour of all.

Only then did I look up to see where Dad was. It must have been a fraction of a second, but it seemed as if many minutes had passed. He was lying in front of the tent, his eyes closed, one hand clutching his thigh. A strange moaning sound escaped from his grimacing mouth.

I stood, keeping the gun trained on him and a good few feet between us. Even now, though he was injured and down, I didn't trust him. When his eyes opened, I could see the rage still boiling behind them, together with a strange, desperate look I couldn't place. A dark stain under his hand was spreading across his trouser leg. I stared with horrible fascination as it grew along the khaki cotton and trickled into the grass beneath.

"Fuck! Look what you've done, you stupid little shit! You've shot me! Fucking — do something!" he yelled, grabbing his thigh. Blood streamed from the wound, soaking his trousers in seconds.

I'd hit the artery, as I intended.

As I looked at his tortured face I felt nothing but sadness — but not for him. Tears clouded my eyes as I remembered a childhood destroyed, a mother's life in ruins. He looked at me with contempt.

"You always were a feeble little pussy," he said.

I stared at him, letting the anger rise from deep in my belly, relishing the moment. At last I felt more powerful than him.

"And you were a loathsome father," I said, my voice hard with pent-up emotion. "This is your reward. For what you did to all of us. You ruined our lives, me, Mum — and Leonora. Yes, Dad, I know what you did to her — your own daughter. You're disgusting." I spat the word out. "I'm being kind to you. You deserve to die in a filthy ditch with a mouthful of shit, not in a beautiful place like this."

I watched as the contempt fell away, replaced by surprise, then horrible realisation. And then, sheer terror.

"Yes, Dad," I said, as I turned away. "This is for Leonora."

CHAPTER FIFTY-THREE

Leonora

She wakes into silence. Only the emerald-green buzz of London traffic pierces the quiet of her room. For a moment, an image of Claire's smile flutters into her mind, but then she remembers: it's been a while since Claire packed her bags and went to live with her boyfriend. She glances at her watch and allows herself a few more precious moments in bed. A feeling of utter contentment wafts over her. It's happened a few times recently, but the novelty has yet to wear off and she can feel a lightness about herself that still surprises her.

No longer does she wake in the morning with her chest tight, because Ricky is lost and she has nobody. Not only is he back in her life, but he's happy, doing a job he loves, working with animals. He's sharing her flat and she sees him every single day.

At first, they talked a lot about the past, sitting at the kitchen table for hours, often well into the night. It felt cathartic, as if they needed to relieve themselves of their memories of those lost years. For each, though, the burden of pain and guilt did not transfer to the other as they spoke, making the weight of their own suffering even greater — instead it floated away like a trail of mist, dissolving into nothing. They were able to lift and dispel each other's load, leaving an unfamiliar space and lightness that made them giddy.

At work, people remark on her transformation. They ask what she's done — lightened her hair, lost weight, come into some money? She smiles, and they smile back, but she doesn't tell them. It's not a story that's easy for people to understand. Rob knows, and understands, and that's enough. He has become a regular feature in her life and he and Ricky have become firm friends. She's happy to see what transpires. For the first time in her life, she's living in the moment.

They are going to sell the brooch. It reminds her too much of the past, and represents another burden, another source of guilt. Together with the money from the house and the investments, they will both have enough to feel secure, perhaps to buy a place of their own one day.

To her relief, Ricky isn't going back to live in South Africa, though they will both visit Luke and Sally and the children when he feels ready. He owes them that, and while it will bring back dark memories, he wants to keep them in his life, as Leonora does Maria, Pete and Jack.

It's still early, but she stretches and throws back the bed-clothes, padding in bare feet across the room to draw back the curtains. She squints into the brightness, then opens the window and listens to the sounds of London.

A ripple of magenta glows and fades as a blackbird sings its fluting song in the bushes below, while the silver-grey rumble of a double-decker bus rises and falls like the mist in a valley. She breathes in and lets the colours wash over her.

THE END

ACKNOWLEDGEMENTS

I'd like to thank everyone who helped me with this book.

The Lost Brother brings many ideas together, including some that have been in my head for a long time. I wanted in particular to explore a tradition that many families used to follow of educating their sons differently from their daughters, and of sending boys away to school. I have always thought this strange and am glad that things now seem to be changing.

South Africa seemed to me the ideal place in which to set the school. I knew there were exceptional private boarding schools there, albeit, sadly, only for the few. Many thanks to John Roff, for his insights into school life and the fantastic flora and fauna of Kwazulu-Natal.

My research trip, as you can imagine, was particularly special, and I have my dear friend from university, Carolyn Thorp (aka Topp) to thank for hosting me and showing me round, as well as for her thoughts and advice on my story. My love of Africa and its wildlife is largely down to her. I was incredibly lucky to be writing this book during the hot, sunny summer of 2018 — appropriate temperatures for writing about South Africa — and I moved my writing desk into my garden and enjoyed my local wildlife in the process.

I must thank Dr Jamie Ward of the University of Sussex, one of the world's leading experts on synaesthesia, for his helpful comments and for his book, *The Frog Who Croaked Blue*. I have always been fascinated by synaesthesia and thoroughly enjoyed this part of my research.

Many thanks too, to Mandy Rigby, for her openness and readiness to answer my rather ignorant questions on homelessness. Her insights were invaluable. Thanks, Joy, for putting me in touch.

To all my early readers, thank you for reading, for your patience and your helpful comments.

I'm so grateful to Emma Grundy Haigh at Joffe Books, for seeing the potential in this story. Many heartfelt thanks to all at Joffe for their support.

ALSO BY SUSANNA BEARD

THE LOST BROTHER
THE PERFECT LIFE
WHAT HAPPENED THAT NIGHT
THE GIRL ON THE BEACH

Please join our mailing list for free Kindle crime thriller, detective, mystery and romance books, and new releases!

www.joffebooks.com

FREE KINDLE BOOKS

Thank you for reading this book.

If you enjoyed it please leave feedback on Amazon or Goodreads, and if there is anything we missed or you have a question about, then please get in touch. The author and publishing team appreciate your feedback and time reading this book.

We're very grateful to eagle-eyed readers who take the time to contact us. Please send any errors you find to corrections@joffebooks.com. We'll get them fixed ASAP.